TOMBOY

TOMBOY

THOMAS MEINECKE

Translated by
DANIEL BOWLES

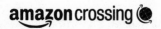

Tomboy by Thomas Meinecke was first published in 1998 by Suhrkamp in Berlin as *Tomboy*.

Translated from the German by Daniel Bowles.
First published in English in 2011 by AmazonCrossing.
Illustration by Michaela Melián.

Published by AmazonCrossing
P.O. Box 400818
Las Vegas, NV 89140

ISBN-13: 9781611090574
ISBN-10: 1611090571
Library of Congress Control Number: 2011901806

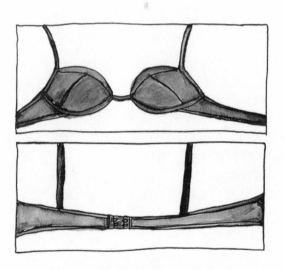

The rock quarries glowed pink from across the nearby Odenwald. Had that artificial encroachment into nature become an element of so-called natural beauty? Had Vivian not just risen from her workspace, had she not stepped toward the window with almost somnambulant resoluteness precisely because the quarries glowed so very especially pink, electric pink as it were, on this sunny late afternoon? Vivian was slightly embarrassed that the mountains, and a scarred low mountain range at that, were even capable of exerting a kind of sensuous charm on her, and so turned away from the window and plopped herself down on the couch for a moment to examine the run in her stocking that had been drifting up her right ankle since the late morning. In the supermarket just before the checkout, a hulking lout, almost six-foot-seven, had shoved a gigantic twin stroller into her heel. Would Vivian's run, like the rock quarries of the Odenwald, ever be able to be read as sexy? Or was the unscathed synthetic fiber fabric itself already a textile euphemism and therefore to be classified as an artificial amplification of nature corresponding ambivalently to those highlights the evening sun draped upon the Odenwald rock, laid bare and furrowed by stonemasons? Did the accent of those (men, Vivian knew) who had once invented women's synthetic pantyhose lie in the garment's transparency or more in its nevertheless gradually veiling function? Vivian Atkinson felt like making a note of this question, rose from the couch, and returned to her workspace; doubtless, transparency was completely inconceivable without its material foil. Just then on her screen saver there appeared, from the right, the words Vivian Atkinson's Screen Saver. The student pressed a key, and again before her eyes stood the text she had abandoned temporarily, on account of the pink-glowing quarries. She had hardly sat down when she noticed with irritation that a long-playing record, namely the new one of the group Bikini Kill, entitled Reject All American, was spinning in its lead-out groove, possibly for a considerable amount of time now. So she stood up yet again and turned the record issued by Kill Rocks Stars in Olympia, Washington, onto its B-side.

Like Bikini Kill, the Riot Girls had intentionally put runs into their nylons since time immemorial. Vivian, however, had accused her supermarket dude of typically masculine carelessness whereupon the latter had felt himself empowered, completely nonsensically, to make reference to the breathtaking grace of—as he expertly deemed—the perfectly feminine curvature of her calves. Thanks for the legs: with these idiotic words he had catcalled at Vivian when she exited the only moderately busy self-service store. But nothing else occurred to the young Ms. Atkinson to say to this, and so she kept her mouth shut, a mouth which the horny gallant would surely have commenced to praise next as the most beguiling in the world. A few weeks before, Vivian had read in Marjorie Garber's book Vested Interests about the Hasty Pudding shows at Harvard University, in which all roles were played by men. In 1917, shortly before the USA entered the war, the Boston newspapers had been full of detailed reports about a dispute between the local censor and the university after the genetically male dancing-girl performers had allegedly refused to wear silk stockings on stage. The Boston legislature, however—with sufficient duplicity, Vivian found—had strictly forbidden revue girls from performing on stage with bare legs, for which reason the stern censor found himself compelled to enforce ex cathedra the wearing of slinky stockings, even by the lady imitators. Vivian was already sitting at her computer again. A boy in a dance dress—in 1917 in Boston, shortly before his being drafted into military service—was regarded as a girl to such a degree that even his bare leg was interpreted as that of one, for which reason, sheerly bestockinged, it was actually put to which gender determination? A doubly feminized one? And had the signifying function of clothing thus accrued a quasi-tautological quality, or had its dialectic been put to the test instead? The young collegian's head buzzed; to her the feminine seemed to be nothing more than a veil, a costume, a pair of transparent stockings. Yet in this scenario what categorical significance would a genetically female dancing girl without tights have? Such a professional girl, in the service of the world of men, has probably never existed; Vivian concluded her scientific catalog of inquiries for today.

Last fall it had cost the student some powers of persuasion before she had convinced her professor that she ought to be allowed to formulate the central line of thought of her master's thesis exclusively as questions. For hours upon hours she had read aloud to him in various Heidelberg cafés—on the banks of the Neckar, too, when the weather was nice—from the more or less deconstructionist works of younger, primarily American feminists, thereby even accepting that the lecturer might believe she was crazy about him; but the post-Lacanian scholar with whom Vivian worked on the tricky triad of having, being, and seeming obviously had no interest in women, so autistic, as it were, did he come off—

3

not even gay—before he had realized that precisely the strength of many young, not-yet-canonized feminisms lay in their truly revolutionary interrogations. But at least compose your headings without question marks, pro forma, the sallow teacher had relented, lingering on the Neckar's dusty towpath while sucking on a silly lollypop, and Vivian Atkinson finally had a green light to match, and possibly outdo, Otto Weininger's misogynist ripostes with some intelligent questions that wouldn't even demand cheap answers. No uncomfortably direct questions, scout's honor.

The master's candidate had offered her hand to her professor, pulled him up out of the dirt, and dusted off his gaunt shoulders so that in the lecture hall he wouldn't look as if he had slipped while catching tadpoles. The professor had actually once left behind a stinking jar of tadpoles standing in the cafeteria, half-dead creatures he had fished out of the boggy water meadows of the Neckar on his way in to work every day, for he always rode his bike—in absolutely any weather—down the Philosophenweg and then, taking a sharp left, along the river up to the old Karl Theodor Bridge, extolled not least by Goethe. In more youthful years he cycled up the Philosophenweg from the Institutes of Physical Sciences, above which he occupied a small garden house, only then shouldering his bike high above the Old Bridge to carry it down the breakneck Schlangenweg. Then the professor had received a woman's bike as a gift and was forced to realize that women's bikes, without the necessary middle bar, were as good as impossible to carry on one's shoulder. The American Allen Ginsberg had once stood at the top of the Philosophenweg and composed a Beat poem on the spot about the whole, mostly hazy plain stretching out before him, even incorporating into it the chemical factories in Ludwigshafen. Vivian's mother could recite the following lines from it from memory: Highdelbergh below, orange roofed, misty under grey cloud flowing over oak ridge, across the red stone bridge, over brown Neckar waters, flowing west to the Rhine plains: supporting BASF. Not long after the divestiture of IG Farben—Vivian's father could report—there were even BASF factories located on the lower Mississippi, and of course there is even a little Heidelberg in the state of Mississippi. Vivian's professor wrote absolutely no poems at all, but supposedly he once went beer-drinking with Judith Butler in one of the Heidelberg watering holes worn shiny over the centuries by student buttocks. Hopefully he didn't then possess the habit yet, the college girl thought today, of tucking his shirt so super conspicuously into his underwear. But probably so.

Despite all unintentional humor of general male conduct, Vivian and her female classmates did not want to live in a world entirely without men. Though one of them, Frauke Stöver—just now stepping off the OEG, a kind of overland railed tram whose track network described a triangle between Mannheim, Heidelberg, and Weinheim—had as a teenager sworn off physical love of the male sex. Frauke sauntered around the small train station building amid a languid little gaggle of locals and made her way to the old tobacco warehouse, converted in the nineties into a block of apartments, where her friend Vivian—heterosexual by compulsion, as she deemed—lived and worked at Daddy Atkinson's expense. Beside the stairs to the entrance—she had already buzzed—Frauke found a stack of official flyers, dodgy, greasy slips of paper carrying the headline Call to Witness, subheading: Sightings of British Tarmac Gangs in the Municipal Area. But then the buzzer buzzed, and Frauke let the flyers be flyers. Up at the top by the elevator stood Vivian, freshly combed, flowery smelling—how unfortunate, Frauke thought—and yet both, who had met each other in 1995 studying Weininger's Sex and Character, had found a common hobby since the previous, mostly rained-out summer in listening together to seditious girl-punk-rock records of the American Northwest with delicate jasmine tea or strong Eichbaum beer, depending on the time and mood of the day. The brick tobacco warehouse had in fact since been upgraded so solidly that both women could listen to their records, undisturbed, with the volume dial maxed out to the right. Frauke gave Vivian a perfunctory kiss and opened her backpack. In it was jammed Vivian's beloved Team Dresch LP Captain My Captain that Frauke had borrowed after both had already listened to it together at Vivian's place, because Frauke Stöver, several years older than her record-crazy friend, lived with three teachers in an unusually poorly soundproofed shared flat at the commercial periphery of Handschuhsheim where she, for years and simply without ever coming to an end, had been writing her dissertation on Jesus' foreskin. This very record craze of Vivian Atkinson—rather rare for women—had been a fallacious indication for Frauke that her pretty classmate must likewise be lesbian. After pulling the record from her sack and steering her host to the sofa, the platinum-blonde Stöver, born and bred on the Baltic Sea, also pulled the inner sleeve out of the cover and translated awkwardly—it was of no use that Vivian insisted with irritation that she knew it more than adequately already—the facsimile of the fan letter of a certain Ann to Kaia Lynn Wilson, one of the two singers and a guitarist of the all-girl group.

7/7/95. Dear Kaia, OK. So here I am in the middle of the woods in Northern Minnesota. I'm having so much fun here. I'm working (for no pay) at a tiny little Girl Scout canoe base in the middle of the woods. I already know all this, interrupted Vivian, who had jumped up impatiently, smoothed out her corduroy dress, and let the tone arm of her professional Technics record player—the thoughtful gift of a celebrated Ludwigshafen House DJ—hover over Sleater-Kinney's Call The Doctor LP, Frauke, you still won't bring me around with this epistle. We go in groups of eight or so and we paddle and portage about ten miles each day, Frauke continued, it is very quiet here and the water is so clean we can drink directly out of the lakes, but let me just skip over a few paragraphs, Vivian, where she talks about the hick town nearest to the Girl Scout camp: A few days ago, four of the guides up here were walking along the main road and they had an encounter with a strange man. The guy said to one guide, Hey! If you were a man with any kind of sense you'd marry that lady (pointing to another guide). It was soooo funny because first of all, they are all women, second, two are dykes—the two he was talking to—and finally, since when does a person go around telling people who to marry? Exactly, Vivian remarked, dropping the tone arm, where-upon, preserved amazingly true to life, Carrie Kinney and Corin Tucker began to sing their Call The Doctor, but the doctoral student wasn't done yet, because Ann the fan had written two letters, the second—likewise a facsimile—to the entire band.

Vivian Atkinson sat down at her workspace. Around the middle of the circuitous document, Frauke Stöver—now almost hoarse thanks to Sleater-Kinney's thundering roar—slowed her reading tempo and declaimed in a solemn tremolo: we carry big canoes across portages and through mud and we make fires and hang our food so that bears don't get it. So anyway, I had been at the canoe base that summer for a week or so when I realized that I had—and here she comes completely out of the closet, Frauke said—a huge crush on another guide. She was so awesome—it really says that, Vivian—and there was something about her—perhaps I should translate it with something was in the air, Frauke gasped—that made me feel all...tingly, hyphen, squishy. She writes: and it wasn't like one of those boy-crushes. A few lines later again: it's so exciting to be out in the woods, far from any civilization, for ten days with only a pair of pants, a shirt, a sleeping bag, a tent, a tiny bit of equipment, some food and a canoe and six other girls. I could talk about it for hours and hours. Says you or says Ann, Vivian asked wearily. Ann's writing, Frauke said, continuing once again: there's a group of us—about twelve girls who are age sixteen and twenty-four or so and we run the whole canoe base. It occurred to Vivian how Frauke had once dragged her to a retrospective film night with the movies of Doctor Fanck, gloomy, erotically charged mountain flicks in most of which wild child Leni Riefenstahl frolics across the slopes and in front of the camera. Actually, she carped, as Sleater-Kinney's I Wanna Be Your Joey Ramone blared from the speakers, why couldn't Luis Trenker be lesbian? Time to open the first couple of Eichbaums, the older but slightly shorter woman answered with noticeable gruffness: the greatest female blues singers, though? All lesbians.

As a matter of fact, Luis Trenker—who had to kiss the sinewy Leni for Doctor Arnold Fanck and soon began making very similar mountain films himself (while the undead Riefenstahl, Vivian said, was until recently still focusing her camera on virilistically heroized racial bodies)—had been a blood-related forebear of Giorgio Moroder, who with his stimulatingly repetitive Munich disco tracks of the seventies had helped one or the other gay (not just deck-) party to unforgettable climaxes. And didn't Moroder's most famous female protagonist, Donna Sum-

mer—African American, discovered for the German version of
the musical Hair—live in Mannheim with a German man, not
far from the Judo Club between sketchy établissements like the
Texas or the Dallas Bar, where the young Vivian Atkinson had
learned to defend herself, self-defense as it is called? And hadn't
Donna Summer, whose early records graced both Frauke's and
Vivian's antiquarian collection, later ungratefully had the nerve
to engage in gay-baiting? If Vivian, so-called army brat, having
grown up in the American barracks near Heidelberg, stood at her
little OEG train station, she could decide if she wanted to take the
electric train to Heidelberg or the one to Mannheim. The one to
the right led purposefully in the direction of Mannheim—that
was seven miles—the one to the left headed for Heidelberg only
some four miles away. Sometimes, mainly during semester break,
the college girl took the first best train, regardless of where, but
sometimes she was struck by an enormous desire specifically for
disreputable Mannheim, the generally so-called ugly Mannheim
that appealed to her—when all was said and done—more (she
admitted it freely) than cute Old Heidelberg. So she let the OEG
whoosh past to the left and waited—though it might rain cats
and dogs and the meager waiting room might be barred shut—
for the red-and-white railcar to Mannheim; just as she had done
back when she was thirteen, coming from Heidelberg, fleeing the
recreation center, heading toward the Judo Club, where her very
first crush, Joe the Greek from Schwetzingen, coached children
and adolescents. In those days, hardly out the front door, she had
bound her budding breasts; baggy Jockey shorts swirled about
her pubescent womb.

Thinking herself liberated, listening to Doors records round the
clock, Vivian's mother, however—a German Miss Miracle by the

name of Gerlinde—would have liked most to run topless (stripped to the waist, that is) through the Patrick Henry Village, the mirrored clothes closet full of gossamer blouses through which the off-duty GIs enjoyed staring at her bosom. In the U.S. she would have landed herself in jail immediately with such transparent rags. Only at the end of the eighties did her gangly only child learn to deal with the role of women and replace the Protestant breast bandages with a Catholic brassiere. But the tripped-out mommy certainly didn't want to acknowledge this undoubtedly ambivalent garment as a sign of sexual maturity, maybe even of adulthood. She condemned the Hole records Vivian had begun collecting soon afterward just as she did those of Madonna Ciccone which the guest worker's son Joe regularly came by with, and soon after Germany's reunification, Gerlinde Atkinson jetted off to Atlanta, Georgia, along with all her crap and a very young, very German Siemens engineer—about a year before her forsaken husband who still had to wrap up a few things, including the American army of occupation between Rhine, Main, and Neckar (obsolete since the end of the Cold War), and who would later end up in Washington, D.C. Thus Vivian Atkinson (now of legal age, entirely without family aside from sporadic attempts at contact from her grandmother in Hanau) had remained behind in Germany—in whose American Sector she was born in 1973 and whose complicated native tongue had become second nature to her—and had enrolled at the Ruprecht-Karls-Universität Heidelberg outside the barracks, erstwhile preferred target of anti-imperialist West-German guerrillas, and there, before sticking herself to the philosophical heels of Judith Butler, had initially set herself to work on the historically objective safeguarding of the Socialist Patients' Collective.

You look really different, somehow changed. Hans Mühlenkamm twisted awkwardly at the buttons of his UPS jacket. Not that he had ever worked for the worldwide package service, but he loved their brown uniforms and had to expend a little criminal energy to acquire one; jacket and pants alike, though, had been attained strictly separately. Vivian contended briskly that she wouldn't know in what way she might have changed. In her mind, though, a light went on: in her enlightened circles, was it considered socially completely impossible to give explicit compliments about the physical attraction of—Korinna's newest favorite expression— body islands, or Leibesinseln; had Hansi Mühlenkamm basically slipped through a loophole of extraparliamentarily corrective legislation? With his latently ingratiating allusion (obviously meant appreciatively) to Vivian's grown-out short hairdo, he had replaced the (in many respects) hierarchizing praise of body-specific beauty, always under suspicion of sexism, with the initially positively understood category of an—albeit here expressly indeterminate—deflection, thereby replacing quality with difference, the courteous construction with equivocal empiricism. The twenty-four-year-old woman—the clueless Hans had just gone to pee—would wonder at her own pace, perhaps even wish to write down a few open questions about this point. On the other hand, no problem whatsoever when Vivian then, in an unequal countermove, praised the happily returning friend's highly fashionable getup. She had gotten to know the twenty-year-old part-time physician's receptionist last year, up at the castle, at an event for the independent record label Source. Both were crazy about its sonorous, instrumental releases, which is why Hans Mühlenkamm also couldn't understand why in the world his new female acquaintance still bothered with such text-heavy records like those of Bikini Kill. Which was a bit pretentious, because Hans had, after all, been excerpting lyrics regularly for several months like (just yesterday) Jeannie C. Riley's He Made a Woman out of Me in order to be able to convey them, verbally, to feminist studies. But even Vivian Atkinson, a regular and enthusiastic visitor of smaller house and techno clubs, had frequently already noticed that abstract electronic pop music was produced primarily by men while bands of the nineties had very radically feminized and thereby overcome their inherent phallocentrism via (so to speak) castration. That may be true rudimentarily—Hans Mühlenkamm had replied on a walk to the Molkenkur—even if not necessarily for your ultimately phantom-schlonged lesbian combos from the Pacific Northwest. On the other hand, hardly anything had ever sounded so unphallic to Hans as the gentle electronics of RO 70 from the Source label.

What kind of men were they—new men with a capital N mayhap—who produced this fascinating music? Even Elvis Presley, descendant of the Palatinate Presslers—as the heirs of the artist tellingly also called The Pelvis had recently found out—had once been (aside from having worn eye shadow in the Grand Ole Opry) just such a New Man when he had—Vivian knew—stuffed an empty toilet paper roll in his underwear before his performance, thereby demonstrating—really only seemingly masculinized by the removable piece—the availability of the roll/e of men too, in the truest sense of the word: at least for himself and his personal circle. And most especially for the exegetes comprising the public, or rather for the female exegetes, added Hans, who knew this ambivalent anecdote in that insignificant modification according to which the hollow, loose cardboard roll had been replaced by a massive steel bar sewn into the fabric. The man as male impersonator? Actually female impersonator, Vivian thought, because only a woman would avail herself of an ersatz penis. And soon legions of intuitive Elvis imitators of all races and genders had appeared on stage. The small underwear intervention as a giant leap for human knowledge, the part-time physician's receptionist punned, and for a brief moment the tinge of a feeling befell Vivian Atkinson that the world armed by her parents had improved a tiny but significant bit. Very tangibly, Hansi Mühlenkamm also remarked, seeming to feel at the same moment, however, nothing more electrifying than to sit next to the army brat with the grown-out bob in this Handschuhsheim pizzeria, frequented by predominantly female students recruited by flyers, while waiting for Frauke Stöver (who claimed to have already begun a presentation twenty minutes ago about the lesbian in more recent pop music).

Stöver is always late, Vivian knew, as did Hans, with whom Frauke, during the course of affairs, had once almost even had a fling in 1996; at the time amateurishly manufactured Ecstasy pills had transported them both pretty much immediately to the sexual finish line, and while they were still dressing one another the following morning, Frauke had sworn up and down never again to sleep with a man, even a nearly hairless one like Hans, whom Frauke had dubbed Hansi Pompadour. I am so terribly sorry. Frauke Stöver—who really did just live right around the corner, adjacent to the industrial park—stepped in from the rain into the trattoria, sopping wet. The country singer k.d. lang—of whom Madonna's remark was rumored: I saw Elvis, and she was gorgeous—once allowed herself, dressed as a man, to be lathered up in a barber's chair for a shave, nay, as if for a shave, by the photo model Cindy Crawford for a cover spread of the magazine

Vanity Fair with which the magazine, oriented toward a female heterosexual readership (Frauke with a note of triumph: heterosexual by compulsion), managed to book a surprisingly large commercial success. Nothing new for the magazine market, this kind of gender-transgressing consumer behavior, explained the female lecturer, whose bathroom was flanked by towering stacks of old Playboys, but who, then, had acquired this Vanity Fair issue in such huge quantities? Sapphic reader circles? Upright men who had always been deeply receptive to the sight of lesbian ensembles? Along with their coquettish wives who were devoted to noncommittal lesbian chic? Here numerous hands flew wriggling into the air. Cool Frauke had addressed her difficult concerns to the muggy microclimate of the room so suggestively that she was barely capable anymore of reconquering the floor. Finally, however, the specialized audience calmed down again, someone tipped open the window to the courtyard, and Frauke Stöver from Travemünde continued lecturing: Phranc, an austere folk songstress with a crew cut, had enjoyed some subcultural success with her song I Enjoy Being a Girl, the collegiate-cute Jill Sobule a smash hit with her I Kissed a Girl; the boy in the back transcribed everything neatly. Frauke had put off all potential female questioners until the end of her remarks.

One of the three female teachers with whom she lived together in the north of Handschuhsheim had possessed the maiden name Schitthouse, or rather this name had possessed her, and that to such an extent that the then–student teacher had married a dodgy tenured secondary school instructor from Leimen named Schulze quite early—far too early, Frauke thought—in any case before she had become aware of her predisposition toward the same sex. After three truly hellish years of marriage as well as the nightmarish birth of her son Hartmut, Mrs. Schulze, cheated on in every possible way, filed for divorce and chose to readopt her maiden name, at which point the full villainy of grade schoolers descended upon her, who missed no opportunity at calling the teacher—in mocking barks and unassailable—by her ridiculous name. In short—Frauke ran her fingers through her platinum-blonde hair—Schitthouse went to the government office and had her name changed to Schoolmistress so that the vile student body might henceforth address her only as Mrs. Schoolmistress. In an of itself an awesome move—Frauke concluded her true story, the da capo of this evening in the lesbian pizzeria—especially since Hartmut, now twenty-two years old, got to be addressed as Schoolmistress from then on, too. Ilse Schoolmistress, sitting upright beneath a horrid mural in oils of Capri fishermen, clapped her hands first. She loved it when her housemate told of her onomastic history, and she had also not yet entirely relinquished the hope that had ensured Frauke a solid roof over her head for almost twenty semesters now, namely that one sunny day she would be permitted to emerge from a cute Heidelberg civil registry office as Ilse Stöver.

Frauke, however, who had stumbled upon the Savior's foreskin during her studies of the Catholic singer Madonna Ciccone as a postmodern embodiment of Sigmund Freud's phallic mother, had for years been showing her annoyance with Ilse Schoolmistress and so tonight preferred in all seriousness to go for a walk around the block again in the rain rather than have to converse with the always far too early roommate. Things didn't look much better with Genoveva and Pat, two dismal tribades from the Darmstadt area who had been subletting from Ilse since 1980, who in turn had rented the apartment (at the edge of the freshly conjured industrial area) immediately following the divorce—at first with her little Hartmut: spuriously still under the discarded name Schulze. Frauke, who had hardly ever taken girls with her to Handschuhsheim herself, recalled that the precocious Hartmut had been able to lure a whole slew of attractive women into these premises, dampened though they were with the mist of melancholy. But last summer Ilse's son had moved out and into the new German capital where he, as Frauke would regale her next class, worked as a dominatrix in the diplomatic quarter. Which of course was a heap of didactic lies, for Hartmut Schulze-Schoolmistress—as Frauke Stöver had gotten to know the boy nine years her junior—would, in spite of all evident attractiveness to the opposite sex, rather make his own pilgrimage to a commercial female disciplinarian than be able—much less harbor the desire—to embody one convincingly himself. That the boy from Handschuhsheim had found a job in the new German Reichstag and straightaway rose rather high (for his young age) into the upper echelons did not fit at all into any of Frauke Stöver's stories for public consumption.

Vivian and Hansi had taken their leave of one another; at the Heidelberg central train station the politically active cavalier had transferred to the tram, his intransigent female friend remaining in the OEG, for Oberrheinische Eisenbahngesellschaft, the Upper-Rhineland Railroad Company. It was entirely possible that the two wouldn't set eyes on each other for another three months. Without Hans Mühlenkamm's prior phone call the college girl would certainly not have traveled to Handschuhsheim today either. Indeed, ultimately, she wouldn't have even been jealous for a second had Hans switched over Frauke in 1996 during their joint Ecstasy high. As she sauntered down Edingen's obsolete train station road to the tobacco warehouse towering above in the darkness with its modern apartments—Frauke disparagingly called them lofts—Vivian heard the street lamps buzzing vividly in the humidity. Enchanted, she paused for a moment, circling around. Obviously the clouds had dumped all their rain on the Odenwald, and from the West an inky-black night sky cleared slowly, which for some time now had been wreathed each evening by the tail of a comet that only passed by the earth every two thousand years. Spring was just one hour old; thus the Roman Catholic church bells first jingled politely in the distance, followed by the Protestant ones on Hauptstrasse, which Vivian had been approaching in the meanwhile, since she too counted the warehouse erected in the olden days not far from the Neckar as her address.

Several days later an entire sect in the U.S. had blown itself to kingdom come in order to travel intergalactically with the lucid comet. In the meantime the superstitious bunch had left behind their mortal remains in a Californian luxury subdivision. Just underneath it, Courtney Love—Hole singer, Kurt Cobain's widow, in Hollywood, the dream factory—grinned from a virginal white evening gown she could have worn at Monaco's royal court: Vivian Atkinson couldn't make out even a single run in her stockings, pensively folded the Mannheim newspaper together, and dissertated further on her topic. Did wearing of transparent pantyhose, regardless of who wore them, signify female impersonation per se? Beyond this: how could this Anglo-American term be translated into German? Damenimitation wouldn't quite be the right word. And can female impersonation ever be feminist impersonation? Even before her erstwhile idol Courtney Love, Vivian had also begun wearing ladylike clothes, playfully, as she adjudged. Where, however, did fashion's earnestness begin?

From which point did the soldier's daughter, who had been called attractive, succumb in this perhaps only putative game to the (proverbially) barely veiled interests of male couturiers? And how could it come to pass that these so-called fashion designers, like shamans, were considered barely masculine, even effeminate, when at the same time they were not only subservient to the dirtiest male fantasies—as a rule fantasies of violence—but also, as it were, gave them color and contour? Was this one of the rottenest tricks of long-established male hegemony, to instrumentalize gay tailors for their presumptuous strategies of rape? Time for Vivian to go out with a boy again she actually is in love with. On the telephone, connected with Handschuhsheim, it sounded like this: to celebrate my studies, which are scarcely flattering for the so-called strong sex, dear Frauke, I ought to put my compulsory heterosexuality to the test again, too. Frauke, however, who had hunkered in rage the entire day over Slavoj Žižek's misogynist ode—dressed up in pseudo-Lacanian garb and recently published in Vienna—to (the two female students as with one voice:) Otto Weininger, was in fact at that moment less able than ever to agree on this point with her ardently revered girl friend, and thus swiftly rattled off a short if oversubtle Navratilova anecdote, and both telephone receivers soon hung again on their hooks.

Vivian recalled her first private encounter with Frauke in the tobacco warehouse. Back then they had crossed paths over a song obsessed with velocity called Miles Per Hour, included on the debut album of the group The Third Sex from Portland, Oregon, and the already then-eternal doctoral candidate had finally managed to win over the budding master's student with a typically German-French anecdote in which the French philosopher Jacques Lacan loaded the German philosopher he so highly revered, Martin Heidegger, along with Heidegger's wife into his white Mercedes-Benz and floored it enough to make his two passengers immediately begin to fear for their lives. Another time, in 1962, Lacan had sent a Soviet Russian psychologist into a flying rage by maintaining that there were no cosmonauts because there is no cosmos; the cosmos, he argued, is nothing more than a perception of the mind. A stroke of genius, Vivian had cheered, who, by implication, considered absolutely everything possible, to which the child of the Baltic Sea had replied there are no such things as geniuses. And Vivian had also really planned to relegate questionable terms to questionable guys, in this case that of the genius to Weininger and his male-society sort. Mnemonic: concepts able to be used by the wrong groups are precisely the wrong concepts. Frauke Stöver was brimming with such anecdotes in any case. Instead of worrying about the Savior's earthly, unascended prepuce, she accumulated all sorts of ideological gossip in her memory. At this point Vivian Atkinson decided, for the time being, not to go out tonight after all, not to indulge her inner slut, scribbling a spate of words on the narrow margin of her daily newspaper only to cross most of them out again anyway: redress, distress, duress. A good dressing-down. And finally, in fair copy, that is, into the eagerly buzzing electronic notebook: From National Dress to Fashion—Two Hundred Years of Gender Polarity. The college girl leaned back with satisfaction; this heading might please her professor.

In 1789 the bourgeoisie had been focusing its considerable energy on distinguishing itself, even outwardly, from the deposed courtly rabble that had been discredited as pompous, denatured, namby-pamby, and effeminate; 1793, then, was the year in which Rousseau had issued his memorable ban on trousers for women. With the monarchy the time of powerful female regents had likewise run its course, for the citizenry was a manly thing through and through and was supposed to be thus until its end; in 1990 Luise F. Pusch was still capable of causing consternation with a book entitled Alle Menschen werden Schwestern, All Men Become Sisters. From the French Revolution, it was necessary to inscribe glitzy femininity as exclusively as possible into generative female bodies, for the woman reflected decoratively what the man was; this, Vivian thought, would probably make a worthwhile cross reference for her as-yet-unfinished excursus on the haute couturiers. The student could not entirely afford, apart from all the adventurous, interdisciplinary cross-country, to lose sight of the ludicrous Weininger, whose degrading conjectures about femininity had, after all, helped determine the subtitle of her master's thesis. High heels, skirt, belt, corset, and girdle submitted, even subjected the feminine to the racist classifications of the honest man's aggressive gaze, Vivian Atkinson noted, laying aside the fountain pen and briefly considering whether she should have once again written sexist instead of racist, or even biologistic; on the other hand, she recalled, her classmate Korinna, an impassioned tennis player who drove an old Czechoslovak Tatra sedan, had once even gotten a fair amount of mileage out of the term colonialism in a similarly vexing feminist context. Yet again the quarry; Vivian would have to buy curtains. She ran to the bathroom, sat down on the toilet, and observed the barely perceptible fuzz on her forearms. Did the Lord God, she had wondered as a pubescent teenager, want to play with her as a man? Had it already been the domain of female imitation when she once shaved her armpits for an American lover from the Patrick Henry Village, a nephew of the GI who had been buried under a Coca-Cola machine by the Red Army Faction bombing of 24 May 1972? And thus her mother's pastel-

colored Ladyshave electric razor (in accordance with regulations)
a despicable utensil of transvestites? A bad joke of world history,
which supposedly unleashed its greatest emancipatory potential
with the good middle-class storming of the Bastille? And anyway
had it even been proven that God was a Lord God?

The raucous girl punk-rock records from the North American
Pacific coast were little suited as background music for such
considerations. So Vivian again pressed the start button on her
Discman in which Curd Duca's switched-on wagner—based
ironically on Walter, now Wendy, Carlos' famous Switched-On
Bach—had been spinning since the early afternoon. Poor Walter
Carlos had once had his primary sexual organ cut off and since
then was allowed to consider himself a female organist. Time
and again, however, feminists had managed to raise substantive
objections to so-called gender reassignment—a classically male
invention, Frauke said—and to Vivian, too, it seemed incomprehensible how a person, as the final aim of his or her fixed-gender-
transcending behavior, could wish to have precisely those
ostensibly vanquished categories confirmed once more—and
confirmed as forgery-proof—with a new ID, for instance. Even
bilingualism allegedly led directly to transsexuality. Had Vivian,
as the daughter of a German mother and an American father,
once bound her breasts for that reason? No, at no point had she
ever wanted to alter her body drastically, having learned rela-
tively early to conceive of it as a social effect instead, and she
also couldn't remember ever having even pondered a change of
anatomical gender. Now and again she may have allowed others
to mistake her for a boy, which she enjoyed, and while German
civil registry offices required given names with absolutely clear
gender determination, the ambiguous name Vivian actually

admitted of both gender attributions in the Anglophone world of the barracks area. She herself, however, had always been certain of her biological gender.

So far, so good. But what did that mean now? Before Vivian's fountain pen dried out: where did the subsets of anatomical and social gender lie? Why, precisely, could Luis Trenker not have been a lesbian, plain and simple? Frauke Stöver, thirty-one, had actually tacked up this flippant remark of her recalcitrant darling behind the mirror for herself. When in 1993 with Martina Navratilova's abdication entire bands of insolent sports reporters had augured the fresh ascent of female tennis players in sexy, frilly lingerie and womanly perfume, Vivian and Korinna had ended up—back then they hadn't yet met Frauke—in a violent dispute over the political assessment of underwear as such, with neither of the two being able to surmise which style may possibly have been that of the young Leni Riefenstahl. And what were union suits exactly? At that, Korinna had even written the controversial and in fact still feisty ancient woman in Upper Bavaria a letter concerning this matter—a juicy one, Vivian thought—to which—big surprise, Vivian said—she received no reply whatsoever. Telephone. Someone in Cuba wanted, in fluent German, to speak with a member of the Hanseatic Bremen tobacconist family that had at one point used this building in Baden for commercial purposes and was completely clueless that the beautiful old warehouse had been converted into a modern apartment building. The renter politely provided the unknown caller on the line with several telephone numbers, among them that of the building management, and had soon involved him in an instructive chat about Havana's current subculture as well as the—in her opinion—self-evident (less so in his) compatibility of communism and Catholicism.

Posters for Faust in the Untere Strasse. Would the gnomes of the Odenwald descend into the winding lanes of Heidelberg's old city to hear the primeval krautrock formation in concert? Rodney Atkinson had had in his possession a considerable collection of such odd West-German records, his young daughter very quickly developing reverent respect for legendary creatures like the Elektrolurch of the Odenwald shroom-smoking combo Guru Guru; Vivian could remember having smuggled a secret LP by the Cosmic Couriers into her childhood bedroom at a tender preschool age. Later, as a tomboy, after her regular evening forays with Joe, little Atkinson tackled very different records of her parents, never though—cross my heart, Hans—the awful Doors of her mother. The spherical sounds wafting through Hans Mühlenkamm's tiny attic apartment now brought back recollections of the smells of her early childhood, the dried fly-agaric-filled strongbox of her parents, who were embroiled in the Vietnam War. Hans was happy to see his downright vernally dressed female friend again already after so few days, for he was just as hopelessly in love with her as Frauke Stöver was. He had just shown Vivian his newest handbag, in crinkled electric-colored patent leather. Hans Mühlenkamm—and for Frauke therefore Monsieur Pompadour—collected historical purses since one of his favorite bands was named after this object, and his lady visitor, who had never owned such a sac herself, who basically abhorred purses, had been coquettish enough to issue a backhanded compliment about her friend's new find and his thereby increasing store. Mind you, the part-time physician's receptionist never appeared on the street with his purses, much less in the medical practice, but he had nailed them all neatly to the wall above his improvised bed. At the same time, there could be no talk of fetishism; all the diminutive clutch purses that in so-called real life had frightened ash-blond Hans, as so many men—and which not seldom had also, like Pandora's box, killed off love—served for him merely as a profane illustration of a hedonistic sonic trace called house music.

Meanwhile Vivian's gaze had been ranging over her admirer's disheveled berth and finally came to rest on a book lying on a pillow and bearing the title Critical Male Studies, subtitle: New Approaches in Gender Theory. Hansi had bought this light reading in a men's bookstore, and it constituted in his mind a first male contribution to the previously female domain of gender studies. Vivian had read an anonymous discussion of this reader in a new Munich magazine lying around in her women's bookstore in which—with good reason, Hans concurred—someone's attempt here to develop a distinct, decidedly male perspective toward this objective social problem of domination had been fundamentally criticized: a standpoint, albeit a minority one, that was even represented in the compendium itself. Also worth reading, Hans said, was an essay about man's so-called womb envy— which at least ought to be given priority over the ubiquitously discussed penis envy—which Freud had proverbially strapped on women, and which—Vivian Atkinson added with a degree of condescension—had in fact unleashed entire world wars. Even the naming rights by which the husband may at least affix the paternal family tree to his offspring is of course, Hans said, nothing more than (pardon the expression) an intellectual birth of womb envy. Sounds logical, Vivian remarked, nevertheless knitting her brows. She considered for a moment whether in the final analysis revanchist attitudes again must be hiding behind such theses. The twenty-four-year-old asked her host to please photocopy this text for her sometime when he had a chance and arose from his foam mattress. Internally she was rather unsettled about Operation Critical Male Studies and a bit worried, too, that Hans might frivolously betray his prior, ultimately honorable autodidactic feminism and cross over to the male side, which was time and again devastatingly concerned with its power. Was it scheming of her, therefore, when she planted a kiss on the crown of his head and immediately invited him to have Ethiopian with her for lunch?

A few hours later—the sun had already set and winter had made yet another surprise return—Vivian was again sitting at her workspace, being too lightly dressed for an evening of flânerie anyway, bringing a word to paper with her fountain pen here, hammering an entire sentence into her laptop there. The reflective jacket of a GDR road maintenance crew draped over his shoulders, Hansi Mühlenkamm had, in the end, strolled by himself up to the castle ruins whose rosy sandstone—most picturesquely laid to ashes by the French Sun King—had inspired many a German Romantic to typically German sentimentalities of doom. Had the castle been triumphantly defended that once, even Hölderlin wouldn't have been able to bawl his eyes out about it so fashionably, or so ran Ilse Schoolmistress' commentary to this effect; why then even, the collegian speculated quietly to herself, did droll Hans feel drawn to the old red exploded powder tower whenever he had just linked arms with his female friend? Why thousands upon thousands of Japanese and American tourists? Mark Twain? Sissi? Aphex Twin? The Source label? Out of a longing for death? Lovesickness? Mineralogically catalyzed melancholy? Lines of inquiry with which Vivian had once again ended up near her (from this perspective, just as banged-up) red and yellow porphyry rock above Schriesheim, which dozed gray in the dark of the breaking night. Vivian Atkinson's Screen Saver again. If she had let her admirer dash off again, then at least a couple clever questions ought to be hewed into the liquid crystal.

How had it been able to come to pass that the masculine, as a deafeningly blaring principle of identity formation, had merely granted the feminine the quiet supporting role as its diffuse Other? Or rather: did not the quality of the feminine lie precisely in its identity-subverting function? A political promise, so to speak, that transcends the theoretical? And when would women be able to make good on it finally? Would men, too, take part in this project? Hans Mühlenkamm, for instance, whose dandyish way of life subordinated being to semblance, might possibly make a pretty Marianne of the feminist cultural revolution—a crying shame, Vivian thought, that Hansi's high-fashion-laden body is capable of exerting so little sexual attraction on me. She called him quickly and asked whether he had gotten home safely. Clothed in a Steigenberger Hotel bathrobe, Hans was sitting in his kitchen, having just brewed himself some linden blossom tea. It's been sleeting for hours in Edingen, too, said the brunette, now swathed in one of Frauke's comfortable lumberjack shirts, in attempted consolation to her buddy. On top of that Hans' stomach hurt; for the first time in his life he had partaken of Abyssinian for a main meal. But as a part-time physician's receptionist, he had a kind of tea in his pantry to combat this too, so then, Hansi Pompadour, have a nice evening; and with that a rapid return to the half-asleep, cozily whirring Texas Instrument. German Gemootlichkeit, Vivian said quoting her daddy with a smirk as she crossed through her large, dimly lit room to her work area, a battered and possibly historically valuable tabletop from the Palatinate Rococo that her mother had scared up, which rested on four legs that a former lover—then as now a house music DJ in Ludwigshafen—had built for her from discarded twelve-inch vinyls. How many times now had Hans crept around the four pitch-black, auspiciously lustrous towers of records, but to this very day Vivian had not permitted him to raise the Rococo plank that sealed them; he would assuredly hit paydirt, and Vivian couldn't continue working on an underlay that was wobbly or too low. There were still other visitors who envied her the antique pink, ornate table. Its owner herself felt her desk somewhat excessive but for various reasons couldn't help but cherish it; one of which being the reading of General de Maistre's two masterworks, just as sentimental as they were deeply affecting, A Journey Around My Room as well as A Nocturnal Journey Around My Room, during her light-hearted move into the tobacco warehouse.

The following morning Vivian received an excited phone call from Korinna—which in recent weeks, particularly since she had begun dating Frauke, was a rare occurrence (only Frauke called her persistently)—and Korinna reported that Genoveva had been arrested, that a room in the shared apartment in Handschuhsheim—for how long she wasn't even sure herself—had freed up. Turn on your fax machine, Viv, and shortly thereafter the following headline noodled its way out of the machine: Tear Gas Used on Store Clerks. Handschuhsheim Teacher Claims Persecution. As one could distill from the corresponding newspaper article, Genoveva had stuck six ridiculous deutschmarks' worth of wares from a Weinheim supermarket into a plastic bag she had brought with her, which she then tucked away in her leopard-print satchel. It read further that the forty-two-year-old school instructor all of a sudden, and supposedly to protect herself from, quote, a feared chemical attack, drew a so-called K.O. spray from her bag and sprayed three supermarket employees, who promptly tumbled aside, stunned out of their minds, and had to make their way immediately to the nearest hospital. What kind of chemical attack, Vivian asked with astonishment after she had retrieved the handset, no clue, replied Korinna, who had already packed all her things to move in with Frauke, Pat, and Ilse.

Shoplifting alone would have been nothing special in Vivian's Bohemian circles; Hans, for instance, at apprentice age, had even cobbled together his very own gay science from pocketing by selective snatching. Genoveva's lunatic demeanor upon her arrest, though, provided food for thought. Vivian recalled that Frauke had frequently related the monstrously rapturous conspiracy theories of her two roommates from Darmstadt, among which the one where the CIA had developed the AIDS pathogen was still the most plausible. Pat, for example, had installed a so-called fixed crow's nest above the Dossenheim rock quarries in the hard-to-reach undergrowth, from which she spied out—predominantly at night, with the help of diverse optical analysis gadgets—the truly staggeringly foul-smelling Baden Aniline and Soda Factory (BASF) on the Western horizon. It stinks—as even Gerlinde Atkinson had always phrased it—whenever the Patrick Henry Village ended up in the odor trail of the heavy emitter BASF during a westerly wind. Then the wind had always changed directions suddenly, and it stank in the Pfälzerwald for the French occupation forces who had taken over the IG-Farben giant from the Nazis and controlled it until the fifties—local history for Vivian's German playmates Martin and Torsten. But not everything that the Ludwigshafen factory produced stank to high heaven, a large portion—one could read regularly in the newspaper—being channeled straight into the Rhine. Genoveva and Pat weren't in fact professed ecologists at all; what, then, could this drivel about a chemical attack have meant? Vivian thought it remarkable that Korinna seemed not to waste a single thought about this, thus coming off as positively intent on moving in with Frauke and her two old prunes right away.

Korinna, the fifth daughter of a Karlsruhe high magistrate, had always been a bit peculiar. A few years ago, following Michel Foucault to an exaggerated degree—who had articulated that sex is a cruel, fictive instrument of domination incapable of developing any kind of critical force against the current regime—she had (temporarily at least, but over a longer period of time) not been in love with anyone at all. Having sliced open an avocado for herself, Vivian was now sitting cross-legged on the floor spooning it out, under the large map of Ohio (which had hung in her childhood bedroom) and in front of a pile of rare old books she considered consulting for scientific purposes because of various significant passages—The Science of Woman: On Woman's Well-Being and Man's Power, Hattenheim: Psychokratie, 1927; In Search of Charm, Rüschlikon-Zürich, 1964; Helga, Wiesbaden, 1968; The American Woman 1988–89: A Status Report, New York, 1988; Luise Büchner's Women and Their Vocation, Darmstadt, 1855, a precious loan from Genoveva, the arrested secondary-school teacher who had written her dissertation on Goethe's Darmstadt friend, the suicide victim Merck. And a two-volume reprint of the Yearbook for Intermediate Sexual Types which appeared from 1899 to 1923, published on behalf of Magnus Hirschfeld's Scientific-Humanitarian Committee. Important, the college girl found, placing Hirschfeld with his antipode Weininger, who had suggested in 1903 that the sum of two lovers' hair lengths had to

be exactly equal in size. Korinna, everyone thought, had pretty
weirdly crimped hair, appreciated manly women, and in com-
memoration of the great Navratilova drove a white Tatra sedan
from Czechoslovakia. As a McJob (her words), she had posed
last summer as a slinky model for a dodgy community college
course called Perfect Girl Photos that Frauke Stöver, in yet again
nearly perfect miscalculation of its ulterior motives, had taken.
Frauke loved feminine women and actually wanted to learn how
to take pretty pictures of them. Naturally she had not reckoned
with an asshole as colossal as the Eberbach community college
instructor Gisbert Gimmel, who, hour after hour, primarily in
light of his new photo model—the old one was to be deported
next week to Bosnia-Herzegovina—let himself get carried away
by ever greater, not solely technical impertinences against womankind, upon which alone he had been directing his throbbingly
erect lenses—zoom lenses—in exceptionally subjective fashion.
Interestingly enough, Korinna had quit on precisely the day (the
third day of class) that Frauke had fallen in love with her.

Both women, each for herself, hated Gimmel with every fiber of
their being, but they had thought they could derive their own
respective use from the course. The topic of the hour in question
after which Korinna was never to return to the wobbly podium
of the girl photographer was called, quite innocuously: Outdoor
Shots by the Water. Korinna, a daughter from a good family, wore
a solid-colored T-shirt belonging to her recently bygone lover
Jens, and Gimmel taught the (all except for Frauke) mustached
course participants that they must pay special attention to the
nipples of their models, for these ought to stand out—the teacher
said at the chalkboard just next to the rusty sink—ought to show
as clearly as possible under the T-shirt. Pointed to his illustra-

tive model, turned on the tap, held a yogurt carton underneath, and sloshed it on poor Korinna's chest. Even the very thought of cold water, Gimmel boasted, having taught this course of studies yearly since 1981, can cause girls' nipples to become hard within seconds. In his studio in Eberbach he is capable, he said, of simulating the great outdoors with props deployed most economically; however, to lend the bared bodies of girls the deceivingly genuine appearance of being in the real outdoors, Gimmel said, it is sometimes necessary to use the following trick; the Eberbacher winked: just before shooting the photograph, the photographer rubs the model with an ice cubelet—the obese Gimmel actually said cubelet—across the areolae of her breasts. Question interposed from among the participants: how is it even possible to get a model, sexy like Korinna, to open up, or rather to break her will (Frauke's heckling interjection: unwillingness). Gimmel: just yesterday two girlies, cute as a button, ran past me at the Heidelberg swimming pool. I didn't have to do anything but put down my bottle of tanning oil, follow them, and convince them of my honest, that is, honorable intentions. Lots of girls these days are interested in becoming popular, and every lady, Gimmel said, feels flattered as soon as she is chased after. Visit beaches—Gisbert Gimmel had fixed his gaze on, of all people, Frauke—or just have a look at those young ladies—Gimmel was actually scratching his balls—who work in the cosmetic departments of large department stores. Behind the Eberbacher's back, Korinna had meanwhile turned away crossly and wrung out her wet T-shirt as well as she could over the dirty sink of the community college.

In the eighteenth century there had once been a whole shipload of people from the Odenwald who hadn't disembarked on Pennsylvania's shore, but who, because the destitute backwoodsmen hadn't been able to pay ransom for their passage, were sent back to the Old World straightaway in the same floating coffin. Gisbert Gimmel from Eberbach was descended from these people. Even the Eisenhauers had once set off from the Heidelberg area—more precisely, from Eiterbach in the southern Odenwald—for the New World, and one of Rodney Atkinson's superiors in the Patrick Henry Village was a direct relative of President Eisenhower. There ought, however, to be Eisenhowers from Schriesheim as well, where the central uplands rise out of the lowland plains. An American major named William Beiderlinden, descendant of an emigrated Rhenish Vormärz revolutionary, thus supposedly preserved the city of Heidelberg from devastating bombardment in the final days of the Second World War. Whereupon an Odenwald shroom smoker by the name of Werner Pieper had, in the eighties, tried in vain to find out why Heidelberg, the future European headquarters of the U.S. Army, had so very blatantly been spared from all Allied carpet bombs. Pieper had developed various theories to this effect in his brochure Heidelberg at the Zero Hour, because apparently the diaries of the Seventh Army had gone missing in—of all places—the Pentagon; the most probable of these was that Dwight D. Eisenhower, the Supreme Commander of U.S. military forces in Germany in 1945, had wanted to protect the historical hatchery of his house. After the gratifying capitulation of the German Wehrmacht, the Yanks requisitioned the so-called Landfried House not far from the train station, P. J. Landfried's old tobacco factory where cigarettes and cigars from local as well as Turkish tobacco had been produced; today Heidelberg's Child Protective Services and two budget supermarkets were located in it. In the immediate postwar period cigarettes had—like chewing gum or nylon stockings—in fact become a fixed currency in occupied Germany, and while BASF fabricated

Perlon (the IG-Farben equivalent of American nylon) in the neighboring French sector at full steam, the GIs in the Landfried House were so generous in giving out American cigarettes that the Germans soon only smoked Virginian tobaccos anymore, requiring in the end that even the old Edingen tobacco warehouse be converted into an apartment building.

The beginning of a physical, romantic relationship between the lesbian Frauke Stöver and the bisexual Korinna Kohn had still taken several months (and also Vivian's persistently adamant recalcitrance toward Frauke's advances). At the time the platinum blonde hadn't even begun shooting perfect girl photos yet, instead turning her whole photographic attentions, as she had for years already, to the documentation, in ideologically critical detail, of boys beating the shit out of each other, making her, at just fifteen or sixteen years old, a point of discussion on the numerous schoolyards of the Hanseatic city of Lübeck back at the beginning of the eighties; it was pretty obvious how all boykind was attuned to absolute nothing but contestation, the bloodthirsty erection of rifles, the violent ejaculation of munition. In Hansi's recapitulated theses on womb envy this meant that the son's failure-bound identification with the life-giving mother caused him to degenerate into a death machine. See also the adult male's dichotomous philosophy of global annihilation: femininity equals nature, masculinity equals culture.

It hadn't been Frauke's idea for her girlish lover to move in with her, and Korinna hadn't even lived in Handschuhsheim for a week before Genoveva was released from custody. On which point the current headline of the North Baden tabloid read: Chemical Clubbing of Clerks. Teacher Unfit to Stand Trial? As it turned out, Genoveva had complained to the criminal and judicial authorities about all those conspiracies she found herself exposed to daily since her mother participated in the primary development of liquid crystal at Merck, Darmstadt. Time and again they had poured chemicals on her head, she claimed; everywhere terror is dumped upon her by the proverbial bucket. Furthermore, it is particularly fashionable in Weinheim for food to be sprayed—by the bank, the accused claimed—with chemicals, for which reason she had put her purchases in the supermarket into an opaque plastic bag as a precaution before checking out. To be able to defend herself against the nasty daily chemical attacks, she carries a small Soviet tear gas club with her at all times. Who (besides the two clerks of course) would ever be so hard-hearted as to blame her if she had finally made use of it for the first time, the pedagogue concluded her verbose self-defense. In the near future a sworn expert witness in forensic medicine in Handschuhsheim was supposed to turn up to adjudge the degree of her criminal liability. Naturally, it fit exactly into Genoveva's system that her political case was answered by a pathologizing psychiatrist. But now first get the hell out of here, Korinna Kohn. Pat Meier, in a speckled camouflage outfit that Genoveva hadn't seen before, loitered about sheepishly in the corridor, seeming for the moment to be embarrassed for having allowed Korinna to move into the private digs of her comrade without a second thought. The relationship of the two women from Darmstadt had cooled considerably in the course of recent years anyway, and not twenty-four hours after her release had Genoveva Weckherlin vanished, without a trace and beyond reach. Because of this, Pat like the other three gave no sign of being distressed and henceforth spent all the more time in her crow's nest while Korinna and Frauke were once again able to spread themselves out comfortably over two rooms.

Ilse was sick with jealousy, and the neurologist showed his face perhaps four or five times and never again after that.

Around the middle of April almost all the trees had turned green, and Vivian Atkinson was sitting in an equally green pantsuit at her electronic notebook. She had bought this terrycloth garment in an African American junk shop two visits ago to her daddy, not far from the Pentagon, primarily because she very much liked the giant zipper with which the tight-fitting one-piece was symmetrically closed. A classmate of Vivian's had gotten so used to saying African American that he constantly referred to his Nigerian paperboy—in spite of being frequently corrected— as his African American paperboy. In actual fact the glamour and gloom of the USA lay immediately adjacent to each other in Washington; Lincoln's murderer himself had jumped from the back window of the posh Ford's Theatre directly into the sketchy Rat Alley. Having, being, and seeming; Vivian Atkinson had been sure to remember these three vocabulary words since last semester. Under which circumstances (to whose detriment was clear) had the notion of seeming, which is to say, of Beautiful Semblance, namely that of the domesticated fair sex, been linked with the surface, the purely external, and this latter word once again with negative terms like masquerade or deception? Or rather: why did being, associated with the masculine principle, represent allegedly non-misleading, so-called real existence? A typical male chimera, the collegiate woman found; what, however, was to be thought of that purportedly feminist vision, according to which there is a chance to subvert the political body in precisely this duality of masculine being and feminine semblance?

Where did this loophole beckon that promised the ability to slip through the various fingers of the fatal dictates of fashion? And would Vivian Atkinson, twenty-four, five-foot-eleven, even really want to escape the sweeping canon of fashions? Hadn't the participatory observation of fashion simultaneously been offering the very best opportunity for political orientation for two centuries now? Walter Benjamin had written that fashion is the eternal return of the new; in spite of this, would there be motives of salvation in fashion? Clearly, yes. Thus the master's candidate ruminated while playing with the oversized ring on her African American zipper, lost in thought. No, Vivian was no uncritical follower of fashion, and actually, she thought, political dissidence could indeed be expressed in a vicious Benjaminian circle by aesthetic difference. To what extent, however, this individual explicitness was in the position to lead to social reception history she couldn't say right now; the army brat wasn't even sure whether she would step outside onto the sallow streets of sleepy Edingen in her green pantsuit. And why in the world was a women's suit called a pantsuit whereas a man's suit was simply called a suit? Because pants were originally a feminine article of clothing? And if the blouse was supposed to be the female counterpart to the male shirt, for whom then had the shirtwaist dress actually been tailored? At the end of the day, hadn't Hermann Göring's uniforms also been one hundred percent drag? Magnus Hirschfeld had learned that officers especially liked to slip into women's clothes outside their barracks. In light of all these proliferating lines of inquiry, Vivian decided to drop by her quirky professor's office hours again sometime soon.

A few days later she was sitting on her American mountain bike and pedaling the four miles to Heidelberg along the southern bank of the Neckar. In Wieblingen the student changed from the bike path to the old Bundesstrasse 37, the highway connecting Heidelberg with Mannheim (actually Mosbach with Kaiserslautern), bought herself candy at a kiosk, and biked further toward Heidelberg where she soon passed the Ernst Walz Bridge, the thermal baths, and the clinics of the university founded in 1386; these Vivian had once inspected in conjunction with her lively interest for the SPC, the legendary Socialist Patients' Collective of the years 1968 to 1976. When Mark Twain had come here for an extended period in 1878, Germany had borne the reputation of the world's hospital. Not that all Germans had been sick; they had instead erected a cozy spa town in nearly every corner of their empire for the international convalescent-elite. Today there was not only a Mark-Twain-Strasse in Heidelberg, but also a Mark Twain Village—abbreviated MTV among the GIs—in Rohrbach's former Nazi barracks, and Mother Atkinson had once taken a cute picture of her only child in front of the barracks sign that identified Twain as a nine-time visitor of Heidelberg. At that time Vivian had still been an innocent schoolgirl, Gerlinde Atkinson by contrast a fervent admirer of Twain's, especially his revolutionary remarks on masturbation. As Vivian now pedaled through Heidelberg's historic district, the most random recollections popped into her memory. Her ruinous job at the secondhand store of the German-American Women's Association, for example; or how she had once come upon a throng awaiting Swedish Queen Silvia during a stroll through the city with her grandma who had traveled from Hanau.

An uncanny hissing could suddenly be heard emanating from one of the sales stands glued to the side of the Church of the Holy Spirit. At that, Grandma Hanau—who was so named because in

Cincinnati there was still a Grandma Cincinnati—had stepped into the dimness of the narrow booth, undaunted by death, and had been able to make out the heavily panting store owner leaning against a shelf with porcelain figures. Come in, she had said with only a deathlike rattle, thrusting a stack of Queen Silvia postcards into both the grandma's and her little granddaughter's hand. Organize them was the nervous asthmatic woman's next order, for between the portraits of the monarch—born Silvia Renate Sommerlath in Heidelberg in 1943, head hostess for the Olympic Games in Munich in 1972—were stuck countless silly motifs that didn't belong here at all and were thus to be sorted by Vivian along with her grandma: pipe-smoking dogs with gamsbart hats, pretty gypsy women, Adolf Hitler. Grandma Hanau had become totally soaked with sweat in no time at all; the tourist rip-offs in the shelf behind the chalk-white business woman had clinked balefully. Only at the moment when Silvia of Sweden, née Sommerlath, had already come within sight with her whole retinue had Vivian and her energetic grandmother completed their volunteer work, and without a word the heavily beleaguered sutler had plunged—with her last ounce of strength as well as, of course, her precious cards—into the dense royalist tumult of people.

Only once had Vivian visited her grandmother in Hanau, a fascinatingly dismal city whose nuclear industrial undertakings continually made it the subject of headlines. Grandma Hanau actually always preferred to travel to the Patrick Henry Village in order to withdraw again into her contaminated widow's apartment loaded down with barbecue sauces, synthetic whipped cream, and perfumed root beer, which she, rudimentarily acquainted with American English, called mein Wurzelbier. And here was Vivian's professor already, as agreed, waving his little cap on the street corner. He had again preferred not to hold his office hours with the interested American-German student at the university, but in the fresh air. Vivian Atkinson chained her mountain bike to a street lamp, promenaded down the lanes along the Neckar beside her politely chattering instructor, and crossed to the other bank, the Neckarwiesen, with the small passenger ferry. The gangly docent had a beige-colored book sticking out of his likewise beige-colored linen jacket, which turned out to be the English edition of the memoirs of the hermaphrodite and suicide victim Herculine Barbin, born in 1838, found dead in February of 1868, introduced in January of 1980 by Michel Foucault, whose famous foreword to the English edition the nutty professor now began to read aloud with his typically ataxic pronunciation: Do we truly need a true sex? Vivian, standing directly at the water's edge, angling with a fresh willow branch in the brown water of the Neckar, laughed aloud: if that doesn't get to the heart of the matter, and fished her own far too many questions out of her backpack. But Michel Foucault—whom Hans, because of his often detached-seeming coldness, had pigeonholed right next to Niklas Luhmann and whom Ilse, a Habermas pupil of the Jewish faith, even chose to lump together with Carl Schmitt—had also formulated an exposition of more than ten pages to his suggestive question, which it had not even occurred to Vivian's professor not to stutter off as well. The college girl vaguely recalled having read in Nancy Fraser that Foucault had regrettably been incapable of rebutting the specious Habermasian accusations against him. Modernity versus postmodernity, dialectical critique versus negativistic critique, humanism, rejection of humanism; should politically progressive action be permitted from one of these platforms in 1997? Isn't that actually from Betty Barclay? A middle-aged passerby had dropped these words, at which the lecturer even lowered

Herculine Barbin into his lap in order to rivet his scientifically august gaze upon Vivian's skirt hem in question.

When the American textile company Betty Barclay had ended its business in the USA, it had been reincarnated at the edge of the Odenwald near Heidelberg, West Germany, as Betty Barclay Kleiderfabrik, GmbH, current address: 69226 Nussbach, Heidelberger Strasse 9. Thousands of North Baden workers, men and women alike, had found employment there, some of Vivian's girlfriends and boyfriends even having worked part-time there. The historic miniskirt that she wore today hailed from the house of Betty Barclay in fact, but the brunette just answered brusquely: wrong, sir, from Herculine Barbin. Afterward she was irritated that she had not heckled the learned gentleman—now leaning on a river navigation sign not much farther downstream and repeatedly staring over at her—regarding her question about the shirtwaist dress. But for a brief moment the professor had twisted his wan face into a kind of crooked smile and then continued on: Brought up as a poor and deserving girl in a milieu that was almost exclusively feminine and strongly religious, Herculine Barbin, who was called Alexina by her familiars, was finally recognized as being truly a young man. Judith Butler had later found fault with the fact that in the final analysis Michel Foucault still always assumed bodies which preceded their cultural inscriptions. Vivian Atkinson, finding it remarkable that the noun hermaphrodite, at least in German, possessed a masculine article, once again recalled Nancy Fraser's defense of Foucault against Habermas: humanism had emerged as a central hinge for the pejoratively dichotomous oppression of women; for it pitted the mind against the body, understanding against feeling, will against nature, and thus male autonomy against domesticable femininity, projected as its Other. Even the docent sitting on his rock found that humanism, beyond both Habermas and Foucault, would have to be assessed in light of feminism and nurtured anew like Betty Barclay in Heidelberg. And yet: When Alexina composed her memoirs, she was not far from suicide; for herself, she was still without a definite sex, but she was deprived of the delights she experienced in not having one, or in not entirely having the same sex as the girls among whom she lived and whom she loved and desired so much. Two underage female canoeists, perhaps even male canoeists, who had watered their boat nearby and now paddled past Vivian and her professor, waved over affably to them. Björk's Venus as a Boy rattled from a portable cassette player. And a few kilometers upstream lay Ziegelhausen with its textile fabric museum, founded by Betty Barclay's new German manager Max Berk. Had this man potentially also developed, invented, or discovered the shirtwaist dress?

When Vivian was still little and had heard the word unisex from her forward mother Gerlinde for the first time, she initially thought it was about sexual practices on campus. Look at my blue jeans, Gerlinde Atkinson had declared, taking up a goofily salacious pose, blue jeans are unisex. But Vivian had long since noticed that the fly of her mother's pants opened to the left, and that of Rodney Atkinson's, conversely, to the right, and the granny from Cincinnati even wore jeans in the family photo album whose fly was sewn, wholly impractically, onto the side on the hips. All of that—Vivian had agreed with herself back then—still can't be unisex; no more than these skirts for men that pass through the magazines every few years, stiff, cone-shaped wraps as if from cheap Italian gladiator films. No, the humanist guild of fashion designers had always, one-sidedly, made sure to celebrate the ever-so-small difference with dichotomous repression; no man had ever made his career in a pant-skirt, not to mention in a shirtwaist dress. On the other hand, what was meant by the chic men's suits tailored to a woman's figure, with which thirty-year-old women cruised through the executive floors of various businesses? Had the globe thereby become more masculine or feminine? No gentleman would ever fit into such a woman's suit, Vivian's professor nitpicked, and how are the things even buttoned around? He himself had worn only light Tuscan summer suits since 1982.

Wrinkly, fusty ones with stains, Vivian thought with amusement in a pale-blue miniskirt, almost daring to regale her university lecturer, who had suddenly become personal, with how she had bound her breasts during puberty. But only almost. Do you know Anna Muthesius? The master's candidate did not know Anna Muthesius. The professor commenced thus: that she had written a book in 1903 called Woman's Own Dress, worth reading, in which she appealed to contemporary womankind to choose clothing independent of the fashion dictated by the patriarchy, which would enhance their respective physical merits or, as the case may be, mitigate any extant handicaps. The definition of these qualities, of course, resided with the world of men, in 1903 as in 1997, Vivian added with interest, but a nice concept nonetheless: Woman's Own Dress. Especially as it superseded the concept of the reform dress, Ms. Atkinson. What had actually become of the Berlin Society for the Betterment of Women's Dress from back then? All of them, ultimately, models condemned to failure from the childhood years of social democracy, Vivian's teacher summarized from atop his boulder. The student was thoroughly aware that her brassiere was showing from underneath her T-shirt;

already at a young age she had learned from the Italian-American sex bomb Madonna that taking to a bra could unleash a virtually emancipatory brisance. Even the maturing schoolgirls of the Bunsen Gymnasium—until the seventies strictly reserved for boys—conspicuously wore their (to use Anna Muthesius' term) physical-asset-enhancing bras while camping out in the grass right beside the student and her professor, doing their homework at volume ten. Vocabulary to be untangled etymologically in this regard: atomic boobs, bikini; Vivian wrote them down with a pen on the back of her left hand. And to what extent, if at all, had the historical topless movement contributed to the advancement of women? A brassiere, the professor noted—just think of Godard—signifies anything but the opposite of bared breasts, of course.

From what point on were breasts even considered bared? Korinna Kohn, whom Vivian (just home) had on the line, had been working on this problem for some time now, in particular with regard to her investigation, beginning with Hermann Schmitz, of colonized body islands. On her regular, empirical excursions Korinna had gotten to know women, supposedly housewives, who in the Mannheim Rosengarten with bared torso and nothing but rubberized stamps stuck to their nipples had not felt naked in any respect, as well as female artists, professional dancers, who had sidestepped the striptease ban of certain establishments with a string between their cheeks that fixed a little rhinestone star on their mons veneris. Speaking of colonized body islands, Korinna—Vivian cut off her animated classmate, believing to hear a detonation coming from the rock quarries—I desperately need materials on the Bikini Atoll. OK, sure, right away, the fairly reliable magistrate's daughter, about three years her senior, promised promptly, but then she simply didn't come over with the

copies, making excuses about this and that, even about the failure
of the postal system. When three weeks later the inquisitive student from the Edingen tobacco warehouse finally wanted to pick
up the files promised her in person in Handschuhsheim, Korinna
Kohn, completely unexpectedly, burst into bitter tears at the door
to the apartment, and shortly thereafter both women were walking together through the Odenwald. The bisexual tennis player
was very obviously going stir-crazy in Handschuhsheim, but at
first there was no getting her to say a single word about what was
feeding this sudden gloom. Instead she spasmodically recounted
to her worried girl friend the talkshow television program of a
single day. SAT 1, 11 a.m.: Trouble with the Help. Noon: Your
Poverty Makes Me Sick. 1 p.m.: Why Does No One Want Me? Pro
Sieben, 2 p.m.: I'm the Best in Bed. RTL, 2 p.m.: Everyone Wants
to Sleep with Me. 4 p.m.: Wild Young Things, Ambitious, Successful, Erotic. And so on and so forth.

Only beyond the misty Heiligenberg when the Nazi open-air
stage came into view did Korinna move from generalities—that
namely, according to Mona Lisa, the women's program on ZDF
(even though according to current knowledge a young man had
posed for Leonardo's paintings), fifteen million virtuous German
women excreted daily and by the ton so-called estrogenic contaminants—those who take the pill—Korinna (who didn't take
the pill anymore) explained to Vivian, who had seated herself
in the mossy round of the amphitheater and didn't take it anymore either, because of which (for no such efficient wastewater
treatment facility could cope with this) the entire, not just environment (which is the usual word), but rather the world itself,
says ZDF, is becoming feminized—to the particular, that namely
a feminine character from the Po Basin by the name of Angela

(who was actually named Angelo) had been working in the lesbian pizzeria in Handschuhsheim for a few weeks and had sidled up to Frauke when she held an event (to which Vivian had not gone) on the Feast of the Ascension, Father's Day, about mariolatry, Madonna, and Lourdes (which was also the baptismal name of Ciccone's daughter). The androgynous creature kissed Frauke's ass by projecting onto the wall, completely unbidden, some faded slides of northern Italian Marx-Engels monuments and finally striking up the Ave Maria with the entire bar. Who would have thought that, of all of us, Frauke Stöver would be the first to get married, wailed Korinna Kohn, a name technically of Jewish derivation, but what Jew in the Federal Republic of Germany could have ascended to the rank of high magistrate in Karlsruhe?

This had been one of Vivian's first thoughts after Korinna had introduced herself to her; but now she was just as gobsmacked as her comrade that Frauke and Angela—in this case Angelo—had gotten engaged only three days after the Father's Day in question, on Mother's Day 1997: that very same night Frauke and Angela rocked across the Canal Grande. The leaseholder of the pub, a resolute Magdeburger named Heidemarie who, in keeping with her dialectical style of dress, called herself Heidemario, had assumed the sad role of notifying Korinna, and it had also been Heidemarie who had subsequently carried the collapsed bisexual in both arms to her ex-boyfriend, the industrious law student Jens. Jens in turn, in a fatal miscalculation of Korinna's condition, had then penetrated her all night long from every angle until, when Jens was finally no longer able to continue, she called a taxi and had herself driven home at daybreak. Frauke not there, Pat still with her infrared gadgets, and Ilse had to leave early in the morning—Korinna wailed, her whole body trembling, and leaned her crimped head of curls on Vivian's shoulder—so all my desperate tension only drained away when of all people you, the compulsorily heterosexual Atkinson, stood at the door. Vivian, in the presence of the imitation Heidelberger Thingspiel site, awkwardly brushed a strand of hair from her brow: did they literally say estrogenic contaminants on ZDF, Korinna?

Over the Pentecost holiday Hans Mühlenkamm had been at his parents' in Offenbach, and the entire Mühlenkamm family—which also included, besides Hans and his parents, his sister Grete—had, as they did every year, undertaken an excursion into downtown Frankfurt to be present at the so-called Stadtgeläut, the great Frankfurt city-wide pealing of the bells, Frankfurt and Heidelberg being the two most Americanized cities in Germany, though in contrary ways. When they passed the Paulskirche, the Christusglocke, or Christ Bell, weighing nearly two tons and cast in 1830, having sounded in 1848 for the first German National Assembly, coincidentally loosed itself from its ball bearing, plunged toward the concrete floor of the historic tower, and was, with unmusical din, shattered to pieces by the eight-and-a-half-ton Bürgerglocke swinging below it, whereupon not only was the entire bell cage shifted, but the Dankesglocke—which only tipped the scales at just over a thousand pounds—also jammed in the timbers. The day after, Vivian had read in the newspaper—which a love-struck neighbor used to leave for her on her doormat every morning after his usually hectic departure for BASF—that the likewise devastated director of the German Bell Museum in Castle Greifenstein had proclaimed that now with the Frankfurt Christusglocke a, quote, German national monument is destroyed. But as if that weren't enough, Viv, Hans Mühlenkamm continued: for below in the nave there was growing unrest about an unpopular traveling exhibition on the crimes of the German Wehrmacht during the Second World War. In no time I had gotten into a scrap with my parents about the lousy connotations of German citizenship. Even as a child I was disgusted whenever my grandfather from Koblenz would stop his Mercedes-Benz to take scores of ridiculous photographs of Grete and me in front of martial monuments of so-called German division or unification—fearsomely petrified mercenaries, the sinister prince Bismarck, the armor-clad Kaiser Wilhelm on horseback—in front of only perfunctorily abraded swastikas or milestones, massively chiseled into granite, showing the distance to Kaliningrad or Wrocław. Do you have any clue, Vivian, how it feels to be a German citizen? The old bell had hardly been shattered for a moment when my father—an active member of the Green Party, mind you, a union member since 1966, mind you—began to jump on this very bandwagon by babbling on about the bitterly irreplaceable nature of the national monument, just as he had at breakfast about the unavoidability of forced cuts in social services; you can imagine that the Mühlenkamms' Pentecost holiday went to hell in a handbasket within a few short minutes and that I only came to when I was sitting on the train home and paging through the men's Vogue I had quickly pilfered at the Frankfurt central train station.

But then Jessica, a nine-person girls' saxophone orchestra, plopped down in the open car, and I couldn't concentrate another second on my reading, Hansi Pompadour said from a Mannheim telephone booth on his way to a club called HD 800: the women— I find it hard to say girls—all wore unkempt updos, sweaters, and garish elastic pants on their legs; I wouldn't have wanted a single one of their repulsive handbags to be given to me. In the train car, which was full to bursting, they wagged the newest edition of a tabloid hysterically, in whose gossip column—which they actually even had the nerve to read aloud to the poor conductor—the main item was a Bonn gala event including Jessica. Above it was flaunted, visible for all passengers, a large color photo of the lady band, insipidly dressed to the hilt, in front of nothing but old horny sods, the female musicians—probably already thirtysomethings, Hans said—tooting around on their brass instruments, in garish plastic miniskirts and stiletto heels. One of them, somewhere around the Biblis Nuclear Power Plant, returned from the payphone and reported breathlessly that her own mother had not recognized her the night before on television, no, what a difference such professional makeup and real TV-show costumes made indeed. Some like it hot was the succinct commentary of Vivian Atkinson, who preferred to know who was DJing tonight in HD 800. Of his sister Grete—a stewardess for Austrian Airlines—who apparently still lived at home with her parents in Offenbach, the dainty physician's receptionist had never actually given a more detailed account; this too, Vivian thought, was worth an occasional inquiry. But today she wanted to go dancing in Mannheim, the sinful grid city, where the Rhine and the Neckar flow sabulously into one another.

The following morning Frauke Stöver stood in front of the tobacco warehouse and buzzed her friend Vivian Atkinson awake. Under her arm the woman from Travemünde was carrying a stack of long-playing records by Sylvester, RuPaul, the New York Dolls, the Leaving Trains, Wayne Country, Divine, as well as several other testimonials, immortalized on vinyl, of male constructions of femininity on one's own body. Into her bottle-green leather jacket was tucked a copy of the film Paris Is Burning by Jennie

Livingston, which Frauke had already rewound to the beginning when the GI-daughter Atkinson, until just moments ago half-asleep, stepped rather jauntily from the shower; in spite of her hot liaison with Angela, Stöver had still insisted on bursting into Vivian's bathroom to dry off her crush's back. Shot between 1987 and 1989 in Spanish Harlem's drag houses, Jennie Livingston's documentary film about gender-related having, being, and seeming for some years had constituted a rather central reference point of feminist gender studies; and Frauke's twenty-four-year-old female friend really didn't want to have to see it again for the ninety-first time on this gorgeous May morning. But then the thirty-year-old had by now let it rip: first off, dearest Vivian, is what drag queens call realness—how am I supposed to translate that, and how do I even translate drag queen—in Judith Butler's coordinate system of performatively dematerializing repetition, parody, and irony? Whatever, let me instead skim through what New York University's Peggy Phelan had to say about it: a represented woman is always a copy of a copy. The real of the woman, or rather the real woman, can't even be represented exactly because her function is to represent the man. She is the mirror and therefore, logically, never to be seen in it. Vivian dried her hair, walked to the window, and gazed upon the Odenwald rock quarries still lying in the morning shade and christened, in cocky common parlance, the Dossenheim Dolomites.

Then there's some guy there, the platinum-blonde lesbian continued her introduction, called Willi Ninja, a bearded queer, a prominent voguing dancer—you do remember the voguing dancers of the eighties, and the brunette at the window sill recalled them well—this guy teaches young women, and budding top models at that, how to walk like women. Once again, Vivian, exactly: a man teaches a woman how she should walk, and she in turn reproduces this walk so that yet again a man, in our case Venus Xtravaganza, one of the countless female impersonators in Harlem's drag house balls, can imitate it. It thus embodies another man's idea of how a woman moves and, Vivian, ultimately, what a woman is. At some point we'll only ever recognize a woman by how she comes tottering in like a transvestite, the doctoral candidate exclaimed excitedly. Now I ask you: does this signify a constructivist or a deconstructivist perpetuum mobile? Still only half-dressed in a Cat Power T-shirt and fresh underwear, Frauke's classmate turned around slowly, twisted her pale-blue terrycloth hand towel into a turban, walked in a straight line as on a catwalk toward her disconcertedly lecturing visitor, then turned toward the map of Ohio, and picked up off the floor a pair of ripped blue jeans that she then slipped on. At that Frauke Stöver for her part finally let go of the pause button on Vivian Atkinson's Korean VCR.

What subliminally irritated both women about Jennie Livingston's flick—which was otherwise dominated by, as they deemed it, an almost symbolist beauty—was that the field of sexual ambiguity in it, as in so many motion pictures too, was cast as African American, Hispanic, and thus according to racial difference, and that it therefore possessed a probably unintentional undertone of what was still by any other name structural racism. Furthermore, the filmmaker had quite obviously fallen in love with Octavia St. Laurent, one of her phallic female protagonists, without, however, in any way reflecting upon this subliminal dismay of hers (ultimately, according to Frauke, the meddling of a white lesbian in the feminization of the formally macho Latin lover): also problematic. Other questions that came up while Paris Is Burning ran and Vivian made a pot of black tea: if the natural sciences themselves—as it was phrased in the work of cyborg-theoretician Donna Haraway—represented nothing more than a specific form of social narration and thereby a cultural practice of the production of meaning, what, then, was heralded by Angela's impressive cock? To what extent were the natural sciences a continuation of politics by other means? Could the objects of the natural sciences in turn act performatively? Was Vivian's vulva a material-semiotic node of production? Frauke's breasts nothing but the mandatory outcome of an exclusively discursive construction? Vivian and Frauke didn't really know whether they could align themselves with the Californian Professor Haraway's theses on proverbial science fiction without betraying those of the erstwhile Heidelberg scholarship student Butler. Shroom smoker Rodney Atkinson had owned a double album that appeared with the Cosmic Couriers in Vivian's birth year by Klaus Schulze called Cyborg, whose individual movements—each lasting an entire side of a record—were called Synphära, Conphära, Chromengel, and Neuronengesang. If I could take only one double LP with me to an island, right now I would choose Kunststoff by Move D from Heidelberg on Source Records, Vivian digressed further, while Pepper Labeija, the legendary Mother of the House Labeija, lasciviously recounted her complicated childhood as a boy. Frauke Stöver could subsequently relate that her fiancée Angela Guida had, in tender adolescence, once subbed for a professional Veronese go-go dancer with resounding success after the latter had been arrested at the party congress of the Italian communists because of a narcotics offense. What had the party comrades gotten to see parading before them? What had they seen? Angelo? A woman? The feminine? Could one contend—with or against Donna Haraway—that the esteemed audience had been deceived by Angela's splendid performance or even betrayed? And what would Barbara Duden, feminist antipode to postmodernity, say about it?

When the video cassette Frauke had taped a few years ago from a local television channel was over, Vivian walked to her Discman and put in a CD by the Chicago group Falstaff, which contained a song with the ingenious refrain I gave my cock a woman's name that the master's candidate really wanted to play for her visitor. Amused at this, Frauke whipped out a risqué nude photo of her phallic fiancée from her wallet and emphasized, referring back to the coked-up Veronese cocotte, that the exclusively male portrayers of women on Shakespeare's stages had not seldom also been called boy actresses. What a revealing idiom, which places essence above existence, Vivian said in summary: quite like the term tomboy, which my parents so often attached to me in my youth—and occasionally insulted me with—and yet which is in no way appropriate for using on boys. Frauke Stöver thought she remembered having once received a postcard years ago from a ghost town by the name of Tomboy near Telluride, Colorado. The worst thing about me, my mother thought, was that I didn't smile all the time, Vivian continued, the first thing she said in the morning when she walked into my childhood room was: smile. And: keep smiling. Girls smile, of course, not just American ones (that even the woman from Schleswig-Holstein knew), even Shakespeare's female impersonators had certainly first had to learn—as Leonardo's Mona Lisa in 1503—how to smile. Vivian took the stack of predominantly historical long-playing records by gender-bending artists that Frauke had brought along and handed her girl friend in return Donna Haraway's much-debated German reader Die Neuerfindung der Natur, The Reinvention of Nature. Can you imagine, the younger woman said while showing the elder one to the door, that upon seeing the Odenwald rock quarries for the first time my neighbor from Brunsbüttel announced with total bewilderment that the mountains were completely wrecked?

Thereafter Vivian stood before her mirror and found her facial expression strikingly cold. Was it possible that others perceived her that way too? Or was it not even her she thought she recognized there, inverted in several, perhaps more than just optical aspects? A look couldn't actually encounter itself: what a betrayal. Could it break itself? How many hours had her mother spent in front of the mirrored doors of her wardrobe? Smiling at her mirror image. Only while smiling, she had always stressed, does the complete conflation of one's appearance with one's personality take place. What then did a smile consist of? Stretching out the corners of one's mouth? Vivian stared into her mirror and tried very consciously to lighten her countenance, to don an empty but friendly countenance. A so-called winning smile. What was it again that a winning smile had to win? Vivian had to laugh at the sight of herself. If it was in fact the sight of herself. She inhaled deeply and took a couple of steps toward the mirror. Grandma Cincinnati had always said that girls should introduce themselves while walking, that they were a sandwich made vertical. The front side of the body the one slice of white bread, the back side the other slice. Between them the bread spread which, pressed flat, was fixed in place. She had liked putting on a Liberace record and demonstrating this. While performing womanish hand motions with which she imitated the movement of blazing flames, rustling tree tops, quietly falling leaves, surging to rippled water. Or she had drawn figure eights in the air in all directions with lightly splayed fingers, her upper body a total sandwich the whole time.

Vivian was now trying to reproduce this in front of the mirror. It was utterly impossible for her, but bore a certain similarity to Willi Ninja.

To better zero in on her Weininger, the student had checked out a slew of novels by the Catholic Wagnerian and occultist Joséphin Péladan, killed in action against Germany in the trenches in 1918: The Ultimate Vice, 1884; Feminine Curiosity, 1885; Woman's Initiation, 1886; The Wife of the Artist, 1887; The Androgyne, 1891, with a furiously pacifist, anti-capitalist afterword by the German translator from the early years of the Weimar Republic. As well as an unbelievable essay with the title How to Become a Fairy, 1892. The helpful Heidelberg librarian had unfortunately been unable to locate the novel Gynandria, likewise published in France in 1892 (in parentheses: Lesbos, as the 1923 prepublication notice of the Georg Müller publishing house in Munich disclosed). Many a passage from these books would end up in a file folder that Vivian had from the very beginning of her research labeled with the preliminary finding Contemptuous Worship of Women. In actual fact only very few men of letters in the nineteenth century had succeeded in extolling women in a way that didn't additionally disenfranchise them. Even Gerlinde Atkinson's Duden Dictionary of Foreign Words, published in Mannheim in 1966, defined feminism as physical and psychological feminization in men. Nowadays intellectuals like Frauke Stöver claimed that female-female love alone was capable of expressing genuine respect toward women. Was it really out of the question, Vivian had noted for herself cautiously, that a sexist mishap occasionally befall the homosexual praxis of social genderedness, too? Or did sexism function solely within the constructed differential between the one and the other biologically verifiable gender? Like racism does only in the delimitation that declasses the foreign? Couldn't sexist violence also possibly turn on itself? Politically speaking, an inadmissible line of inquiry, the army brat decided, even though Angela—it was safe to say—could peddle some visual aids as regards the marginalization of the self. Vivian removed herself briefly from her Rococo workspace, which was overloaded with Péladan's cloying epics, and wandered barefoot into the little kitchen to partake of a massive gulp of milk.

The Mannheimer Morgen of her neighbor from Brunsbüttel revealed the bad tidings writ large that Mannheim's Boehringer factories had been swallowed up by the pharmaceutical giant Roche. Once again tens of thousands of jobs at stake; and once again tens of thousands of so-called jobholders would want to waive their salaries to be able to keep holding on to their jobs. A Mr. Engelhorn from the Boehringer firm spoke words of reassurance to this effect. Did he belong to that race of industrialists that had once created BASF, but also the Mannheim fashion boutique Engelhorn & Sturm? In the free fish-wrap that Vivian next paged through there was an article about the considerable increase in so-called military defense readiness among German youth since the German armed forces carried out active—they called them humanitarian—military deployments. Hardly any conscientious objectors left? The student couldn't believe her eyes, took another cold gulp from the milk bottle, got hung up with fresh irritation on a fan profile of the African German pop singer Roberto Blanco—whereupon she briefly considered whether Ernst Neger, the carnival figure from Mainz, had been a pseudonym as well—and was just about to flee back to Joséphin Péladan and his lusty mock-hermaphrodites in the confessional when the mail carrier buzzed and then buzzed again right away, so heavy was the package that Grandma Cincinnati had sent this time. The grand-daughter schlepped it to her sofa and began to undo all the string and tape that held the Lucullian shipment together. Ever since the Berlin Airlift the now-aged Grandma Cincinnati—who herself had never set foot on an airplane—had never tired of sending regular, delicious care packages to Germany, and with the Atkinsons' move out of the Patrick Henry Village, all packages of grub had immediately found their way straight to Edingen, which, according to the simple American worldview like that of Grandma Cincinnati, lay not in the wicked Communist half of the divided nation, but in the good (as she said mindlessly) fascist one. How could Vivian manage to explain to her primordially American grandmother—who also thought that German women still always spread their laundry out to dry on the rocks down by the river—that Germany had meanwhile become whole again and that, furthermore, in this wholeness lay a great corruption in both foreign and domestic policy?

The very same evening Vivian, Hans, Frauke, and Korinna, together and with ravenous hunger, laid into all the tubes, jars, bags, and cans from Ohio: on the floor since the ornate slab still overflowed with Péladan and the kitchen table simply offered too little space for four people. Angela had unfortunately been unable to come, which Korinna regretted less than Vivian and Hans, who were extremely curious about Frauke's fiancée, whom they had only experienced as a waitress—that is to say waiter—in the lesbian pizzeria in Handschuhsheim. When does he get off work tonight, Korinna asked bitchily, but Frauke answered with sangfroid: it could be two a.m. before she gets home. Korinna Kohn nevertheless appeared calm and collected by comparison and ate with great appetite. As Frauke meanwhile left to wash her hands, the tennis player told Hans and Vivian in hushed tones that she had already fallen in love again anyway and was moving in with Heiner, a drug dealer, to the far reaches of the Odenwald this very week. That can't possibly come to anything, Korinna, Hansi Pompadour blurted out, completely unceremoniously, and Vivian could only concur. The drug dealer—who was a true king in his hick town, always dressed in white, as neat as a pin, a white panama hat on his head, snow-white sneakers on his feet—came down regularly to Heidelberg on weekends and was not unknown to either Hans or Vivian. But then Frauke was already coming back from the bathroom, and the topic ought to be changed.

The platinum blonde, who alone from among this circle had not slept with Vivian, whom she desired most of all, was already holding forth as she pulled the bathroom door shut behind her: urinary segregation, thus Lacan's standing expression, denoted one of the central everyday problems, not just for Angela. The symbolic representations of gender on the doors to public privies really spent no time at all dealing with the at least biologistically reliable illustration of so-called genitalia—which after all are used to being lolled out at the urinal—but exclusively with social, culturalistic vexations like bow ties, pipes, ponytails, or petticoats; for which reason Angela, if necessary, albeit somehow hesitantly, always chooses to steer toward the women's restroom. In the temporary security of her stall, the so-called smallest room of the house, she is beset before long by the disquieting apprehension of possibly being able, as she puts it, to be read when leaving the public restroom. Being read, Frauke said, is tantamount to being seen through, is tantamount to the penis under Angela's petticoat. Which, just by the way, marks a social problem we've gotten to know as cultural binarism, and even here it has a decent bias: a woman in pants like we're all wearing tonight—even Korinna was wearing floral bell-bottoms that day—can indeed step through the door with the petticoat with no trouble, a man in a petticoat, however, only heavy-heartedly through that with the pipe. Moreover, a mother can visit the ladies' room with her young son, a father with his daughter, though, neither the ladies' nor the men's room, for on the way to the stalls lies the stinking pissoir, the Shangri-La of every exhibitionist; spare me further details, please. Frauke Stöver hadn't even taken a seat on the floor again but was pacing back and forth in the spacious room, her breasts heaving: already in elementary school there's no greater infringement of the rules than infiltrating the strictly segregated sanitary spaces of the opposite gender. And yet no greater adventure either, Korinna Kohn objected obstreperously. Until not so long ago, Vivian Atkinson knew furthermore, urinary segregation in the American South had also meant, though, that there were separate bathrooms for blacks and whites. No one could answer, on the other hand, Hans Mühlenkamm's not uninteresting question of whether there had been, at the respective localities, four doors— that is, variously colored pipes and ponytails too—or whether, with the always delimiting emphasis on race, the emphasis on gender had been somewhat interfered with, indeed had vanished. The quadraphony had been unable to assert itself against the stereophony.

For the second time on the same day, Frauke whipped out the risqué nude photo of her fiancée, handed it to Hans and Korinna as well, and, gesticulating nervously, took off: whenever I go walking in the Odenwald, I have to squat down to urinate like you, Vivian, like you, Korinna, while Angela just goes to the next best tree, pulls her dick out of her pants, and, rain or shine, standing upright, pees into the scenery. Like Hansi. Biological mechanisms that came under suspicion of biologism time and again and were all too well known to all those present; but Frauke wanted to get at something that did not belong to the wealth of experience of the normal female citizen. Not even to that of the normal lesbian citizen. Thus she cleared her throat, her hands by now sticking in her pants pockets, and began anew: dichotomizing rules like those that girls pee sitting and boys standing have both marked the social difference of the sexes and accentuated the hierarchical differential between them. Now, concerning the male-canonized ranking of the sexes, this can be leveraged, semiotically as it were, Frauke said, in that I, possibly in the sense of the Chicago band Falstaff, reinterpret Angela's (as they would have us believe) primary sexual organ, which is to say, rename it. Whenever Angela has penetrated me, there is no longer any clarity as to which of the two of us has the penis, and whenever she pulls it out again, it possesses a name that we cannot find in any biology book in the world, if you all understand what I'm trying to say here. I really have puked on dicks before. Vivian, Korinna, and Hans may have stared awkwardly into the empty cans on the floor, but they thought they had understood roughly what they had already read in Judith Butler: namely, that organs, too, were, at the end of the day, nothing more than words or—as Hans put it at this moment with near solemnity—fleshy agents of sketchy social agreements.

When around three in morning Vivian accompanied her amiga/os downstairs to Korinna's Tatra glowing in the moonlight—amiga/os with the slash-o, for with Hans among them there was an amigo too—the magistrate's daughter inconspicuously slipped her an address at the far edge of the Odenwald where the forest imperceptibly disappeared in the East, leveling off quite flat, toward Franconia, and where there were supposedly only hick towns, one of which being where Korinna's newly minted lover organized his machinations, come visit us anytime, Vivian, Korinna said, the window rolled down, Hans buckled in next to her, Frauke sprawled out in the back seat, wondering why Korinna had said us. The German-American only child waved after them a bit as the Czechoslovakian sedan turned onto Hauptstrasse, which became Heidelberger Strasse after one or two hundred yards, took not the elevator in the tobacco warehouse but the stairs, aired out her room, and shoved the enormous pile of accumulated packaging trash into the hallway. Before she undressed, she briefly consulted Caroline Walker Bynum's book Fragmentation and Redemption, translated into German in 1996, in which the medieval beginnings of an autonomous female, that is, conventual science grew around, of all things, Jesus' foreskin, and thereby the only body part of the Savior that did not ascend to heaven. The Virgin Mary's umbilical cord added to this, the Christ Child's milk teeth neglected. Frauke had already told Vivian several times about the Landsberg abbess Herrad and her attempts to find out whether dead fetuses, amputated limbs, and even clipped fingernails and toenails would also rise from the dead. Late twelfth century, if Vivian remembered correctly. For a while now she had been meaning to read this very primary secondary work on Frauke's dissertation topic for herself; now, since her girl friend had spoken the entire evening about the so doubtful primalities of the genital area, she was at least taking it with her to her pillow. No less interesting when opening it for the very first time, though, was the bibliographic reference to an earlier book by the American medievalist that might possibly lead somewhere: Jesus as Mother.

Vivian turned out the light, listened a bit into the quiet night, curiously felt her so-called private parts, and considered whether she was capable, in all earnestness, of understanding her vulva—like Frauke Stöver in adaptive gender unity with Angela Guida—as a scrotum, her clitoris as a glans, and her vagina (into which she now slid her index finger) as a penis. After all she, too, had at times had the human, all too human experience of having asked herself in front of the mirror: that's supposed to be me? Into the eighteenth century the penis and the vagina had in fact been seen as one and the same tube and—turned to the inside or the outside—merely as the gradual difference of a gender determination which even then was a pure male one; there was nothing more imperfect than a woman. Even the view still held today that sexuality only ever arrived at its purpose when the man stuck his sword into the woman's sheath could be imputed to this scenario of organs turned inwards and outwards or, as the case may be, drawn inwards or outwards. As the pièce de résistance of the Enlightenment, the woman was then pathologized and, according to Hansi's photocopies, dissected by gynecologists, womb-envious male specialists in femininity. By now Vivian had inadvertently aroused herself autoerotically. Foucault was right, she thought, in that he had relieved human sexual desire of any trace whatsoever of a natural, precultural inevitability and unmasked it as a perfidious bio-plaything of political powers. Gynecologists had tolerated female masturbation solely because it provided female performance training—considered anywhere from welcome to necessary—for the sexual optimization of male lusts. Should the twenty-four-year-old grant herself her at once an imminent clitoral climax on these grounds? No way.

On Corpus Christi Vivian stood with her neighbor from Brunsbüttel on the observation tower erected by the Heidelberg Odenwald Club in 1906 atop the Weisser Stein mountain near Dossenheim, and he, the recent newcomer, pointed out to her BASF on the horizon, where he was supposedly working his way up in a dizzying salary spiral, to the right and left of it the monumental cooling towers of the Biblis and Philippsburg Nuclear Power Plants whose respective worst-case scenarios he feared irrepressibly, and closer to the front in the lowlands the little tobacco town Ladenburg (which is worth seeing), where Carl Benz, having fled Mannheim, had tried to work out the infuriating difference between ignition and backfiring. Mr. Petersen from Brunsbüttel may have proved himself a rudimentarily amusing storyteller, but one could, without a great deal of imagination, envision for him more grateful listeners than Vivian of all people, who simply hadn't been able to say no to the lonely man standing at her door beaming, a packed picnic basket in hand. Mr. Petersen drove two motorcycles, a brand-new Japanese one and an ancient Bavarian one with a sidecar. The latter was apparently in the shop, so Vivian had to press herself up against the athletic body of her neighbor, nearly fifteen years her senior, clasping him tightly like a sweetheart—for instance, while overtaking at terrific speeds—but as a motorcyclist Petersen knew that he ought not presume anything about such embraces.

At the Strahlenburg castle of the weak-willed Käthchen of Heilbronn, the world-famous Heinrich von Kleistian marionette (Kleist also as author of the gender study The Schroffenstein Family), they had parked Petersen's crotch rocket and gone on foot to the Ölberg, the Mount of Olives, at which point it occurred to the college girl that the Christian trinity in fact constituted a form of existence in which the one exists at once in the Other. Definitely make a mental note for Frauke, or as the case may be for Korinna too; Mr. Petersen would have no use for it. Frauke and Korinna were actually going to have to reconcile themselves with each other, owing to the clear parallels in the scope of their academic work, Vivian thought. Weren't they very much body islands whenever the Savior's wounds attained figurative representation far outside his body? In fragmentation and redemption, so to speak. But what had Korinna alluded to recently with her approach that supposedly led further than Plessner, Schmitz, and Plügge to so-called inner colonization? Now and again the girlish tennis player managed to develop an almost mysterious air, in marked contrast to Frauke Stöver, who, with everything that popped into her mind, flailed about downright wildly. And now? The virile Petersen wanted to know what direction they should go. To the Weisser Stein, down to Dossenheim, and over the Schauenburg back to the Honda, Vivian commanded.

Not far from the Schauenburg, however, soared one of those breathtakingly gigantic rock quarries that was finally supposed to be decommissioned in 2000 and above which Pat Meier had mounted her professional day- and night-vision devices against BASF. Mr. Petersen, as the older one, had long since offered Vivian the use of his first name, but the brunette college girl with the grown-out boy-do simply couldn't accustom herself to using the informal mode of address with such a seasoned fellow as Bodo Petersen. So she automatically continued to address him formally while he, clearly in flames of love, arrogated for himself every opportunity to use her first name. He nevertheless turned rather quiet and ashen when Vivian then prowled with him through the undergrowth immediately above the steep escarpment of the rock quarry. In Brunsbüttel, which lay at sea level, he had been unable to rid himself of a fear of heights, Petersen whimpered; once when he saw his brother-in-law, a Greenpeace activist known on TV, climbing on the smokestack of a nuclear power plant along the lower Elbe River, he lost his lunch straightaway. Holy fucking shit. What are you doing here? Pat Meier, in camouflage, was taken by complete surprise after Vivian bent aside a few branches of the thicket and revealed her cute American-German face. May I introduce, Vivian said impassively, Mr. Petersen, Ms. Meier. And before long the two had maneuvered themselves, addressing each other formally, into a first cautious, then passionate dispute about the boon and bane of the chemical industry.

Pat Meier—birth year 1954, by her own account conclusively political since the chemical workers' strike of 1971 that had been betrayed by the unions, on the occasion of which her two older sisters had laid stones on the train tracks of the Merck factory—was quoting, among other things, some passages from a 1972 RAF polemic against the major chemical corporations that she carried in her breasts as well as (from memory) the notorious telegram of the Chilean Hoechst subsidiary to the synthetic dye company Farbwerke Hoechst AG in Frankfurt, alongside BASF and Bayer the deconcentrated heirs of the National Socialist IG Farben, in whose prefascist administration building the leadership of the U.S. Forces, European Theater, as well as the CIA, settled after the war and which had been handed over to its Frankfurt alma mater (in English nourishing mother) upon the departure of American occupation troops: Santiago de Chile, September 17, 1973. The long-awaited military intervention has finally taken place. In the future Chile will be an increasingly interesting market for Hoechst products.

Bodo Petersen, who was quite visibly several years younger than Pat Meier, merely remarked: so what. At that, she, perceptibly upset, summoned forth Ernst Bloch, who had written that the eye of the law sits in the face of the ruling class. The Brunsbütteler, once an apprentice at Bayer, didn't contradict that either and in return began to enumerate quite masterfully all the civilizing achievements of the chemical industry, in particular of Ludwigshafen's BASF; in 1882 it had received telephone connection number one in the Kingdom of Bavaria of which the Palatinate, an exclave, was then considered a part. In 1897 the trailblazing invention of synthetic indigo took place, in 1913 the groundbreaking for the earth-shattering production of nitrogen fertilizers, in 1927 the sensational extraction of gasoline from bituminous tar, and from 1930 on the explosive development of newer and newer plastics by the Baden Aniline & Soda Factory. Back in 1936 already it recorded the London Philharmonic under Sir Thomas Beecham in the Ludwigshafen Feierabendhaus with the BASF Magnetophon, invented only a year before. The knight Beecham was deeply impressed, and by the beginning of the war BASF had already manufactured thirteen million yards of magnetic tape. After the war only six percent of all factory buildings had remained unscathed, but the great victory march of polystyrene could not be stopped, and Bodo Petersen had arrived at his favorite topic, the glorious production of plastic. Possibly another major industrial materialization of male womb-envy, surmised Vivian, who, at the feet of the two debaters gesturing with increasing agitation in the early summer air, had taken a seat on the exposed grass edge of the western Odenwald, letting her long legs—ogled especially by Mr. Petersen—dangle with visible recklessness above the tremendous precipice of the quarry.

In 1966 when I began school in Brunsbüttel and got my first
chemistry set, the sales program of BASF encompassed around
five thousand products, Petersen explicated in a trenchant voice:
plastic assortments for the most various fields of application as
material for processing by injection molding, blow molding,
extrusion, calendering, deep drawing, molding, foaming, and
sintering such as Lupolen, Luparen, Oppanol, Luran, Terluran,
Polystyrol, Styropor, Iporka, Ultramid, Vinoflex, Palatal; plastic
dispersions as performance products for the glue, paper, packaging, and textile industries like Acronal, Diofan, Propiofan; pig-
ment resins, Plastopal, Ludopal, Luprenal, Larodur, for example;
plasticizers like Palatinol or Plastomoll; solvents, glycol and glycol derivatives; Glysantin engine coolant; precursors for synthetic
fibers; condensation products for the forest industry on the basis
of melamine-urea-phenol like the hot glues Kaurit and Kauresin
as well as for the textile and paper industries; furthermore, organic
precursors and intermediary products for the pharmaceutical
and cosmetic industries; catalysts; inorganic basic chemicals;
pigments for dyeing and printing textiles of all kinds, for dyeing lacquers, paper, leather, plastics, and other things; in addition
ancillary and performance products for the textile, leather, paper,
mineral oil, and chemical-technical industries as well as others;
technical nitrogen products; fertilizers, for example Nitrophoska
and Floranid; herbicides and pesticides, moreover, like Pyramin,
U 46, Polyram-Combi, Kumulus, and Perfekthion; as well as—
last but not least—the good old Magnetophon tape BASF. When
her heated neighbor was finally finished, Vivian Atkinson had
to laugh out loud, abruptly unnerving, if not insulting him. But
Pat Meier—who in 1975 had written a never-published sonnet
together with Genoveva Weckherlin about how Merck once lost
the Darmstadt world monopoly on cocaine—for the first time

mustered a certain amount of respect for that so obvious connoisseur of synthetic material and undertook the first steps toward staying in this man's favor.

Did he want to look through, she asked him amicably, handing over one of her olive-green photographic devices. As a member of BASF Bodo Petersen was, as they say, prohibited by plant security from taking photographs of his workplace for business-related reasons. Therefore do not take your camera, nor any private belongings with you into the plant, read the Tips for New Employees—which the virtuous Brunsbütteler had scared up secondhand at a junk dealer in Oggersheim—back in 1957: Should there be a particular reason that, in your opinion, is so important that you think you must take private items with you into the plant, then please first consult plant security. They must know and confirm to you what you may take out of the plant as your property. How enticing must it have seemed to the employee then, at least from afar—and even a bit from above—to be able to snap shots of the inside of the optically zoomed factory. Before long he had shot an entire roll of film, and the teacher with obvious terrorist proclivities, on leave for a year now, promised him that she would bring by homemade prints as soon as possible. You do have the address, the motorcyclist said with delight, but in her lifetime Pat Meier had never once been to visit Edingen, much less Vivian Atkinson, whom she, according to Frauke, had always felt to be an avowedly silly, spoiled brat.

A couple of days later one could read in the women's section of the weekend newspapers that the German underwear company Triumph aspired to introduce brassieres and panties made from recycled plastic—in this case sorted old plastic bottles—to the

Japanese market. During a Tokyo press conference, the marketing director of the Munich corporation explained how a soft green underwear set comprising a bra and a pair of briefs could be produced from exactly three and a half 1.5-liter bottles shredded into plastic granules. Even the flowery lace of this lingerie—unavailable in white, in accordance with its base elements of course—was to consist of waste material. Vivian didn't know if she ought to find anything special about this. After all, so-called sophisticated feminine undergarments had been made from male plastics for ages. Mr. Petersen, who always brought by the weekend edition of the Mannheimer Morgen in person—and mostly in his socks—countered vigorously: not male plastics, but virginal ones have been used. The recycling of industrial waste on female skin, be it Japanese, Italian, or German skin, Petersen said, represents in his mind an unacceptable debasement of women. The neighbor, leaning against her apartment door, didn't care to contradict this genteel standpoint at the moment; she at least found it remarkable that Bodo Petersen had stumbled upon the colorful housewife side of things at all, where every weekend genetic women were in fact reduced to ventriloquizing sexual objects. She accepted the tattered newspaper, gave her thanks politely with an ironic intimation of a curtsy, and neighbor Petersen—who the whole time had been yearningly gazing past Vivian Atkinson's shoulder into her private interior—was then able to beat his retreat once again into philistine isolation.

The student closed her apartment door behind her, walked over to a braided clothes box, and pulled out the only bikini she owned. The peculiar verbal equivalence of the military atomic bomb detonation and the fashion-design labeling of feminine corporeality by Louis Réard—the inventor of the scant, two-piece bathing suit that exhibits young women's generative body islands with both revealing and veiling strategies—yet again aroused her suspicion. According to Korinna Kohn's notes, Réard had presented his duds to the Western public in 1946, only four days after the first of numerous devastating nuclear tests that the U.S. carried out over the innocent Bikini Atoll, and had presented them by name as le bikini, whereby the bombarded South Pacific archipelago had been colonized yet again, which is to say, occupied by language. Korinna's handwritten finding dated to May of 1996: the (so to speak) glorified physicality of women in its fatal stigmatization as an explosion, as destructive as it is unfathomably beautiful, produced by targeted, phallocratic aggression. Since reading Korinna's etymological documents, Vivian had realized more clearly than ever why she herself had been so exceptionally afraid during puberty of getting so-called atomic boobs. Thank God she hadn't, but on this Saturday morning her only bikini finally wandered its way into the wastebasket. May some scientists somewhere create plastic bottles from it.

USA, SA, SS. After the RAF's internationalist retaliatory strike on the Heidelberg headquarters of the U.S. Army during which the Coke machine had fallen over—burying under it the uncle of Vivian's fleeting lover for whom she had, in American fashion, shaved her armpits—the resistance fighter Irmgard Möller, who had participated in the globally attention-grabbing operation, had been addressed in a West German streetcar by an older gentleman about how marvelous he had found this bomb attack. Irmgard Möller, who used to take public transportation regularly after her respective operations to gauge the immediate reaction of the body of the Volk for which she was ultimately fighting, had understandably not revealed her identity to the old man. Hans

Mühlenkamm raised his index finger and pointed out that said elderly man had perhaps been an old Nazi anyway and why in the world hadn't the Red Army Faction let loose back then primarily against the legions of Nazis who still controlled West Germany. His best girl friend, Vivian Atkinson—who was wearing a second-hand Lurex top today and who at the time of the Heidelberg attack had, when she added it all up, only just been conceived—could only shrug at this too for the time being, briefly polished her sunglasses, and again picked up Hansi's paperback edition, with book wrapper, of the memoirs of the female terrorist who had been released from prison in 1994 after almost twenty-three excruciating years.

Anti-Americanism had in fact become, at least since her daddy had begun sending home the occupation forces stationed here, an ambivalent topic. Nevertheless—she ended up replying to Hans—in 1972 the RAF was in the right to bomb American facilities inside cozy Heidelberg that lay within the wholly common war of conquest. You're OK; nothing else occurred to Hans at the moment. The midday sun stood steep above the Königstuhl, the Upper Rhine Valley lay in a humid haze, even up here at the Molkenkur no cool breeze was blowing. On the other hand, Vivian continued abruptly, the attacks in early 1972 themselves of course contributed pretty decisively to the polarization among West German leftists and thus to their fatal attenuation; Irmgard Möller says on page forty-one: shortly after our attacks on the IG-Farben-Haus in Frankfurt and the central computer in Heidelberg, there was the conference The Example of Angela Davis in Frankfurt on June 3, 1972. There Oskar Negt called for a Linke party faction that had decided to set out on the Marsch durch die Institutionen, the March through the Institutions, to withdraw their solidarity with us. A few lines further below: Consequently, the teacher with whom Ulrike Meinhof had gone into hiding also promptly reported her to the police. After that she got to march through an institution called the penitentiary, Hans noted, shaking his head. To this day his parents assumed that Meinhof and her comrades, in 1976 and 1977 respectively, had all—each and every one of them (not including of course the thus especially despicable Möller)—killed themselves in their cells. Now looking upon Irmgard Möller's photographically diffuse face on the wrapper of her memoirs, Hans couldn't resist a certain erotic fascination for this aging revolutionary, which caused Vivian to prick up her ears again: had the woman with the gun, at least psychoanalytically speaking, not always been the woman with the phallus too?

Since first reading Otto Weininger two years ago, the college girl constantly came across psychoanalysis and its (not also infrequently) bothersome spawns. Weininger, 1880–1903, an Austrian Jew who had decided to become more German than the Germans and on the day he received his doctorate solemnly converted to Protestantism, had admittedly fought against the softy (same thing: effeminate) coffee house culture, against so-called mixed feelings that he hated, and yet at the same time struck a blow, proverbially, for the so-called theory of bisexuality, which proceeded from the relative mixed-genderedness of every individual. Having divulged this in confidence to his patient Hermann Swoboda, a close friend of the diligent doctoral candidate Weininger, the father of psychoanalysis, Sigmund Freud—when Weininger's expanded dissertation was published with the title Sex and Character and immediately became a bestseller in 1903—got into the deepest of trouble with his Berlin colleague Wilhelm Fliess, who had developed this theory of the innate bisexuality of all living creatures in peace and quiet, confiding it to his Viennese friend Freud only under the pledge of utmost secrecy. Otto Weininger, meanwhile, had shot himself in Beethoven's last residence only months after the publication of his misogynist tome and began a posthumous career as the scientific object of psychoanalysis, along with Daniel Paul Schreber—son of the inventor of allotment gardening and of masturbation's very greatest opponent—who suffered from obsessions as insanely religious as they were gender-bending.

In actuality Schreber's Memoirs of My Nervous Illness had appeared the same year as Weininger's unequally popular work Sex and Character. From his revulsion at the Jewishness and the feminine in himself, Weininger had distilled the paranoid equation that the Jew is a woman and thus even managed to make the young Hitler his fan. Jesus Christ was a Jew too, but only, he claimed, to overcome the Jewishness in himself absolutely. The Jew is a communist procuress, and so forth. Vivian knew the closed system of Weininger's obsessions practically by heart; after all it was pretty overwhelmingly in line with Western common sense from the first half of the twentieth century. In his final diary entries before he met his early end, he had acknowledged of himself, though, that hiding behind the loathing for women there is always an as-yet-to-be-overcome loathing of one's own sexuality. In his literary remains Vivian Atkinson had found the following aphorism: the good man goes to his death when he feels that he is becoming irretrievably bad. Still manages to hand his father the scuffed leather case for his glasses (now if that isn't a blueprint for the psychoanalyst, the student thought), rents himself a musty room in Schwarzspanierstrasse 15 where sixty-seven years prior the dead Beethoven had also been carried out, and blows his brains out. At the cemetery personalities like Stefan Zweig, Karl Kraus, and Ludwig Wittgenstein, all of fourteen years old, supposedly followed his casket. In 1931 the latter would write excitedly about Weininger: It is his enormous mistake which is great. Wittgenstein's oft-photocopied adage had been serving Vivian Atkinson for several weeks now as a bookmark in her 1947 edition, the twenty-eighth printing of Sex and Character, acquired secondhand in 1995 in Heidelberg, down by the Neckar. But then she had thrown the slip of paper away anyhow, into the Neckar, having adjudged that Wittgenstein was mistaken in his appraisal of Weininger's mistake.

What Vivian at this moment still recalled, up at the Molkenkur, while the equally breezily dressed Hans continued reading from Oliver Tolmein's very personal conversation with Irmgard Möller: the occultist Swede August Strindberg sends a wreath to Otto Weininger's funeral and composes an obituary in which he blusters on about the unalterable fact that a woman is nothing more than a rudimentary man; exhilarated, Karl Kraus will print this text in The Torch. In his correspondence with Weininger's friend Artur Gerber, the half-benighted Stringberg regards the so-called woman problem as solved by Otto Weininger and professes on December 8, 1903: I now believe that I have done wrong before I was born. I, like Weininger, became religious out of a fear of becoming a monster. I even deified Beethoven, having founded a Beethoven club where only Beethoven is played. But I noticed that so-called good people cannot abide Beethoven. He is an ill-fated, troubled man who cannot be called heavenly: otherworldly, certainly. P.S. Do not publish my letters before my death. At which point a smile stole its way into Vivian's still very concentrated features, Hansi immediately inquired attentively why she was smiling, and thereby educed from his lady sidekick, three and a half years his senior, the almost classic female answer: oh, nothing. A cable railway car, built in 1907, came crawling and creaking down from the Königstuhl, and Hans rubbed his back against the red sandstone cliff they were leaning on. Other prominent first-generation admirers of the self-proclaimed genius Otto Weininger, more than a half century before Slavoj Žižek, who now came to the master's candidate's mind: Heimito von Doderer, Alban Berg, Walter Serner, Alfred Kubin. The French Germanist Jacques Le Rider would later write that Weiniger may not have been a genius, but was a symptom of genius; for this reason the question poses itself as to what extent his psychopathology was not simultaneously the Ratio of his time. Thus the twenty-three-year-old Viennese had already been accused during his lifetime— those few weeks he permitted himself to live to see his fame—by the Leipzig professor Paul Julius Moebius, author of the enormously successful public blockbuster Über den physiologischen Schwachsinn des Weibes, or On the Physiological Debility of Woman, of plagiarizing his ideas. And years after Weininger had taken his own life, the aforesaid Wilhelm Fliess was still raving, wherever anyone would listen, for the same reason (Sigmund Freud, anyway, never at any point being ready to concede to his friend in Berlin the full creative rights to the idea of the innate bisexuality of all living creatures). Once again Karl Kraus was the third party here who rejoiced and reviewed this fruitless dispute, pro-Weininger of course, in his journal The Torch.

For Kraus, the articulate chief of the tightly-knit circle of Weiningerians, Sex and Character had provided a topnotch anti-Freud compendium since its celebrated publication. The suicide victim's anti-feminist theory of genius served Karl Kraus, Heimito von Doderer, and Ernst Jünger as a verbal command post against abhorrent psychoanalysis until Hitler dumbfounded them all. And yet the famous Dr. Freud had been quite revered by the still-nameless student Weininger, having even given the inquisitive neuropath a couple of tips on his thesis as well as having later judged him to be, quote, a highly gifted, sexually disturbed young philosopher who assailed Jews and women with the same hostility and the same male opprobrium. This Vivian had read in a Freudian footnote cited by Jacques Le Rider on the Analysis of a Phobia in a Five-Year-Old Boy, where she had also found and copied the following words of the first psychoanalyst: The castration complex is the deepest unconscious root of anti-Semitism, for even in the nursery boys hear that Jews have something cut off their penis—a bit of the penis, they suppose—and this gives them the right to despise Jews. Likewise, there is no stronger unconscious root to men's superiority over women. According to Jacques Le Rider, Sex and Character represented a singular harried song about castration, whereby the work— as Frauke had already expressed last summer in the Weininger seminar—did in fact, at least phenomenologically, lurch along in close vicinity to schoolmasterly psychoanalysis. Where Otto Weininger had claimed that woman possesses no ego, even that woman is nothingness, one could read in Freud's exegete Jacques Lacan: la femme n'existe pas. Since Oedipus, the phallocratic world had apparently known only one leitmotif, the eternal castration complex. Could Weininger's insanity thus ultimately be understood as Freud's truth, Le Rider had written, Weininger as ultra-Freud? At this Frauke Stöver and Vivian Atkinson had gone to the Marstall together, the university cafeteria, for the first time.

Just a few things, Hans Mühlenkamm abruptly interrupted Vivian's mental recapitulations: did you actually know that Irmgard Möller had initially only sent leaflet missiles into American barracks to invite the soldiers there to desert? And that she was arrested at a kiosk in Offenbach just a few hundred yards away from her parents' house? Do you believe the legend that the RAF didn't even know that the mainframe computer that coordinated all the bombing raids in Vietnam was located in the Heidelberg headquarters? Which they then, however, destroyed with their two car explosions, creating two, three, many Vietnams as Che had demanded, or rather, in the words of the Pentagon: bombed back into the Stone Age? No clue, the college girl replied, you read the book, not me. But the part-time physician's receptionist hadn't yet finished it by a long shot and plunged back into his reading again. A year after the so-called German Autumn, in 1978, Judith Butler showed up in Heidelberg; as an American scholarship student with European ancestors of the Jewish confession, she had begun her search for old Jewish cemeteries and vestiges of Jewish resistance to German anti-Semitism, swallowed Fassbinder's feature films whole, engaged in debates with her new German friends about Germans, Jews, history, politics, and sexuality, and studied Hegel's reception in France at the university. Finally the logical move to France. Hegel: The system is closed when philosophy turns toward itself and reflects upon the means and methods of its language. Query: Could there be a femininity outside of language? Even in 1993 the female philosopher—philosopher equals feminist—professed her amazement in her essay Überlegungen zu Deutschland: One Girl's Story at being characterized in the Frankfurter Rundschau as a nice young man, perhaps of Italian derivation, as it reads. Butler's commentary: The assumption of Italian heritage, here moreover the site of vexation at the loss of gender and racial boundaries, testifies to a still-prevalent illegibility of the Jew in Germany. Joe, the Mediterranean, as they always said in the Judo Club, because Germans by their nature were Nordic. Difference, according to Georg Wilhelm Friedrich Hegel, appointed to the University of Heidelberg in 1816: A distinction that both connects and discriminates, and thus binds. Vivian Atkinson's favorite part in Überlegungen zu Deutschland: One Girl's Story: Can there be a notion of difference that does not revert back to a notion of identity?

The student fished a slip of paper out of her bag and wrote down: measure Joan Rivière's 1929 Womanliness as a Masquerade and Judith Butler's current concepts of performance and parody, respectively, against the memoirs of the Abbé de Choisy. She then arose, climbed agilely over the cliff, and was for Hans as good as vanished: off to use the phone. A quarter of an hour later she returned and warbled a song into her friend's ear that the actress Ann-Margret had had to sing in 1963 as a pubescent bobby soxer in the Hollywood film Bye Bye Birdie, a year before getting to perform with the hotly idolized male player Elvis Presley in Viva Las Vegas: How lovely to be a woman, the wait was way worthwhile. How lovely to wear mascara and smile a woman's smile. How lovely to have a figure that's round instead of flat. Whenever you hear boys whistle you're what they're whistling at. No way, Hans laughed, who wrote that? Charles Strouse and Lee Adams, Vivian replied, though Lee can also be a girl's name; anyway, the paradigmatic model of gender impersonation, and it gets even better, since the B-section goes: It's wonderful to feel the things a woman feels. It gives you such a blow just to know you're wearing lipstick and heels. Or a top as funny as yours, Hansi Pompadour teased his girl friend, who was four inches taller, who did you call? Frauke Stöver, and she's getting the car, Vivian answered, beaming. She had induced Frauke to plead with Ilse Schoolmistress for her Ford Escort so they could all ride to Munich for a day where Judith Butler herself was supposed to be visiting with the Americanists at the university the day after next; Korinna Kohn with her somewhat more spacious Tatra sedan had, as previously announced, zoomed off weeks ago to the far reaches of the Odenwald. All righty, Hans said, if you all can fit me, Viv, I'll come along, leapt up, and intoned, only a bit deeper than the original, She Acts Like a Woman Should, a really crappy self-abasing hit that Marilyn Monroe had once had tailor-made for her highly remunerated self. And sometimes all women became like men, D. H. Lawrence had noted, so that men didn't need to be manly anymore. And sometime, obladi, oblada, all men became like women, and so women no longer needed to be womanly. The Kinks had recorded a popular song called Lola about that. And sometimes, oh so seldom, men remained men and women remained women, and they came together in their difference and were very happy. But in the end, men had to remain men and women women because D. H. Lawrence, author of these thoughts, had learned to love complicated, contradictory love affairs.

On Thursday, June 12, 1997, Frauke, Angela, Vivian, and Hans— plus a Luxembourgian auditor named Maurice—sat in Ilse Schoolmistress' bright yellow Ford Escort. The holder of the vehicle's registration was not on board; she had to teach in the Odenwald. Frauke, who had gotten her driver's license ages ago in Travemünde, proved to be an inexperienced but not unadept chauffeuse, and after only four hours on overcrowded highways, amid multiple, thunderous listenings of a cassette of Sleater-Kinney's brand-new album Dig Me Out, which sped up time, the five amigos—or as the case may be amigas—rolled into the Bavarian state capital. Angela Guida had dyed her dainty shock of hair platinum blonde like Frauke Stöver, an idea the two fiancées had run across during an enthusiastic reading of Ernest Hemingway's unfinished novel The Garden of Eden, in the plot of which the newly married hero, a lyric I called David (possibly Hemingway himself, Frauke said) is gradually molded by his spouse, the madcap Catherine, into her image. Already by the honeymoon the man has to serve as a compliant girl in bed, the woman approaches him as a resolute boy, as Frauke also liked to do, which, in turn, the phallic Angela could tell people a thing or two about.

Maurice, who was sitting next to Angela, looked aside awkwardly. Just now the mighty Schloss Charlottenburg rolled past the Escort; even the Alps could be made out in the distance, as sharp as a pin. And yet The Garden of Eden is only available, for reasons absolutely incomprehensible to me, in an edition—just imagine, you all—abridged by more than a thousand pages, Frauke said, complaining about this thus doubly unfinished, somewhat risqué posthumous work by the suicide victim. All this doesn't really fit with the rumors about Hemingway's chest toupee, Hans Mühlenkamm determined thoughtfully while Frauke threaded Ilse's car through Munich's evening rush-hour traffic. It kind of does though, countered Vivian, who had read in Marjorie Garber that Ernest Hemingway and his older sister Marcelline had as children been dressed by their mother as same-sex twins, today as boys, tomorrow as girls, how the mother had generally liked to call her son her summer girl—which a famous song of the same name testified—and that, furthermore, the poet's youngest offspring ultimately professed to being a cross-dresser. Probably a coincidence, Garber had written, which put an additional spin on the fascinating, in any case complex Hemingway (hi)story. Maurice, who had positioned his left arm behind Angela and Hans on the rear window shelf, not least because of the crampedness of the Escort, ran his hand through his seatmate's bleached hair and said quite simply: charmant. Vivian, who had been sitting up front since Augsburg, had a city map unfolded on her thighs, which peeked out from Oshkosh overalls she had cut off shortly before the departure. Hans leaned his head out of the open window. There might well still be a thunderstorm coming today.

An hour later everyone but Maurice, who had only been brought along for his contributions to fuel costs and wanted to visit a reprobate girl cousin of his in Munich, was sitting in a lecture hall at the Munich university. In no time at all it had been filled to such a degree that the entire assembly got to move next door to a larger room. For a brief moment Hans was ashamed of his gender, of which, proportionally speaking, strikingly few specimens were present. Then Judith Butler entered, immensely congenial, winsomely refined, Hans found. Vivian's heart was thumping like crazy as the American woman then stepped to the podium, was asked by an older, obviously local female Americanist who was to give some introductory remarks to have a seat first on a chair readied for her, and finally approached the microphone herself, but ten or twelve feet in front of Hans and Vivian. Frauke and Angela had slipped off into the back row right away; they were truly incapable of refraining for even a minute from fumbling around with each other obscenely. For which reason Angela, by majority decision, had also had to spend the entire trip to Munich in the back seat. Judith Butler's talk was about Antigone in particular and in general about a definition of family kinship. When toward the end of her text the author shifted over to the German translation on a whim, it occurred to Vivian again how extraordinarily circuitously her bulky mother tongue functioned. Daddy Atkinson had once strictly forbidden himself from learning even one word more than the most rudimentary phrases in German: Where may I do my laundry, please? I would like to dress my own salad. I have come to ask for the hand of your daughter in marriage.

Even Hansi Mühlenkamm, whose first foreign language was French, had understood Antigone's political claim as explicated by Judith Butler somewhat better in the unfamiliar idiom of English than in the synonymously meandering translation into German. Did you know in fact, the ash-blond part-time physician's receptionist asked the brunette sitting next to him after the presenter had finished and the entire lecture hall—including Frauke and Angela, who had even leapt to their feet—had burst into frenetic applause, that Judith Butler, as I overheard from the row behind us, has a more or less bourgeois small family with wife and kid, the puritanically American dictates of which, on the contrary, she so vehemently opposes, even in the essay we just heard on Antigone, Daughter of Oedipus? And so what, replied Vivian, who didn't care either if communists drove Mercedes. Hans, however, felt a certain jealousy rise up inside him; he would gladly have changed places with Judith Butler's enviable girlfriend under the California sun Brian Wilson sang about. An inner stirring of which the American-German college girl immediately took note, by all means with relief, for the young Offenbacher's up until now so exceedingly exclusive infatuation with Vivian Atkinson had placed upon her, despite all her fondness for him, a not inconsiderable burden in the course of the preceding months.

A couple of pointless questions from the audience as well as the pathologically recognition-craving incest blather from an obviously Freudian female Americanist rounded off the evening's event, the university porter was already rattling his key ring, and around half past nine the ground-floor lecture hall was emptied into Munich's Schellingstrasse. At which point Hans in fact weaseled his way up front for a second, past the staff, to ask the theory star whether she would be back in Heidelberg again in the foreseeable future. Unfortunately not, answered Judith Butler, who knew how to speak pleasantly fluent German, she gave the same talk yesterday, just in Berlin. Which I enjoyed enormously, Hans Mühlenkamm stammered in English, for which the American woman in turn thanked him amicably. And thus: end of the performance. The fan bolted away overjoyed; his travel companions had observed the scene from the elevated rear ranks, not far from the exits. Crazy, Frauke Stöver squealed, drumming with both fists on Hansi's shoulders, you actually spoke with her, for that I'm going to give you my only handbag (a heinous piece from the eighties that the collector wouldn't even want thrown at him). But he said nothing about it—for Frauke would have forgotten about the matter tomorrow anyway—and asked instead: pizza or McDonald's? In fact, all four were ravenously hungry, and so before long they were feasting in a vile pizzeria in Schwabing, the inquisitive Angela masticating Butler's amazing theorems, her cheeks full. A miracle that the entire lasagna didn't fall out of the temperamental peroxide blonde's painted face: my beautiful cock, nothing but the result of political agreements made flesh? At which point a lively debate flared up about whether Frauke's and Angela's engagement should be classified as homosexual, heterosexual, or even heterosexual by compulsion. And whether—in case the protagonists of post-Fordism, all men, didn't better themselves—compulsory homosexuality should be imposed upon the world. At any rate, the waiter, getting nervous, brought the check before the noisy circle had even come close to finishing the food.

Even on the Autobahn Angela Guida refused to accept that her feminine gender impersonation, universally considered perfect, was to be judged a parodic repetition of discursive practices of signification, a subversive act for the higher aim of a revolutionary multiplication of genders, namely beyond the—as all those in the Ford thought—absolutely scrappable binary system. By the same token, Angela in no way wanted to get rid of her penis (which, according to Frauke, answered to a woman's name), stridently justifying this with the Cartesian separation of body and mind, but Vivian Atkinson called to mind that even Simone de Beauvoir's differentiation—originally read as emancipative—between sex and gender, i.e. anatomic and social sex, had been produced discursively, and that wholly reactionary biologisms were ultimately codified in the hierarchizing separation of both categories via phallogocentrism. Sex in particular was, according to Judith Butler, always already gender. Lacan had once pointed out the impossibility of the prediscursive. To denaturalize absolutist chimeras of science like the body, identity, and the subject was today's slogan, the master's candidate said excitedly. And as for Descartes, Angelo, she added insidiously, is it actually even consistent with your Catholic faith to conceive of the mind as the inner world and body as the outer world? Poor Angela was completely lost and put on a disgruntled face. Below the Dossenheim rock quarries, however, she had had a vision during a rising full moon only a few weeks ago (or rather, according to Frauke, thought she had one) that, if she was honest, pretty much transcended any Cartesian worldview. During the night afterward she had dreamed she was a blonde-locked, lascivious abbess seeking the earthly whereabouts of Jesus' foreskin in the Middle East and, while dreaming, had thrashed about so wildly that Frauke Stöver, who pantomimed this incident in Ilse's bright yellow car, came away with a black eye.

There wasn't much happening on the Autobahn when around two in the morning the Escort purred over the Swabian Mountains with the Heidelberg clique. In the car's interior the heated conversation about Judith Butler and Angela Guida had totally lost its way. The Italian flipped sulkily through her Monika, a Catholic women's magazine to which she had subscribed since 1995—to the great amazement of her travel companions—and ultimately became engrossed in a womanly travel guide to the island of Corsica. Ganz einfach Frau, simply woman; this motto of the glossy, published in 86601 Donauwörth, had one day fluttered out of Ilse's TV guide on an advertising leaflet that opened with the disarming doctrinal lines: simply being woman is the new womanhood's attitude toward life. Today's woman self-consciously embraces her typically feminine qualities because she has been emancipated for quite some time. She works hard for a harmonious life and rediscovers Christian virtues. She adheres to her life's work, and she expects more from her magazine than just fashion and cosmetics. She likes to read, and she reads Monika. Even the fine print Angela had found extremely promising: Yes, I'd like to get to know Monika. Send me the next two issues at no charge and with no obligation. After receiving the second issue I have ten days to decide if I would like to receive Monika regularly at twelve issues a year. Only if I am convinced, and so on, delivered free to your door for thirty-eight marks and forty pfennigs. The phallic Catholic girl had promptly subscribed, and so the enthroned

Playboy in Frauke's, Ilse's, and Pat's—and now her—communal bathroom had found in chaste Monika a sinful partner.

Simply woman is of course nonsense, Angela, Hans Mühlen-kamm said, trying to snatch the sulking girl next to him from her escapist reading; in vain, she had perhaps glued her gaze to a single letter. And so Frauke had to feign slamming on the brakes dangerously in order to regain her bride-to-be's attention: Lesley Ferris, she began, remarks in her essay on Goethe, Goldoni, and Woman-Hating, published by Memphis State University in 1990, that the German poet revered in the femininely dressed Italian castrati of his time not the thing itself but its imitation. Whereby the thing would have been the woman—your monthly Monika, Angela—just as the man-loving French poet Cocteau, on the other hand, had almost managed to restructure himself as a lover of woman in his hymn to the Texan transvestite and trapeze art-ist Barbette. Makes sense, said Hans, Cocteau as cock, Barbette as barbed woman. And Goethe's thing in itself as woman, Viv-ian added with amusement, but Frauke Stöver still wanted to be a bit more explicit about it: if both the misogyny of the alleg-edly heterosexual Goethe and the veneration of women by the gay décadent Cocteau had drawn upon male representations of so-called femaleness, then essentialist lines of argumentation like those from Donauwörth about being able to be simply woman are simply shit.

Hans scratched the back of his head. A really stupid question, he said: if in fact, according to Judith Butler, the body is a text and the subject as such doesn't exist, and one is instead to proceed from—to use your expression, Frauke—a perpetuum mobile that both manifests and exhausts itself in one, I'll say, incessantly chattering process of meaning-making ranging from the gestural to the verbal, then of course the so-called female is also an effect of this praxis. And if, as it says in Meret Oppenheim, men project their contingent of femaleness onto women who, like satellites, revolve around this patriarchal central orb, then women represent an outsourced partial quantity of what we once misunderstood, that is, overestimated as the male subject? Or a vestige of what, prior to Judith Butler, would have been called the object? In Luce Irigaray both the Self and the Other are already coded male. Yeah, so what is a woman then really, Angela Guida butted in again all of a sudden, with striking impatience, almost suggestiveness, and what is deep down inside her? Frauke Stöver, whose face, seeming distinctly alert for the late hour, was illuminated at this moment by the gleaming reflection of a rapidly approaching sports car in the rearview mirror, slammed the palm of her hand on the steering wheel, partial quantities, partial men, male parts, she ruminated with a short, shrill laugh, but then posed the surprising counter question: what is a picture, Angela, and what is in it? At this the proud female hermaphrodite again fell silent. Hans, too, again abandoned his more difficult train of thought for the time being. What would the difference be exactly—Vivian mused to herself instead in the front seat—if the body weren't even a text but a picture, the very picture of a woman, the very picture of a man? On top of this, a distinct sympathy for Angela crept over her. However candid her pretersexual globetrot made itself out to be, Vivian Atkinson felt herself reminded time and again—if she observed this successful reconstruction of a waitress, who was sexy by traditional conceptions—of Butler's critical remarks on Foucault's almost bucolic estimation of the ultimately suicidal paramours of Herculine Barbin. Outside of horror films,

the heroes who died for science were hardly ever scientists themselves, the budding female academic thought.

Was Angela now happier than Angelo ever could have been?
Could she, lounging lasciviously in the Escort, actually be characterized as a cross-dresser, at once subject and object of the
gaze? Was Angela not Angelo? Her image of woman not his male
fantasy? Alias Carmen, Medusa, Salome? Back there in the rear
seat with Hans, did Angelo's dick not cause a pretty enormous
bulge in Angela's chic wrap dress? If she had gotten a nose job,
why not, to be blunt, a penis job too? What was Freud actually
getting at when he wrote that only one set of genitals—the male
ones, that is—played a role for both genders? And Lacan again,
when he stressed that the phallus, which no one could possess
anyway, is in no way whatsoever the organ it symbolizes, neither
penis, nor clitoris, but the pure representation that completely
cancelled itself out in the presence of what it represented? The
student with the straggly transitional hairdo stretched herself in
her front passenger seat as well as she could while buckled up
(according to one of her professor's anecdotes, even Habermas
had failed miserably at Lacan), folded out the vanity mirror, and
looked into the back seat, realizing that the sinful Italian had
fallen asleep; her little head lay on Hansi's shoulder. He, flash-
light in his mouth, engrossed in Irmgard Möller. The Escort at
full speed. Was there perchance a male hysteric hidden away in
Angela Guida like Baudelaire, Flaubert, Huysmans, Mallarmé,
Péladan? Whose respective self-feminizations had signified not
a devotion to women, but rather, Vivian knew, a usurpation of
femininity in their own interests. Just as she had learned to conceive of the invention of the femme fatale as a phantasmagoria of

an indubitably male female existence. Woman as an obsession. Mae West and Madonna both as genetically female drag queens. Gender (grammatical) and genius. Key words that Vivian wrote on her right thigh with a pen from Ilse's glove compartment. A mosquito had mistakenly found its way into the car's interior. Frauke squashed it to death near her carotid artery, and from the back Hans asked how far they still had to go. The four individuals, thirsty for knowledge, each exhilarated differently, thus drove through the stormy summer night and finally reached the Upper Rhine Valley at the break of dawn.

The overseer struck the Hindu with the whip in the middle of his face. With this sentence the Nazi author Karl Aloys Schenzinger opened his 1936 historical novel Aniline about the Baden Aniline & Soda Factory, with which he was able to build somewhat seamlessly on Hitler Youth Quex, his big hit of 1932. Pat Meier had organized a small private reading at home in Handschuhsheim to which Bodo Petersen had also been invited. And since he had just picked up his archaic sidecar from the Ladenburg repair shop, his pretty neighbor definitely ought to come along too (to which end he violently buzzed at her door), which meant sitting in the coach with wheels on one side which Petersen had just screwed on to his BMW motorcycle. Vivian agreed because this way she could give a whole stack of borrowed records back to Frauke Stöver without lugging them around, but actually found herself (for Frauke and Angela had headed out who knows where) again sitting Indian style in front of the gruff Pat Meier on a foam rubber cushion that was in the process of falling apart, between Ilse Schoolmistress (who had made gallons of tea), and Mr. Petersen (who was not at all used to sitting on the floor), as well as a handful of grungy anarchists whose giant dogs romped around in the corridor.

At the beginning of the summer semester in 1858, a very young man strode excitedly through Heidelberg's lanes and sought, as he said every chance he got, someplace to live, Pat read aloud. He had already viewed the castle. What had had the strongest impression on him was the view from the terrace out onto the city and the Neckar Valley. And here it comes, the reader said: he just couldn't warm to the structure itself. He just preferred a whole structure to a destroyed one. Isn't that awesome? The hostess, the rare hint of a smile about her mouth, turned twenty-three pages further into the year 1865, where a sentimental gardener by the name of Klingele narrowmindedly threatens to prevent national progress in the guise of BASF by boasting impudently of Herr Engelhorn's magic potion shop, and that his cabbages will probably soon taste like sulfur, his universally renowned apple wine like chlorine. And what an unsavory sharecropper he was for Karl Aloys Schenzinger, who writes: Here the garden master took a break. He finally had to wipe his brow and see that he got some air. Besides, it was important to see what the effect was of what people were saying; direct quote, Schenzinger, Pat said. The good mayor's vigorous counter-speech: What you just said, Mr. Klingele, seems to me to be the salient point of your whole approach. Fear for your own benefit—which, incidentally, is unfounded—causes you to distort the entire issue. Mr. Engelhorn is a man with almost genius business sense. He tells himself that aniline dyes are a German invention, but there isn't a German factory that exploits them. Pat Meier wanted to page further, but the mayor of Ludwigshafen wasn't done yet: Mr. Engelhorn most certainly reckons with the fact that the new factory will have to be enlarged mightily in the very shortest time, and that requires space, space, and more space. A factory without room, so to say, the reader commented, and the anarchists nodded; in their view the fatal realization of a militant corporation like IG Farben needed to be analyzed in detail from all angles. Bodo Petersen from Brunsbüttel shifted his weight to the left butt cheek. Where, pray tell, had he ended up here?

For her last get-together Pat Meier had read aloud Serve the People/Red Army Faction: The Urban Guerrilla and Class Struggle, the famous RAF writ from April 1972, dated one month before the Heidelberg car bombs. Its content briefly: corporations and the state; West-German domestic and foreign policies as the domestic and foreign policies of the corporations; the multinational organization of the corporations and the national parochialism of the proletariat; the urban guerrilla as the connection between national and international class struggle; the exemplary meaning of the chemical workers' strike of 1971, militarization of class struggles; the objective reality of the social question (read: poverty) in the Federal Republic of Germany; by contrast, the subjective reality of the question of ownership; reformism and the difference between the CDU and the SPD; the role of the Springer Press; possibilities and function of the urban guerrilla; furthermore, remarks on treason, liberalism, bank robbery, and solidarity. A super text by the RAF that almost everyone assembled on the floor greeted rapturously even a quarter century after its publication. Schenzinger, on the other hand, had extolled the heroic rise of BASF to its violent expansion in a kind of futurist epic whose most significant howlers Pat Meier insisted upon reading even after the second intermission: The other came. The new. The supplement. It came inevitably. The reflection joined the idea. Out of the idea arose tangible form. Out of invention pushed forth practical application. Out of theory emerged practical value from valorization, the commodity. In the test tube lay the milligram. The milligram girdled the fruit of a mental process. Pat's guests jeered. The milligram girdled the fruit of a mental process, she repeated. Consumption demanded the kilo, required the hundredweight, screamed for tons. Even Mr. Petersen, who now lay on his back, could hardly contain himself any longer and found it—as he readily assured Vivian—unfortunate that he didn't yet know Pat Meier four weeks ago when she was concerned with the RAF flyers. Sounds like it could be a pretty fun club, he whispered to his neighbor. Was it possible that the hobby biker had never heard of Baader-Meinhof, Irmgard Möller, and the Red Army Faction?

This was the foundation, the woman from Darmstadt continued reading in the meanwhile. This was the factory. The beginning was difficult. The chemist stood in the empty factory building. He had no prototype for this. He lacked all experience. The methods he brought with him from his laboratory failed miserably here, the instruments he had used up until now seemed dollishly delicate, even ridiculous before the magnitude of the tasks that had been set for him here. Everything was to be rendered a thousand-fold, a million-fold. Pat Meier looked earnestly into the assembled circle, took a sip of tea, and kept reading at the bottom of page 244: The chemist stuck to his guns. He became completely absorbed in his new task. He became a technician. At his side was a specialized worker. From his schooling this worker brought an active intellect, from his military service the discipline for work. Running the factory demanded military order—and got it. It had now become very still at the reader's feet, chills running down the spine of even the good-natured BASF employee Petersen. Pat Meier flipped around a hundred pages further, toward the end of the book, Schenzinger's present, the German past, still not overcome in 1997. Sixty thousand tons of gum elastic per year for German tires, it read. No sources of naphtha, no oil, no rubber in our own country. No colonies. Dangerous sums threaten to flow off abroad. We are cramped, geographically, economically, politically. We want to live; exclamation point. The demand for synthetic material grew louder and louder. Petersen had never seen it from that perspective before. Today synthetic material determines the future of the German nation. Synthetic material has become the vital question for Germany.

And don't forget, Pat Meier said, walking her guests to her front door along with their dogs, who had been sleeping, that the Baden Aniline & Soda Factory, according to Ludwigshafen's greatest son, Ernst Bloch, lies, so to speak, in the middle of our Song of the Nibelungs. The anarchists had already climbed into their old VW bus when from Pat Meier's wide-open upstairs window Blochian phrases were still zipping past both their ears and those of the two adoptive Edingers: on Germany's most solemn river. Between Speyer and Worms. In the middle of the Song of the Nibelungs. One step over the bridge, and the air was different. Germany's biggest factory here. Germany's biggest castle over in Mannheim. The realities and ideals of the industrial age seldom so close together. The dirt as well as the royally built-in money. All around Ludwigshafen the misty plain. Bogs and watery sloughs. The college girl and the employee were putting on their helmets. Bloch: A kind of prairie. No little manors and idylls. Factory walls and fiery chimneys. The song of the telephone poles. Ilse School-mistress tried to pull Pat Meier away from her window; in vain: We lads at the water's edge felt nymphs in the flesh, tree gods on odd evenings, when the waves of the Rhine lay like glass. Here Pat's sermon was interrupted by the roaring of the VW bus, which had finally started after several backfires. Vivian Atkinson called up that she didn't even know Bloch had been from Ludwigshafen. But of course he was, Pat bellowed back, all around there were only industrial buildings, son of a Jewish Royal Bavarian Railway administrator. The Palatinate, for centuries an exclave of Bavaria, even Petersen could report.

Vivian took a seat in his sidecar. She thought she saw the sky in the far west glowing bloodred over the factory. Was it really possible that the chimneys of BASF sang the Song of the Nibelungs? And why had Pat Meier thought this Germanic race of dwarves worthy of comment in the first place? What could the anarchists take away from that? Which nymphs had the young Marxist Bloch felt in the reeds on the riverbank, and what had he set about to do with their corporeality? How in fact had the male construction nymphomania gotten its dubious name? And what did leftist, or more precisely, post-leftist thought actually care about Germanic mythology? Hadn't Vivian even read in a recent declaration of the honorable Socialist Patients Collective of Heidelberg—which had been calling itself the Patients' Front since 1973 and issued its so-called Kränkschriften, or writs of aggrievance, in its own Publishing House for Sickness—a reference to the legendary Odenwald as Wotan's a.k.a. Odin's Forest? Master of sorcery who drank from Mimir's well, god of war, victory, death. The ravens his attendants, Gungnir his spear, Slepnir his steed. Bodo Petersen, who indicated having just now heard the name Ernst Bloch for the second time in his entire life, stepped on the gas; in three and a half hours he would have to get up again and head into the factory. Was it actually OK that he let his beloved business be bad-mouthed by a political extremist? Had he perhaps even developed a crush on Pat Meier? Or vice-versa? Or did she (the single-minded one) only keep him (the clueless one) around in order to retrain him bit by bit as a traitor? Weren't his secret photos taken from the rock quarry already plant espionage, yes, even sabotage?

At home in the tobacco warehouse, Vivian Atkinson did not go straight to bed. She pulled various references works from the bookshelves next to her big map of Ohio and learned that Manuscript C of the Song of the Nibelungs had, with high probability, been written down at the foot of the Odenwald, toward Worms, where it primarily takes place, in the old Imperial Abbey of Lorsch, founded another four hundred years prior by its poetry-writing abbot Sigehard von Schauenburg, 1167–1198, who accordingly let his vertically-challenged heroes hunt in the Odenwald, where many a spring was named for Siegfried, who in turn supposedly also found his eternal rest in the Abbey of Lorsch, where Siegfriedstrasse intersects exactly two Autobahns. Just as—Vivian now on the couch—the dowager's estate of Kriemhild's mother Ute could also be found there. The Lorsch Codex, the curious student learned while day broke outside, contained the entire history of the Odenwald from the eighth to the thirteenth century and was preserved in the Bavarian State Archives. Though the mythical designation Odenwald had been documented since the eighth century. Maps said: there was not just Siegfriedstrasse running straight through the entire Odenwald but, to the great horror of historians, a Nibelungenstrasse as well that—running largely parallel, likewise oriented East-to-West—intersected the former a bit farther north behind the Limes Germanicus in Bavaria. The same picture of the streets of Worms: Nibelungian names as far as the eye could see. Only now did it occur to Vivian that Pat had shown Bodo not only the gas flares of BASF in the viewfinder above the rock quarry on the Pentecost holiday, but, oddly as it had seemed to her then, the towers of the medieval cathedrals of Speyer and Worms, too. That even the knights of the Tiefburg of Handschuhsheim had once been in the service of the Abbey of Lorsch perhaps went too far at this juncture, Vivian thought on her way into the bathroom. In the post-scientific belief that everything is interrelated, many people had pretty quickly gotten bogged down already. Not just Donna Haraway.

Fax from Hans Mühlenkamm, Medical Practice of Dr. Ancelet, 7/4/1997, 3:03 p.m.: Dear Viv, after multiple excited listenings of the current double album of the group Conjoint, centered around the vibraphonist Karl Berger and our Heidelberg hero David Moufang, a.k.a. Move D, who even plays guitar here, I put on the new Sleater-Kinney LP you gave me after our Munich excursion yesterday evening again. Silvia Bovenschen, whose name I likewise first learned through you, investigated in her groundbreaking book Imagined Femininity back in 1979 the noteworthy proportion—I think I may call it disproportion—between the few women who write and the hosts of women who have been written since the eighteenth century. Already in the foreword she pleads for an as-yet-to-be-written history of the lack of female history, which reminds me a bit (allow me this digression) of how you recently announced to me on the Molkenkur your desire to write a never-before-seen history of the present. Bovenschen writes: As the embodiment of the unity of nature, woman is what man attempts to reproduce in the work of art. Yet this affinity does not become a chance for women, serving instead the legitimation of their exclusion from this sphere, too. On the occasion of the formal contrast between Conjoint's instrumental, supposedly intrinsically quiescent sounds and Sleater-Kinney's vocally determined songs, I have now noticed (I can't say with reassurance) how Sleater-Kinney's voices, those of Corin Tucker and Carrie Brownstein, as Carrie Kinney now calls herself, oscillate perpetually between body and text, how in the so-called singer-songwriter, particularly (let me half-translate that) in the songstress-songwriter, neither just she who is written, nor just she who writes can be seen.

In other words, Vivian: whom or what does a sexy female singer-songwriter actually represent? And in what capacity? As authoress? As text? Embodiment of her text? As navel? As a voice calling for reconciliation? Is she subject, object, or both at the same time? Do I go beyond the literary scholar Bovenschen when I conceive of a girl group—whose members may even have written their very intelligent songs themselves—primarily as written women? Whereby the patriarchally condescending, implicitly biased attestation of intelligence itself is already more than problematic because it spreads not only the pestilent blight of racism—according to which African Americans have smaller brains than European Americans—but also that of sexism—according to which you yourself have so often been classified, quite villainously, as a woman who is as smart as she is pretty. In the end, hiding behind male compliments, there are simply almost always very subtle procedures of exclusion. Or have you ever heard of a woman being called a genius? Only the imagined, the symbolic woman is close to art, Bovenschen contends. How can one break through the fact, I ask (jumping, as it were, out of my skin), that woman is understood by man—who eternally defines the Other instead of himself—merely as a creature of nature and species? Oops, I have to close here, the doctor is back from her lunch break, and I haven't even aired out the waiting room yet. Awaiting verbal clarification, H. M.

Oops, Vivian thought too, as she picked up her heavily worn copy of Imagined Femininity again herself, following Hansi's telefax, and got stuck once more on Ernst Bloch's quoted words. The Ludwigshafener had spoken of the half-colonial status of women; that definitely had to be forwarded on to Korinna Kohn right away. A heavy summer rain fell over Edingen. The Dossenheim rock quarries clouded over, an unsufficiently colorized black-and-white photograph. In all of the Patrick Henry Village, everyone always went crazy on the Fourth of July each and every year; today the American national holiday meant nothing at all to the army brat anymore. Rather than as a container of misfortune, Pandora's dowry could be read as a box of mysteries too, even as Pandora herself: The Principle of Hope, first volume, pages 388 and 389; as soon as possible, Vivian noted with amusement, deliver into Hansi's hands, fax to the female specialist Ancelet, MD. Also from the second volume—the title of the chapter in question: Struggle for the New Woman—Silvia Bovenschen had cited a significant passage of Blochian ambiguity regarding the feminine, which was about the frothily half-decisive, wrongly decisive, indecisive jumble and intertwining in woman, as present society delivers her to a future one. About things gentle and wild, destructive and merciful, flower and witch, the haughty bronze and the diligent soul of business. What's more, about the maenads and prevailing Demeter, mature Juno, cool Artemis, Russian Minerva, and whatever else, wrote Bloch, seeking to overcome previous womanhood as a masquerade in a better world for the benefit of an anticipated, true nature of the feminine.

Where in the world does—Angela remarked surprisingly in the Escort at the gas station, somewhere around Degerloch—the questionable boundary lie between radical deconstruction and compulsory religiosity and thus the difference between your and my worldview? After all, even the alleged spherical shape of the earth is nothing more than a convenient convention of sophisticated conduct, a harmless novella, a Harawayian scientific narrative, a projection, proverbially, as even the strictest cartographers of free spirit would confess. That's right, Vivian thought. Exactly, had been Frauke's terse commentary. But why then, Angela, did the Catholic church, Hans had asked, ultimately cave in to the triumphal march of the globe, in contrast to its stalwartly overdue recognition of the (in no way less compulsory, in fact supremely dangerous) construction of Darwinism, as Hans put it, the theory of evolution? In the laboratories of the Vatican, the world definitely does not exist as either a sphere or a disk, the (so to speak) outlawed church ally had thought she knew, recognizing imitation as her possibility of feminine self-representation. No one in Ilse's yellow car, which had long been sweeping over the highway at full speed again, had had anything to respond to that. Rather difficult, Vivian thought, flipping through Bovenschen's seventh printing, anno 1993, and not really any adequate reply to Hansi Mühlenkamm's question either. Having become pensive, she thus fetched herself a pen from her Rococo tablet and, while standing at the window, the Odenwald in her blind spot, formulated the following half sentences which had seemed to their author as she wrote them down hesitantly on a fresh sheet of paper very ponderous, almost pathetic. The Woman in the Mirror as the proverbially vanished woman; no women's magazine had ever been more aptly named. The unashamedly demanding, disenfranchizing, massacring gaze of the invisible man behind her: beyond her shoulder, through her iris. This gaze as a viewpoint that robbed her of her mirror image in which (and thus not: by which) she imagined first having found herself after, with, in her husband's words. Yours, Vivian. To fax something like this to Hans, without a second thought?

Two weeks later in the glowing heat, the student sat in a slow local train, departing from Heidelberg, heading up the Neckar Valley toward Mosbach, across from a very handsome boy from Bremen who recounted to her excitedly how the robot Sojourner, having recently landed on Mars, was awakened and whipped into shape every morning through space radio by the samba rhythms of Coisinha do Pai, which could be translated as Daddy's Pretty Thing. The choice of this little song, unusually frivolous for scientific contexts, went back to the initiative of a female Brazilian engineer who had been allowed to help in preparations for the current Mars expedition with the American space agency NASA. At this it became apparent that the pronounced attractiveness of the Hanseatic boy originated from his Portuguese mother, a famous concert pianist who had brought him into the world on the father's conning bridge three weeks earlier than planned, not far from the Cape Verdean islands and on stormy seas. A gigantic mess, as the strikingly candid Bremer expressed it to his fresh acquaintance, the father's noble card table just as blood-smeared as the first officer's white pants.

Further topics in the sun-drenched compartment: the midsummery weather, the identification of Ernesto Che Guevara's skeleton exhumed from under the airstrip of Vallegrande, Bolivia, Karl Lagerfeld's newest favorite model—therefore Claudia Schiffer's successor—a blonde Dutch woman named Esther de Jong about whom specifically the so-called arrogance of her profile as well as the never-ending length of her neck delighted the ponytailed fashion designer, her (in Lagerfeld's words) spontaneous, uncompromising, total modernity, the Bundeswehr's scandal video, inadvertently made public, in which German conscripts act out the rape and execution of subhuman Eastern Europeans, and the imminent feminist opening of the Catholic Church, as currently circulating in the daily papers, after Augsburg's Bishop Dammerz had declared that the denominational language is pervasively male in a no longer acceptable way. But then wasn't church per se a thoroughly female-coded issue? Talk to Angela about this now and again, Vivian thought, immersing herself in the pleasantly fragrant captain's son's well-thumbed Frankfurter Allgemeine. The line is long, the soldiers all want to mount a woman, said the soundtrack of the Bundeswehr video: after her rape the defiled woman has to drag a wooden cross over the parade grounds, then she'll be crucified. The television network SAT 1 had broadcast the film, exclusively, already twice in one day.

In Hirschhorn, below the castle, the curious brunette got out of the train on the spur of the moment to check out a pub described by Mark Twain with the (she thought) sensational name The Naturalist. A wow escaped her lips as she approached, down the sleepy street in front of the train station, a somewhat unappealing box of concrete whose various markings promised not only the casino to the side, the community center and restaurant The Naturalist in front, but also a Mark Twain Parlor inside. The latter's separate entrance proved, however, to be blocked by a potted palm tree. Vivian Atkinson gathered her courage, stepped into the dining room The Naturalist, said a friendly hello in German, was taken for an American, wanted to be let into said Mark Twain Parlor, which was not possible, however, since it, regrettably, alas (said a man polishing glasses behind the bar), was only opened for groups of a hundred people or more, ordered a Coca-Cola, found absolutely nothing special in this historic, carelessly historicized locale, and dawdled, somewhat ill-humoredly, back to the train station, kicking a peach pit in front of her with her platform sneakers. Had she only continued conversing with the handsome boy instead of impulsively interrupting her little trip, she thought. Oppressive midday heat blanketed the small Neckar town; there the only child would loll about on a shady embankment in the grass until the next Swabian train came and idly page through— in the presence of the Hessian police who resided in the little gatehouse—the travel reading she had brought along, Boyarin's Unheroic Conduct. Twain, anyway, had recommended enjoying the view of the old Odenwald castle from afar: Hirschhorn is best seen from a distance.

Neckarelz: change to the Odenwald Railroad. A nice traveler lent Vivian his mobile telephone such that at the Mosbach train station (Baden once again) Korinna's white Tatra, now with license plate code MOS, sat catty-corner under a pruned sapling in a cloud of blue exhaust, super on-time. The girl from Edingen only needed to get in, and then they both rattled away toward a rather deserted area of the far side of the Odenwald called Bauland. Haven't seen you in forever, said Korinna Kohn, who wore ugly, possibly valuable Versace sunglasses; the Italian fashion designer had only just been murdered in Miami, Florida. Even Vivian thought her reunion with her classmate was long overdue. Haven't changed a bit, she said without really meaning it, for Korinna had, since moving away from Heidelberg, very clearly put on a few pounds. Really? She, freshly crimped, was delighted at Vivian's amicable gesture, took it as a compliment, and took off her sunglasses. Versace, she said solemnly in his memory.

They'd be something for Angela, Vivian remarked, and in no time Korinna wanted to know every detail about the status of the relationship between the masculine woman from the Baltic beach whom she had once so loved and the hyperfeminine man from the Po Basin who had pinched the latter away from her so cruelly. Still not married yet, I think, Vivian answered uncommunicatively, discovering on the floor of the Tatra among all sorts of cosmetics an English tennis trade journal, a hair band, and three cans of dog food welded together, Donna Haraway's new book Modest_Wit-ness@Second_Millennium.FemaleMan©_Meets_ OncoMouse™. Subtitle: Feminism and Technoscience. Not long ago Frauke Stöver had tried to read it and declared it unreadable. Korinna actually seemed to have read it from beginning to end, but did not necessarily care to recommend it, due to political reservations. In the end Haraway would probably be won over by any old piggish genetic manipulation, she said, taking her foot from the gas pedal and kicking, in symbolic disapproval, at the appealingly dressed-up Routledge book in Vivian's footwell. At that the old Tatra sedan lost its speed and could then only be badgered up out of the Elz Valley at a snail's pace.

When the friends finally arrived in the Bauland and Korinna Kohn pulled her smoking vehicle up in front of her new homestead, Heiner's outrageous mastiff immediately jumped up on the car. No dog food tasted as good to it as that particularly hearty kind from Mosbach on the Neckar. Standing on the terrace of his estate, even Heiner, dressed entirely in white, seemed to be happy that a visitor had come; he had already heard a lot about Vivian, and God knows Korinna hadn't promised him too much. Great figure, he called out still at a distance, describing with his plump hands in the balmy evening air the voluptuous contours of a Greek amphora. Before, back in the Patrick Henry Village, the soldier's daughter would have given polite thanks for such remarks, would have awkwardly said why thank you, perhaps even curtsied, yet ever since her scientific engagement with the triad of having, being, and seeming, she was regarded by womanizing guys as markedly frigid. But because Heiner was not just a dangerous criminal, but also her confidante's new lover, she smiled back amicably for a change and called out: likewise, Heiner. The dealer had screwed an acutely insolvent, recently deceased customer— who for his part had inherited it from his uncle killed in action in Sarajevo—out of the white-plastered house with its numerous bricked and forged archways, the colorful flower windows and the industrial-glass stairwell, the two lighted fountains, as well as the generous, lavishly paved southwest terrace. Not a pretty backstory, Heiner said, leading Vivian around the premises while Korinna made coffee, although, look for yourself, an all the more beautiful view, you might even be able to see the Katzenbuckel. How in the hell had Korinna found such a primitive guy? Had he gotten her addicted, maybe with the help of synthetic drugs?

In the guest bathroom the visitor found a text that seemed familiar to her: Appeal for Witnesses. Sightings of British Tarmac Gangs in the Municipal Area. According to police information British tarmac gangs resided in our district in 1995 and 1996. The members of this gang traveled in trailers, trucks, and work vehicles. Through door-to-door solicitations, private persons were allegedly offered cheap yard- and path-tarring. However, work was then carried out unprofessionally and superficially. The remaining tar was disposed of in meadows and forested areas. This constitutes a considerable spoiling of the environment. Furthermore, cases have become known in which down payments were charged for work not done. Who can provide information regarding the stay of members of a tarmac gang in 1995 and 1996? Where were the corresponding tar jobs commissioned or carried out? There followed the applicable telephone number to dial for the appropriate police station, Vivian pulled up her terrycloth underwear, let down her American summer dress, initiated a roaring toilet flush, briefly perused a sticker that suggested to men to sit on the toilet seat to urinate too, washed her hands, wet her face with cold tap water, and examined her eyelashes in the oval mirror over the tiny sink: a lash was caught in her eye and was painfully irritating when she batted them. In childhood Vivian, whose dark, long, naturally curved lashes still garnered admiration today, had once tried to break herself entirely of the habit of intermittently closing the lids, so-called blinking, a monomania she now recalled in Heiner's and Korinna's narrow guest bathroom. With the tip of her index finger she was able to remove the lash and blew it outside through the tipped bathroom window: may Korinna Kohn be freed from this inexplicable imprisonment as soon as possible.

All of them itinerants, Heiner said—you know what I mean, Vivian: itinerants—but no one wanted to press charges against them, from Mannheim to Walldürn not a single charge filed with the police. Inexpert asphalt jobs, all trade law regulations ignored, tar on the shoes of those looking for relaxation, a meteoric rise in bicycle thefts throughout the entire Odenwald—car trailers with vehicle identification numbers filed off were even seized—and still not a single complaint from the populace, the brute ranted, these fuckers deserve to be tarred and feathered, while Korinna, having completely changed clothes, appeared in the patio door with the glass coffee service. One day members of one of these tarmac gangs had even showed up in their—Heiner's and Korinna's—driveway and had made supercilious allusions to this and that from Heiner's precarious professional life for so long that the hard-pressed man of the house had not only agreed to a tarring of the gravel in front of his domicile, but had also even provided a generous advance for it. While the itinerants—you know what I mean, Vivian, said Heiner, from whose lips the following words were issued with reluctance—went to work, I took photos of the wretches (who only had eyes for Korinna's tits anyway and spilled all their sticky tar in the rose beds) on the down low from the kitchen window, several rolls full, which I took to Mosbach to be developed that very afternoon so that the gypsies, eight men between thirteen and thirty-seven years of age—not least thanks to my smooth connections with the criminal investigation division of the police (Heiner said word for word) could be convicted the very next morning before his front door. During their interrogation the wild guys from Liverpool had vehemently denied having carried out any tar jobs in the Odenwald area, and now get this, the dealer snorted as his hairy paw groped Vivian's left knee, they claimed to have their work machinery with them only so that it wouldn't be stolen from them in England, is that not hard as nails, toots? The four legs of the white plastic terrace chair threatened to blow out from under Heiner's booming laughter.

Before she knew it, Vivian Atkinson, against her original intention, had stayed a whole week with her girl friend and her girl friend's boyfriend in the far reaches of the Odenwald. The media reported new details of the Versace murder every day, and the visitor from the plains—who hadn't even brought her own toothbrush with her—worked her way, at first by necessity, then increasingly for fun, through the opulently well-endowed armoire of the Karlruhe magistrate's daughter, who had the same measurements. It happened now and again that Korinna and Vivian had changed clothes three or four times before Heiner—who preferred to handle his business at night—crawled out of bed in the early afternoon. Korinna had apparently taken part in every trend since 1982 and wore, even as a child, as her carefully guarded photo album proved, bikini tops over her flat chest. It's not called a bikini top, there is only le bikini as one and the same article of clothing, as a whole in two colonizing sections, Korinna corrected her friend. I threw away my last bikini not so long ago, Vivian confessed, today wearing a sleeveless tennis dress belonging to Korinna. Was it not already a lie—an arch-lie, even—if a woman said Büstenhalter (breast holder, brassiere) or rather believed the brassiere held the breasts, held them tight and in form? In which and in whose form exactly? The famous female silhouette, who had designed it? Could one, as a woman, ever argue convincingly that one of those delicate brassieres had practical value? So that the breasts didn't bounce up and down when one walked? Why not then just bandage them as Vivian had so liked to do as a young madcap? Do we let our breasts proverbially drop—and where to, Korinna Kohn asked—when we divest ourselves of the bra? Do two hearts beat, alas!, under both Körbchen? In English, by the way, the German Körbchen isn't called basket but cup, Korinna, that is, tasse, tumbler, dish, chalice, goblet. Interesting, interesting. How much significance had resided in the child's helpless gesture when she, in all innocence, had demanded a bikini for those of her body islands coded as sinful, Vivian thought on the third day of the second week of her house call and said: one day I'll definitely have to recount for you the highly unorthodox orthodox California Jewish scholar Daniel Boyarin's theses on the Zionists' colonial drag. I'd really love that, but later, the one with crimped hair replied, turning on the television: apparently Versace's murderer had also wanted to kill Madonna Ciccone.

Eight days prior the Süddeutsche Zeitung had complained about the fact that homosexuals—from Pasolini and Foucault, to Mapplethorpe and Jarman, up to Versace in the recent present (spurned by the SZ as hypocritical)—quite obviously, quote, made better dead people. Thus the Munich feuilleton thought that whoever has to buy young men for love simply enters into the circulation of black money and—sorry, it's an occupational hazard, journalist Willi Winkler worded it—quite simply has himself to blame for his death, in whichever brutal way may have caused it. Sucks for them, so to speak, for the homosexuals, Vivian asked, can that really have been meant that way? Of course, Korinna answered sharply, and unjust luck in just misfortune to whomever might breathe his cowardly last in the noble gutter. Michel Foucault could work as diligently as he wanted to on madness in society; according to the Süddeutsche Zeitung on July 21, he only ever posthumously became an authentic holy man of art by being tortured as a big white gay man in San Francisco's dark rooms. Nope, Willi Winkler, keep your shitty opinion to yourself, Vivian said, sourly taking umbrage after having read Korinna's clipping, for how else besides in an anti-Enlightenment homophobic vein could one read Winkler's cynical summary that gays simply aren't better people and most certainly not martyrs if they die violently or from AIDS?

Ugh, Korinna also remarked, filing the scandalous snippet away again and removing from her wardrobe a daring disco dirndl by the couturier murdered two weeks ago: try this on, Vivian Atkinson. She, however, had taken up her friend's voluminous binder of material in the meantime and opened to a newspaper article about the snapshots by a Bavarian photographer named Ewald Schadt of blonde girls dressed in skimpy lingerie inside a Swabian village church (this last word in bold)—that is, on pews, at the pulpit, and on the altar—that were to be exhibited as high-gloss prints in a (as it was called) super-sexy power show with high artistic aspirations put on by a hobby magician and former insurance salesman named Peki, all this soon in Munich. The Catholic Church showed itself to be—how totally proper, Vivian remarked, how very clever, remarked Korinna, as she had once already when the Vatican determined that anti-baby pills degraded women as the mere sexual objects of men—clearly averse since it understood the questionable photographs, as the relevant ordinariate averred, to be the sexist and misogynist documents of a repressed macho imagination. But the hobby magician Peki, who had intended to crown his event with public body painting as well as—get this— a lesbian performance, countered vehemently that Schadt—this Korinna had underlined with squiggles—creates true works of art from naked girls. Period. The precious disco dirndl which its owner was just tightening at the navel didn't fit Vivian badly at all, almost, its wearer smirked, like a glove sewn by Versace himself, and manifested in her college friend, Korinna Kohn noted with a suddenly unmistakeably teary gaze, a kind of Madonna of almost audacious purity. With disproportionate quiet also, almost parenthetically, the girlish magistrate's daughter's ensuing comment accompanying the stirring of her herbal tea that she had been pregnant with Heiner's child for thirteen weeks now.

At the same moment a pale metallic-green Audi full of noisily blustering Saxons unloaded itself into Heiner's inexpertly tarred driveway. The two startled friends could hear one of them slur:

I'm going to shoot up, and then I'll be in good shape by dinner. Heiner's brother-in-law from his first marriage, Korinna whispered to Vivian with disgust. Her boyfriend had in fact been able to take a large portion of the Saxon drug market under his attentive wing in the first few years after German reunification, even recording a flexi disc with the title I Know Life, back side: O Lord, Won't You Buy Me a Mercedes-Benz. Then though—helter-skelter as Heiner himself said—the entirely unexpected return to the Odenwald, on top of that dirty divorce proceedings with the jilted wife, a barren peroxide blonde from Zwickau; Vivian could not by any stretch of the imagination understand how Korinna had managed to get involved with this man and now even wanted to carry his child to term. Or was it, rather, her child? Had she, twenty-seven at any rate and about to graduate, merely copulated with this (by common standards) well-built backwoods Odenwald guy? In order to fleece him later good and proper? Would her deconstructionist insights hold their ground as corporeal experience against the biological experience of motherhood?

Korinna Kohn had run upstairs to wake Heiner before Godehardt Jablonka (the name of the raucous drunk) could reach the terrace. In the meantime the other Saxons, three in number, stood around smoking in the front yard and cracked lewd jokes about Vivian's flamboyant getup. Then the bedroom window flew open, and Heiner bawled out together with Godehardt, the two arm in arm, Korinna's frightened face behind them in the musty dimness of the boudoir: I Know Life, to a metrically absolutely unsuitable melody unmistakeably derived from the Horst-Wessel-Lied. The Saxons immediately chimed in, at the same time, however, not daring to advance any further onto the premises. Her heart pounding in her throat in these uncannily turbulent minutes,

Vivian Atkinson thought she could make out a rather dark-skinned man crouched behind the front seat behind the tinted windows of the Audi. Why hadn't he gotten out with the others?

On that very same afternoon of July 29, 1997, the events on that property came so thick and fast that its owner ultimately managed to—or rather had to—be marched off by criminal investigators, and in handcuffs no less. As it turned out, Heiner's Saxon brother-in-law had been able to ally himself by way of a public defender with the still-incarcerated members of the British tarmac gang as well as weave an impermeable net of incriminating evidence against the former husband of his maltreated sister and present it to the authorities. Vivian, to some degree distraught, was still in Versace's expensive glitter dress when the patrol cars pulled up, Korinna in a pale-pink-and-beige-striped kimono, thunderstruck, apparently unaffected, observing from the canopy swing with a nearly dispassionate facial expression, as the dealer with white vest over his bare torso was led away without resisting arrest. Gode-hardt Jablonka, who had perhaps only faked his drunkenness, along with his men—now among them the Liverpool witness from the back seat—were meanwhile making sandwiches in the kitchen; they wanted to drive back to Dresden, which they called Florence on the Elbe, that same night. Why in the world, Korinna, Vivian asked when the pale metallic-green Audi had finally absconded, did you get involved with Heiner? I just fell in love with him, came the pitifully meek riposte from the ubiquitously attention-grabbing tennis player, which began, as it were, with a time delay and was stifled in the end by a very bitter flood of tears.

And so the twenty-four-year-old American girl from Heidelberg was supposed to extend her stay with her friend a full second week. It simply wouldn't do for the so promptly abandoned—and pregnant—woman to stay behind in Heiner's lonely house without any succor. There were, in addition, several practical inconsistencies to work out in conversation regarding the gorgeous Korinna's in fact scores of hapless flings; the last three affairs alone—that is, those with Jens, Frauke, and Heiner—had proven themselves to be total busts. Then the two women descended once more, together again, into the enticing theoretical realms of their academic research. So they read Isabell Lorey's disquisition published the previous year in Tübingen, Immer Ärger mit dem Subjekt, The Trouble with the Subject, according to which the subject—totally illuminating, Korinna thought—appeared as an individual, incoherent, and temporary discursive interconnection in movable power structures, in radical opposition to Barbara Duden's support of the reactionary binary by identification, but also unfortunately, however, in relative contradiction to Judith Butler's conception of performance which (in Isabell Lorey's estimation) was ultimately recognizable as a dutiful reproduction of the old-school Cartesian subject. Pooh, Vivian Atkinson huffed, not wanting to let go of Judith Butler so easily; she shut her classmate's edition of The Trouble with the Subject, poured herself a glass of iced tea, and said absentmindedly: I wonder what Heiner is doing right now. Korinna, however, as the fifth daughter of a judge, did not want to hear any more about the jailbird and thus replied: tell me something about the colonial drag of your Californian Jewish scholar instead.

The Bauland lay sallow and hazy in the midsummer midday heat when Vivian began recounting the not uncomplicated achievements of Daniel Boyarin, a colleague of Judith Butler at the University of California in Berkeley, Butler (likewise Jewish) for rhetoric, Boyarin for Talmudic culture, but he also had a very keen sense for Judith Butler's feminist theories and on the front cover depicted a Jewish bridal couple named Ruth Zurom and Hyman Fenster, Catskills, circa 1925, Ruth in the photo on the left, Hyman on the right, which needs to be specified because Ruth convincingly wore Hyman's suit and Hyman, coquettishly, Ruth's blouse and skirt. She with a little stick, a cigarette between her lips, he in her arm, bejeweled, holding the purse in front of his crotch. Subtitle of the book: The Rise of Heterosexuality and the Invention of the Jewish Man. That's really interesting, said Korinna without a trace of irony, after having taken a seat on a white lacquered sunbed dressed in nothing but a pale-blue Cat Power T-shirt. The actual title of the work, which appeared this year from the University of California Press, is listed as—Vivian explained further—Unheroic Conduct and refers to a Freudian anecdote from the Eastearn European childhood of the future father of psychoanalysis; so Sigmund Freud's father is walking through the shtetl, a German Aryan comes along and orders: get off the sidewalk, Jew. And knocks the poor man's fur cap from his head. Which is particularly piquant in light of the fact that the wives of orthodox Jews wore wigs atop shaved heads, Korinna interjected. Freud at this: and what did you do, Father? The old man's answer: I picked the fur cap up again. The son's rather German conclusion finally: This seemed to me rather unheroic conduct. And he thus soon ended up in Vienna. Countering this, Boyarin (somewhere else entirely) turns the discriminating image of the Jew as woman against those who created it and tried to give it a positive spin with the help of his historic heroine Bertha Pappenheim, Freud's (actually his colleague Breuer's) famous Anna O., who, by the by, had referred to Yiddish as the woman's German. The very first sentence of the prologue even reads: As

I reflect on my coming of age in New Jersey, I realize that I had always been in some sense more of a girl than a boy, the two genders each in quotation marks, explained Vivian who—reciting Boyarin, which lay open upstairs next to her mattress, as well as she could from memory, yet not mechanically at all—had fixed her sight on Korinna's dark-blonde pubic hair.

Where may I ask did you get your Cat Power T-shirt? From the same merchandising stand that you got yours, the mother-to-be answered, plucking a shamrock from the lawn that had sprouted visibly since Heiner's arrest. Right; Korinna, Frauke, and Vivian had in fact been together at that concert of the charismatic songstress. There was even a Polaroid Frauke had taken in a Frankfurt hotel bar in which Vivian Atkinson, her big brown eyes turned to the side, showed a striking resemblance to Chan Marshall a.k.a. Cat Power. Her most recent acquisition from the still-slim oeuvre of the conspicuously sensitive, oddly both intro- and extroverted artist who had moved from the American South to New York City's Lower East Side: the CD single release Nude as the News with the second unforgettable song not included on the album What Would the Community Think called Schizophrenia's Weighted Me Down, penned by Alexander Spence, first of Jefferson Airplane, later Moby Grape, possibly from Chan Marshall's parents' record collection. A former boyfriend of Korinna Kohn's was in the middle of writing his doctoral thesis on how the New Right in the USA could be traced back directly to Jefferson Airplane's only reputedly countercultural treasury of songs.

In the evening the two classmates dropped by a fire department ball at the edge of the nearest township that had been advertised on posters throughout the whole district. With their black-rubber platform soles they were taller than the majority of the assembled men, and many of those thus debased seemed to pose for themselves the apprehensive question as to whether these young, confident women would ever descend again from their buskins. On stage in the full-to-bursting party tent between two rubber trees, Heavy Spider, a professional rock band from nearby Amorbach, Bavaria, was performing, oddly enough presenting rock music inadvertently—that is, evidently with utter ignorance—for all eyes and ears as a now thoroughly historical genre. As the musicians swayed their guitar necks to the beat before their bulging lederhosen, the two foreign women had to burst into uproarious laughter. When men still had dicks, Korinna punned, and Vivian added, strictly speaking, such music—since the musicians in the girl punk-rock band The Slits had cribbed their stage getup from the decidedly virile transvestism of the New York Dolls—can really only be performed by females. Totally right, chuckled Korinna Kohn, who had already warmed herself up at home, for upon his arrest Heiner had left behind under the corner bench a whole wad of natural stimulants pregnant women could take. Nothing, alas, for Vivian Atkinson, who, since the (from the disinterested view of a child rather repugnant) hallucinatory experiments of her freakish parents in the Patrick Henry Village, at most permitted herself a little bit of alcohol now and again. That, mind you, was flowing at the fire department ball like water at a firefight.

After several half-pints of so-called Nibelungen wine, Vivian was at that point so full of zip that she would have liked to go around and join in the conversation at every table. But since the two friends didn't know anyone in the party tent and weren't transmitting any locally customary signals that they could be spoken to, they soon landed on the dance floor, a strip of grass in front of the stage left without tables and chairs that was tramped down in no time and frequented primarily by teenage girls, thirteen- to fifteen-year-old Odenwald Lolitas whose bodies seemed to know more than their minds, an interesting, ambivalent phenomenon (and one ought to look into whether it was explicable with the natural or social sciences) of so-called awakening femininity, quite different from the rather stupid scenario of awakening masculinity, apart from Thomas Mann's dreamed-up boy Tadzio in whom a rather fatal femininity had also awakened, which Korinna would have liked to write down for herself; it was just that there was no writing implement in the whole party tent. So Korinna and Vivian continued bopping to Heavy Spider's boogie rock and at 1 a.m. were flabbergasted by Taps—at once quite obviously the town's local hit—in which—beside those two and a small, scattered clutch of recalcitrant schoolgirls—the entire assembly joined singing. A girl was in the forest, not a word she said. There came a German Panzer and shot her dead. 'Cause of the German Bundeswehr there ain't no more girls in there. A girl was in the forest, not a word she said.

The next morning, two ice packs, the fuzzy memory of a trip home in the Tatra that was as erratic as it was risky during which Vivian had insisted on being behind the wheel, and onwards with Boyarin, page 202: In addition to the elements of homoeroticism in the letters of Freud to Fliess, or rather intimately bound up with them, are manifold symptoms of fantasy of pregnancy by Fliess. Here, Vivian Atkinson summarized voluntarily, it's about Sigmund Freud's self-feminization in his relationship with Wilhelm Fliess, whom he, as you know, will betray to Weininger. In the end Freud thinks he's carrying Fliess' baby to term; several times he

writes to him full of inner agitation about walking around pregnant with some such ideas, of having given birth to this or that
thought, and so forth. Whereas Boyarin with Jay Geller wonders
about the fact that, in German, guests are not received but conceived. Then Freud's and Fliess' doubly and triply instructive—
that is, even psychoanalytically instructive—correspondence is
about the alleged relationship between the nose and, you know,
the johnson, and in particular between nose bleeds and menstruation, Vivian—this morning in a red velvet leisure suit Korinna's
mother had once brought back from Saint Tropez—continued to
report. The hostess herself in a whiff of a leopard-print leotard
with an open, obscenely ruffled crotch that she had supposedly
never worn before, she didn't even know where it came from.
It was still unforeseeable when the two girl friends would really
have tried on absolutely everything in Korinna's bafflingly waste-
ful (Vivian thought) wardrobe, which ranged from the exhibitionist to the absurd.

Not only a miscarriage, but even birth itself is, Sigmund Freud
wrote to Wilhelm Fliess, a dirty thing, related to diarrhea. In his
letter of December 22, 1897, he alludes to the common root of
Abort, toilet, and Abortus, the latter being Latin for abortion.
Boyarin cites Geller: These images of befouled or failed birth
conflict with Freud's desire to create. His works are his creations,
his children with Fliess; Vivian had already marked this passage
back in Edingen. Freud did believe—she flipped a few pages further—that Jewish men represented a third gender, namely that of
menstruating men. Oh, knock it off, Korinna Kohn said with suspicion, biting agitatedly on a straw, but the brunette college girl
swathed in purplish velvet from the Côte d'Azur wouldn't dream
of knocking it off: in the fourteenth century the Italian astrologer

Cecci d'Ascoli ascertained that all Jewish men since the death of Christ—inclined to melancholy anyway and like women sexually debauched—suffered under the lash of menstruation. Daniel Boyarin points out that in the reigning Viennese dialect of Freud's day the clitoris was referred to as the Jew, female masturbation correspondingly as playing with the Jew. Korinna had leapt up from her lawn chair and paced barefoot (and Vivian thought: nervously) up and down Heiner's travertine patio. Perhaps she was just cold in her scandalously breezy jumpsuit, for this morning the two women had, on account of their hangover, carried the breakfast table into the cool shade of a pear tree. So in the nineteenth century the Jew appears—Vivian couldn't be pulled away from Unheroic Conduct—from the perspective of gender as a Victorian woman, hysteric, hypochondriac; one section about real and phantasmagorical unmanning, feminization a.k.a. Jewification was even called Freud as Schreber. The nice title of a compendium in this vein that I recently had in my hands: Reading Freud's Reading. A near endless roundelay of mind games, psychoanalytic juggleries, overblown spawns of imagined pregnancies, Korinna. The rejection, dismissal, disavowal, indeed repudiation of femininity—the Verstoßung des Weiblichen, to translate Freud's famous 1937 pronouncement back into German—as the decisive basis for psychoanalysis. Decisive, Korinna burst out laughing, what kind of a word is that, and what does all of this have to do with colonial drag?

The two young criminal investigators were not unsurprised when they caught sight of the blatantly open ruffly crotch of the higher magistrate's daughter. They only had a few questions to ask, it wouldn't take long at all, they said, clearly embarrassed, knees pressed together, soon disappearing into the house's interior, the kitchen, with Korinna, who for her part thought to tie a white oil-cloth apron around the feather-light jumpsuit. Vivian wondered whether her eccentric friend would incriminate or exonerate the detained Heiner with her candid or, as the case may be, scheming answers, perhaps even maneuver her own person into the ongoing criminal case, then, however, paged further in her Boyarin and to the next underlined passage on page 237: Rather than patholo-gizing anti-Semitism, Freud was, in fact, naturalizing it via the castration complex. Followed by an equation with Weininger as well as the baleful rise of National Socialism. Or, as Daniel Boya-rin quoted from the 1995 English translation of Gerald Stieg's study on Franz Kafka and Otto Weininger from Temple Univer-sity in Philadelphia: The uncanny part is that in such writings the most dreadful aspects of the political propaganda of National Socialism seem to present themselves in the most private sphere, internalized to the point of self-torture. To simultaneously have majority appeal as a collective, not so unconscious twilight of the gods: the German's most holy self-destruction. Vivian was happy again in any case to be able to be classified as half-German. Have a good one, the lady in red too, the master's candidate heard as the two inspectors almost effusively took their leave of her class-mate. Interestingly enough, they had come from the basement entrance on the side of the house and walked straightaway, across the lawn, to their unmarked car parked in the driveway. The ten-nis player, still dressed in nothing but her leotard and Heiner's shiny cocktail apron, closed the basement door from inside again and went back out to the patio through the kitchen exit. To her visitor she seemed oddly springy, somehow relieved. Once again Vivian Atkinson could not decide whether she should classify this as a sign of Heiner's imminent homecoming or of his poten-tially longer stay behind bars. At the moment Korinna Kohn (the more Vivian got to know her, the more enigmatic she became) seemed in this regard anything but in the mood for conversation; besides, the twenty-four-year-old Heidelberger owed the twenty-seven-year-old Karlsruher her daring theses on the colonial drag of the Zionists anyway.

Shoot, off you go; Boyarin's white book on Vivian's thighs cloaked in Korinna's mother's red velvet suit: Herzl's Zionism allowed the true German essence of the German Jew to appear. If we prove our manliness to the Germans by becoming colonizers ourself, they will come to see that we are equal. The ambivalence of Zionism thus comes to the fore more sharply in Herzl's fear of Verjudung of Europe, Verjudung in italics, Korinna. On one hand, as I have said, this involves an infamous anti-Semitic stereotype. On the other hand, there is acknowledgment in this fear that Germans may lose their Germanness in the absence of the Other (Other here capitalized) against whom hegemonic identity is constructed. So, if the Jews were to leave Germany—and this is a pretty tricky line of thought now, Korinna—the Germans would have to acknowledge the Germanness of the Jews, thus making the Zionists the true Germans.

Vivian leaned back, shoved her sunglasses into her hair, and closed her eyes. Her suit glowed red in the morning sun. Now lying recumbent on a bath towel, still dressed lightly, Korinna Kohn had in fact also briefly dealt with Theodor Herzl in the course of her intensive study of the colonization of body islands: did you know, she asked Vivian (from the gut, as it were), that at first he wanted to call the future homeland of the Jews Altneuland, Old New Land? And that there is a locality here in the Odenwald called Altneudorf? But her friend had already interrupted once again, quoting happily in American English: As much as it is a reterritorialization of Jewishness, then, Herzlian Zionism is a deterritorialization of Germanness; at any rate I'd never read such a thing anywhere before. And, on the same page, a little further down: This is masquerade colonialism, parodic mimesis of colonialism, Jews in colonialist drag, with regards to my buddy Butler. But what are we thinking, I now ask you, Korinna, and how can we blather on when the Federal Republic's anti-Semitism has been making use of very similar argumentative structures for fifty years now? The interviewee fiddled around with her wipeable apron for a little while: at least no Jewish self-hatred, obviously, in Boyarin's case, she diagnosed carefully, at most a male one; but what is this man trying to get at? He himself says, Vivian said, looking up on page 356: this is a book about male identification with women, a collective one in the cultural history of male Jews but also my own. And: I am a sort of orthodoxymoron, a male feminist orthodox Jew whose interest is the perpetuation of Judaism through an internal process of feminist reformation. One paragraph further: If women and men feminists and lesbigay people learn Torah, the very Torah that they learn will change itself. Aha, Korinna Kohn said, regarding her involved friend from the side. Could it be that Vivian Atkinson was a Jew? At the same moment Vivian Atkinson posed the counter-question: the name Kohn, isn't that actually Jewish? Both had no idea, and it didn't really matter to them either what blood flowed in their veins. And yet it had once again become apparent that talking about race and gender as a matter of course was still nearly impossible in Germany, perhaps in the German language. In such a lacking matter of course, there may lie a chance too, Korinna Kohn thought, stood up, and—kneeling on her all of a sudden—shot a Polaroid of her friend, who once again had to laugh about this almost paranoid-seeming skittishness.

In the middle of August—Vivian Atkinson had already been at home in Edingen again working on her thesis for two weeks now—the German daily newspapers reported on a Hamburg exhibition of Leni Riefenstahl's photographs. Her ninety-fifth birthday imminent, the artist had daringly advanced as far as a hotel near the gallery in question but, because of a few anti-fascist demonstrators—and thereby in opposition to them—had not appeared at her gallery opening. On the telephone, Korinna Kohn once again came to the defense of the aged Prussian woman from Pöcking in Upper Bavaria, whom she liked to juxtapose with the tomboy slash femme fatale Marlene Dietrich: after all, Riefenstahl introduced herself as a sexy wild child and made the climbing freak Trenker seem to you and me like Frauke Stöver's butch dyke. Furthermore she was never at any point in her a life a member of the NSDAP. Although, admittedly, the perfect photos of blacks—never just an aesthetic construction of so-called natural peoples whom the late Riefenstahl had put in the spotlight time and again—were by all means politically problematic to classify, the caller from the far reaches of the Odenwald pronounced. Then she recapitulated an observation by the missing Genoveva Weckherlin according to which the old Nazis—now that few of them were still living—increasingly came into the limelight of publicity: and thereby no longer into the crosshairs of conscientious Jewish Nazi hunters. Though they may indeed seem harmless, Vivian—these thoroughly lackluster grandpas shuffling through our botanical gardens with their neat straw hats—we recognize the Nazi with ever greater certainty, the fewer of them there are left. Suddenly all old people are Nazis; I know the feeling well: the senior citizen's special becomes the Nazi special, you know? Genoveva never wanted to venture out into the street again until all of them were finally dead. In their so-called best years, however, Vivian, today's pale, weak-bladdered men formed the government, occupied all central positions of power, from 1933 until long after 1945, even after 1968, into our grade-school years. I know, I know, Vivian said on the line, but the worst thing here and now are those ruling here and now, who certainly shouldn't be spared, the so-called baby boomers—and I mean those throughout every political party—who finally get to historicize German guilt when they point their fingers at Genoveva's very last, yellowed old dotterers and—Korinna finishing her friend's sentence again—overrun the whole world with German wars once more. Uh oh, it's the Germans again.

The German nation had even produced gruesome Nazi women. Like Hildegard Lächert—called Bloody Brigitte, SS camp overseer in Majdanek, a quarter million murdered—who had let a German shepherd rip the child out of a very pregnant woman. Or her sidekick and intimate friend Hermine Braunsteiner—assistant wardress, the Stamping Mare of Majdanek, proven one-thousand-one-hundred-eighty-one-fold murderess, plus seven-hundred-fifty counts of complicity to murder—whose feared fondness it was to stamp down prisoners with her very own iron-studded boots and who since her release from custody in 1996 lived—with one leg amputated, marked by death, with her husband, a GI—in a Protestant nursing home in Bochum. In 1964 she had been tracked down in the U.S. by Simon Wiesenthal; only almost ten years later did the FRG apply for her extradition. Dirty courts back then, dirty courts today. For now Vivian and Korinna did not even want to acknowledge the designation of Bloody Brigitte and the Stamping Mare as women. And what else? Heiner will likely have to go to hell for a few years, the magistrate's daughter professed, and as far as I'm concerned he can ultimately stay there.

He writes me letters from prison where he asks me duplicitously: what crimes have I committed? Like Leni Riefenstahl you may be thinking, Viv. Then he describes to me for pages on end in the most depressing way how the penitentiary has been infiltrated by backwards-speaking dwarves from the boulder field who aim to tickle him to death at night on his hard pallet; the same gnomes had betrayed him to the tarmac gang with which he now has to go for his boring walks in the barren courtyard. You do know the old Odenwald custom of tickling to death, right? My goodness, no, Vivian admitted, shaking her bob. A stiff draft in the room loosened from the wall one of the pushpins that attached the big map of Ohio. A building crane swung its iron freight past Vivian's window. The rock quarries almost colorless, tending to the yellowish. I'll manage fine, Korinna said (unsolicited) into the accrued silence. Vivian thought that it didn't sound particularly convincing. Did the bisexual disciple of Martina Navratilova perhaps want to carry her baby to term in secret?

Two further distractions from the daily newspaper about which the two classmates also conversed: from the northern edge of the Odenwald, a thirty-one-year-old Austrian man had begun the endless journey for home with his tractor, exclamation point, from Darmstadt to Vienna, second exclamation point, and had chosen for this purpose the German Autobahn A3, third exclamation point. In no time at all an almost endless line had formed behind the tractor, the highway police finally pulling him from traffic near Aschaffenburg. The Lenker—the Austrian term for driver—vehemently denied having driven himself and claimed in all seriousness that his tractor was remote-controlled, the latter in quotation marks. At that he was promptly admitted to psychiatric care. In the U.S. state Alabama an American had bit into a hamburger that had—beyond the customary quantity for mastication—been dressed with a condom. In vain the customer affected by this irregularity had tried to bite through what he mistakenly deemed a pickle, a pickled cucumber. Upon the ultimate discovery that he had chomped around on a vile plastic prophylactic the whole time, he had become extremely ill. Now the sensational case, garnering attention worldwide under the heading Miscellaneous, was before the competent court in Hoover, Alabama, and the dishonored plaintiff, a man named Jeff Bolling, who—Vivian surmised—had probably never had a condom in his mouth before, demanded both a high indemnity for himself from the McDonald's company as well as an (as they say) exemplary penalization of the fast-food corporation. What this was to consist of was not in Korinna's newspaper. Nor in that of Vivian, who, after ending this (as she thought) unsettling telephone call, first closed the windows of her apartment. Should she be worrying about Korinna, even travel back to the far reaches of the Odenwald, return home to Heiner's white house? I am somebody, Jeff Bolling had likely said. Jemand sein, to be somebody. A rather American cliché, Vivian thought.

At exactly four o'clock, as agreed upon not long before, Hans Mühlenkamm rang the buzzer at the expanded and extended tobacco warehouse—in his left hand (as usual) a record bag, in his right a neon yellow mesh bag with textiles—took the spick-and-span elevator up to the revered army brat, and marveled yet again at the means Rodney Atkinson mustered for the certainly not inconsiderable rent for his daughter's attractive flat. For the life of her (to the best of her knowledge, but still less in good conscience), Vivian could not provide him an answer to what her daddy was actually doing at the Pentagon; at the Patrick Henry

Village he had hardly ever talked explicitly about the particular missions of the U.S. Army, not among relatives and certainly not in front of Vivian. Still today deadly planes took off continuously from Frankfurt, fully loaded, only to land again later, divested of their payload, at the U.S. Rhine-Main base. No one would ask during the family's mealtime prayer which city, which country, which people was now going to be bombed back into the stone age or rather into the New World Order. When I think about it, Vivian said, then it's high time I finally earn my rent myself and then maybe move too, by which I mean into Mannheim's square street grid.

Hans was just delighted about how the abruptly clouded facial expression of his adored one merged into her strikingly gaudy getup du jour and wanted to know right away: where did you get that? From Korinna, Vivian answered, adding as casually as possible: it kind of doesn't fit her anymore. Korinna Kohn had strictly forbidden her from even intimating why the bilious green velvet corduroy tube dress no longer fit the tall, slender tennis player in the Bauland (temporarily wouldn't fit anymore). Hans, whose knees peeked out—probably also on account of the still very hot weather—of the short khaki shorts stolen in Toulon, wore on his feet obviously brand-new, downright chunky foam-soled sand-colored Fila sneakers. Vivian thought—and said too—that it looked weird. She had seen such athletic footwear almost exclusively on girls' legs recently such that his in fact rough, inelegant look—glossing over androcentrism with Futurism—had in Vivian's estimation become altogether linked with the feminine. What were girls' legs anyway, though? They ought to be slim and never-ending: a requirement that certainly more men's legs than women's legs fulfilled. For which reason the transvestite's most passable display was, absurdly enough, not seldom his legs. Look, Hansi Pompadour said with compunction, I've obviously torn you away from your work again. And saw her electronic notebook purring half-asleep on the duly tidy Rococo slab. Well, the admired one answered quickly, you may take off your shoes, too.

Hans had a story to tell. On his way to the tobacco warehouse—at its base along the former soccer club right in front of which was the old sports field along with the plant nursery and the whole small-scale industrial area of yore too, partially disbanded, dug up, and transformed into housing plots years ago—he had come into conversation with a friendly middle-aged gentleman, obviously a soccer coach. I had caught an OEG train too early, Hansi Mühlenkamm justified himself, and didn't want to ambush you, Vivian, so I asked the affable Edinger after the whereabouts of his club, what would happen with the old Fulmina building in your neighborhood—they're not going to tear it down, that I can tell you—and learned on this occasion en passant the whole checkered history of your brick tobacco warehouse which, a hundred years ago, was in fact—which you, I think, also didn't know—a brewhouse until the brewer decided to emigrate to America in the early twenties, hocked his precious copper stills, and by the time of his arrival in Bremerhaven's port had nothing but worthless money left in his wallet.

Then, after the disastrous inflation, up to two hundred women at the same time worked in this building, which now served only to manufacture tobacco. In 1938 the Baden industrialist family was slapped with an occupational ban by the Nazis, had to close their business, and surrender the building as well as the surrounding manufacturing buildings, including today's Kling-Malz warehouse on the Neckar, to unidentified Middle Germans who toed the party line. Vivian Atkinson, who at no point had inquired so precisely into the history of the residence her daddy had secured for her two years ago, perked up. More a political conflict than an Aryanization, judging from everything the coach conveyed, her cavalier continued. In 1945 the Soviet army marched into Saxony-Anhalt, and thus the unlawful owners of the building were themselves expropriated, whereby both land and facilities reverted back to the upright predecessors on the Neckar. Soon after the founding of the FRG, they in turn leased out—I'm almost done, said Hans—their tobacco factory to a family from the Bremen area for whom Vivian, on account of her inherited Telekom connection, possessed a few current telephone numbers. A daughter is even married in the area. Now after the executive head of this family had died, the manufacturing buildings, protected as historic structures, stood empty for several years. Two Syrians, finally, acquired the development rights for the upgrading, renovation, and additions still visible today and one or two years ago, as you know, went belly-up. I played a little dumb, Hans said, and asked: who's living in the tobacco warehouse today, its audacious extension, the trim annexes, and up in the penthouse? The soccer coach's prompt answer, Vivian: the residents are pretty multicultural.

Then I went walking along the main street, marveled at the finely chiseled tobacco leaves on your neighbor's front gate, bought myself sherbet straws at the oriental kiosk, strolled down the narrow lane to the Neckar along the so-called harbor area behind the old malt store, saw a boat called Odin moored to the bank, the Odenwald in the background, Schriesheim's and Dossenheim's characteristic porphyry quarries, prowled around the former mansion of the tobacco manufacturer (in which, incidentally, luxury apartments may still be had) observed the kids on the playground next to the warehouse, paged through the weekly paper laid out in front of the entrance, and finally the clock struck one, two, three, four. Besides the copy of your professor's Godard cassette you wanted, *Une femme est une femme*, *Une femme mariée*, and *Masculin féminin*, here you go, the very newest double album from the highly regarded house Source, four beautiful sides, fresh from the pressing plant, by Tim Hutton and Thomas Melchior, who call themselves Vulva. Oh yeah? Really? Yeah, Vulva. Vivian, in green velvet corduroy, completely worn out by her friend's lengthy verbosity, put on side D of the double album: Tiny Ambient Handbag. Direct hit, said the part-time physician's receptionist with elation, the wadded-up termination notice, both generic and without prior notice, from the unbending Doctor Ancelet in his pants pocket. Then it finally became quiet in the room. Vivian and Hans relaxed like the music of the duo Vulva.

Behold then—an enormous black hat of chiffon velvet and black plumes—huge: a smaller hat of silky woven straw, very soft: a complicated Paquin dress of frail, dark-blue, stone-blue silky velvet and purplish heavy embroidery: a complicated whitey-blue petticoat of very soft silk: a voluminous dressing-gown wrap of thin silk and endless lace: a chemise of more lace than linen: two pairs of high laced shoes, of greeny grey thin kid with black patent golosh: who had broken off his unfinished autobiographical novel with these words, with this colon? Hansi Mühlenkamm showed himself clueless; he knew similarly enthusiastically detailed descriptions of female attire at most from Richard Wagner's letters to his modiste. He had never consciously laid eyes on that white Diogenes paperback that Vivian Atkinson, after reading its last page aloud, hid behind her dress, amused. Come on, let me see it, Vivian, what's with the fuss, he griped, reaping instead only laughter, chuckling, and pulled the master's candidate down onto her sofa with an impulsiveness never before seen by anyone, then leapt up again immediately, appalled at himself, and Vivian, somewhat disheveled, whipped out D. H. Lawrence's life's confession Mr. Noon, published posthumously by fifty-four years. Rack upon rack of highly complicated dresses and still more complicated petticoats fluttered about in it through the prenuptial honeymoon of the English writer with his gigantic German bride, Frieda Weekley, maiden name von Richthofen, married first to a professor of the younger (by six years) student D. H., whom—calling her Fritz like their children together in Nottingham, UK—she left for the latter, that is, eloped with him to lush Upper Bavaria and logically further over the Alps to Italy, land of Madonna, holy mother of God. So I hope I shall spend eternity, with my face down buried between her breasts. Had D. H. Lawrence, author of Sons and Lovers, not also wished that his dominant bride wear the complicated dresses of his mother? In fact, complicated was also printed in the English Penguin Book.

And Frieda was supposed to wear a dirndl with puffy sleeves, a laced bodice, a capacious skirt. The poet loved it when his wife-to-be stood on the balcony of their Beuerberg village inn in her scarlet-red apron, the blue Alps in the background, erotically charged to the extreme: The great slopes shelving upwards, far overhead: the sudden dark, hairy ravines in which he was trapped: all made him feel he was caught, shut in down below there. He felt tiny, like a dwarf among the great thighs and ravines of the mountains. Imprisoned in hairy ravines, a dwarf between powerful thighs, Lawrence loved hiking in female nature. Mr. Noon's alter ego, the unfinished novelistic character—Hans now knew, his sister Grete thinking she could recognize herself in Lawrence's female figures—had at all times possessed a more female clientele. Vivian, who had also been reading him since she turned seventeen, had found somewhere that D. H. L. very consciously, in order to keep his female readership in line, wove in the most detailed descriptions of unambiguously female-coded things and performances, particularly from the areas of high dress and couture. Still lying recumbent on the sofa, her feet drawn up, she asked her guest sitting on the carpet: was Wagner really fetishistically inclined? Totally, Viv, Hans answered, but his audience was, I think, primarily anatomically male. One is not born a woman. In German: Man wird nicht als Frau geboren. Vivian Atkinson couldn't shake the feeling that David Herbert Lawrence had written his best texts not only in reference to the world of women, but more generally (that is, primarily), from a so-to-speak adapted (it could perhaps be said) sincerely female perspective.

The joys of physical love that he enjoyed with Frieda (for Mr. Noon: Johanna) during their 1912 week of honeymoon in the pre-Alpine Loisach hamlet Beuerberg his temperamental petticoat baroness had explored five years earlier with the Freudian model student and sex maniac Otto Gross, who in turn haunted Lawrence's manuscript under the name Eberhard. You see, Hansi, no matter what I do I just can't get past psychoanalysis. All her life up to her now dangerously proliferating master's thesis, Vivian had in fact weaseled out of the reductionist primary reading of Sigmund Freud. Why read Freud when Butler read him for us? Hans Mühlenkamm still couldn't muster any direct interest in him: one woman's Freud is another man's sorrow, he was likely thinking at that moment, unemployed, destitute like D. H. Lawrence, yet only three years younger but a knowing four inches shorter than his female friend, who, then as now, showed herself reserved in the face of his advances. As a schoolgirl she had been so tall that her concerned mother had gone with her to the doctor. Vivian's own current diagnosis ran thus: the dichotomous gaze imputes psychic problems to tall women and solves them— instead of through thematizing hierarchical dual-genderedness— preemptively by prescribing growth inhibitors to girls. These Gerlinde Atkinson, thank God, had preferred to flush down the toilet instead.

The Freudian Gross, a Grazer in Swabia, a genius of course—add to that blond, blue-eyed, a morphine addict—had published several much-debated tracts on the joys of the libido and the dangers of repressing it, as well as on the psychological difference of both genders; writings dedicated to the Magna Mater—and as my professor, who read them, related: composed in a thoroughly anti-patriarchal manner, albeit laced with libertarianism for only positively blue-blooded aristocrats, Hans—which, in the spring of 1907, had to be tested out in bed via licentiousness with Frieda Weekley—dishonorable spouse of a linguist, chain-smoking Nietzschian, occasional translator of Schiller into English (and conversely Yeats into German), but above all baroness; Lawrence made Gross continue lecturing in Mr. Noon even during copulation. When the shrink met Frieda, he had just made a daring pact regarding complete sexual liberation with his wife—who ironically enough was likewise named Frieda and had gone to school with Dame Frieda's sister Else—and initially impregnated Else, one of the first women at the University of Heidelberg to receive her doctorate (and summa cum laude with Max Weber at that) and later translator of Lawrence into German, on one of her regular Munich trips. Else was a famous figure in Heidelberg (which had already gone into a liberal position against the Iron Chancellor), had married Weber's colleague Edgar Jaffé and thereby, the biographers of the Richthofen sisters wrote, Heidelberg itself, where she, as a feminist, kept a four-story house as glamorous as it was countercultural. Now Frieda also wanted to become Magna Mater—which is to say: wanted to be inseminated by Otto Gross—and to begin with gave him a ring into which she had engraved three hetaerae, two Friedas, one Else. Otto eventually awarded the contract to, of all the three, the Baroness Frieda from Nottingham, long since spouse and mother there, who (it was said) was exorbitantly innovative in bed. Besotted, Gross called the outspoken woman my Turkish horse and finally felt himself liberated from Sigmund Freud. Are you still following along, Hans?

Where to? Hans had engrossed himself entirely in the frontispiece of Mr. Noon, an oil painting by Tamara de Lempicka from 1933 entitled La Chemise rose. In it one could see an attractive young woman with a bob, brunette like Vivian, draped though and really only attired in a touch of pink camisole, but frame-fillingly large and wide: undoubtedly a person, a somebody so to speak, whom Hans couldn't simply describe as a shirt. But, but, Vivian probed, zealously ready to broach this topic, didn't such things have a tradition in art history? The woman as a shell, again? Had a female article of clothing in 1933 ever been captured in oils without female abundance? Probably not, Hans surmised. Who was this Tamara de Lempicka anyway? The Offenbach boy had cemented his gaze on Mr. Noon's lascivious title girl. Where did she come from, where did she go, this Lempicka? Isn't she that painter of foolhardy Amazons in their dynamic race cars? Vivian went to her bookshelf next to the big map of Ohio, opened a tome she had already targeted in her thoughts, and said before long: exactly; she came from Warsaw, ended up—via Paris, Hollywood, and Houston—in Mexico City, where she died in 1980. At first heterosexual by compulsion, later the greatest lover of her models. Wow, Hans Mühlenkamm said, what a life, Poland, France, California, Texas, Mexico, and I can't get out of Mannheim with the OEG.

Because Else was now pregnant with the doctor's child as he himself was with his pathos and Frieda just couldn't conceive with him—though capable of offering sexual sensations about which Else didn't have the faintest idea—the two sisters, full of resentment, locked horns as once (to speak with Otto Gross) Brünnhilde and Krimhilde. Frieda took a ferry back to England, and Else then also lapsed into a ferocious dispute with the polygamous pasha about his affection. From the first Gross showed himself deeply disappointed: how could such a noble woman as Else Jaffé, who was so proud of her little sister, suddenly become so petty by bringing into the world such narrowminded jealousies. Then, however, Else began seeing another man, and Otto Gross nearly went mad with wounded pride. In the following early spring of 1908, Sigmund Freud began to distance himself from his erstwhile favorite student. At a convention in Salzburg, he spoke about the Rat Man, soon on everyone's lips, Gross leapt excitedly to his feet and in stentorianly Dionysian ecstasy juxtaposed him whom he had actually long since sworn off pseudo-matriarchally (Lawrence didn't care for him anyway) with the Übermensch Friedrich Nietzsche. Annoyed, Freud supposedly replied chillingly: we are doctors, and doctors we shall remain. Whereupon Gross again bombarded him with increasingly mentally unstable epistles from his solemnly decadent love life. Later he had himself admitted to C. G. Jung's clinic in Burghölzli only to escape over its walls again straightaway and coke the hell out of himself in Munich.

The father of Else's little son Edgar Peter Behrend Jaffé ultimately made big headlines in Ascona when he administered a lethal dose of poison to his last flame Sophie Benz so that she would kill herself, which she then did. Nevertheless, Otto Gross did not end up in jail for this, but instead in the hospital and in 1921 croaked, completely uprooted, as a drugged-out wreck in Berlin-Pankow; in her memoirs, Frieda Lawrence rather preferred to have him die for the German Kaiser on a world war battlefield. Edgar Jaffé, having moved with Else from the Neckar Valley to the Isar-Loisach Valley though only seldom at home under the same roof (on the heels of Rilke and Andreas-Salomé, so to speak), eventually became Bolshevik finance minister of the Bavarian Soviet Republic and died the same year as Otto Gross. His idea for a State Ministry for Sexuality, presented in Vienna in 1918, was implemented neither in Munich nor in Berlin. Interesting combination, Vivian tried to imagine: Mühsam, Gross, the Countess Reventlow, and Jaffé at a round table in Café Simplicissimus. What might they have drunk? Beer, cocoa, urine from high heels? Lawrence the Brit did dislike Swabia on principle, preferring to stalk through Irschenhausen, to observe Frieda skinny-dipping in the Isar, to contemplate sexuality at the deep Lake Starnberg. Or, in light of the nation of farmers, at the Beuerberg pond. Or rather up on top of the Schwarze Wand near Eurasburg, the Alps before his eyes. Vivian Atkinson's Screen Saver. It was entirely possible that she, mentioned by name, had become obsessed with a (hi) story here that only peripherally pertained to her work. But on the other hand hadn't she also been enormously inspired by Mark Twain's American-transvestic changeling stories about race and gender that her mommy shoved under her pillow? Well, all right then.

You see: being a virago is nothing for me. I want to remain a woman, through and through, since that's what I am by a twist of fate after all. Just as you men feel a deep, instinctive repugnance toward unmanly men, toward timid, squeamish, conceited people, so do I abhor unwomanly women as a caricature of my own better self. Not just our flaws, but our merits too lie within the barriers of gender, with you all as with us. Adam and Eve will remain Adam and Eve forever. And besides, thank God, this emancipated woman, as she imagines the thoughtless masses, this smoking and bicycling hysterical hermaphrodite in bloomers, is still really only an invention of our fusty comic papers and theatrical farces. But Philistines take their pleasure in precisely such insipid fare. Not you. You are, I'd like to say, a noble Philistine. Something better, more refined. Old-Heidelberg, You Pretty Lass. Novel of a Collegiate Girl, by Rudolph Stratz, 1902, the middle of the opening. A bit later, the same narrator: But these days you men do not know how to knead us into a masterpiece, at best into practicable average wares and among them lots of half-baked, crooked, wayward, stunted things, thanks to this peculiar entity that we call girls' schooling. Magic Marker, come hither. Three paragraphs further on: Why I went to Heidelberg of all places I wish to tell you upfront, because the inducement for it just walked into my room and is sitting and yawning on the sofa; Stratz has her describe this inducement as Meta from Karlruhe, cool, blonde, and bespectacled, frigid if not (between the lines) lesbian, literally: as a man who slipped into a feminine shroud.

It is for her sake that I came to Heidelberg. For she is the only woman pursuing a degree I know.

Thus Stratz's heroine Erna Bauernfeind wrote to her overseas fiancé John Henry van Lennep: Since you, as most men, have never seriously reflected upon the question of women's rights, but have simply taken us as we are today because of you, so it will not occur to you that it is far more moral and reasonable to spend the evening with a good book behind a reading lamp than in a ballroom, heated and breathing heavily, flying from the arms of one strange man into those of the next in a dress with a plunging neckline and a fluttering train as I experienced last winter as the much celebrated belle of the ball. Same page, at the bottom: Just imagine, dear John Henry, you were a girl. Make every effort, as much as it is possible for a sunburned brutal person and self-made man from Shanghai. Et cetera. Finally, ten pages later: And thus two sides of my being that were actually quite different from one another gradually evolved. Here, in the evening, amid society, the elegant young lady, the rich heiress, poor little rich girl and belle of the ball, this is how the world saw me, this is how you got to know me, there, in the morning, a diligent young pupil at Gymnasium who props his head on both hands and flounders about with the secrets of the Ciceronian periods and conic sections. The latter of these was me. Myself. Vivian was of half a mind to read this popular bestseller from the turn of the last century through to the end. D. H. Lawrence, who had always liked getting tangled up in female networks, had the three emancipated Richthofen sisters Else, Frieda, and Nusch—on account of whom he first dabbled as a writer in the female first person—theorize in the feminist idiom in his texts in what he thought was a typically German manner. But in Mr. Noon there was also this: He felt sick of women who talked and discussed and had privileges, of a theoretic life. Oh if only he was with the common soldiers!—the man's reckless, manly life of indifference and blood-satisfaction and stupidity. And oh that a man would arise in me. That the man I am might cease to be. Vivian heard, synchronously with a coughing fit of Bodo Petersen, a bright laugh from the stairwell. Could that perhaps be Pat Meier's voice? Whom no one in Handschuhsheim had ever really heard laugh? Vivian closed the door to the corridor, put a CD in the Discman, and paged further in her photocopies: On a hike through Switzerland, Lawrence had passed himself off one evening as an Austrian doctor, a variation on Professor Doctor Gross, the blatant psychopath and leading paramour of his wife, and did this successfully, so good must his German have been back then. The poet's mail to England, however, soon manifested itself as follows: On 1st July comes sister-in-law from Munich: but speaks good English.

Johanna wore a smoke-blue gauze dress and a white hat, and was, in Lawrence's words, like the landscape. Hans Mühlenkamm had gotten to take the white Diogenes paperback with Tamara de Lempicka's pink camisole on it home with him the evening of his visit and wanted that very night to read about Frieda's and David Herbert's wild Beuerberg honeymoon; he didn't need to show his face again the next morning anyway at Dr. Ancelet's, from whom he had misappropriated a prescription or two, as he confided to Vivian under the door. La Chemise rose had also proven extremely complicated, as Hans had confessed to his friend, for the reason that he found it extremely difficult to pass by a female creature lolling about in lingerie on a billboard as if it were nothing: I inevitably pause briefly, as if pinned in place for seconds, Vivian, but am of course totally aware of all the perfidious political implications of this male-contrived comparison, culpably aware even, and yet I always stop in my tracks, as if entranced, at least slowing my pace and peering—which is even worse—at this both larger-than-life and naturally reprehensible representation of so-called femininity. What can I do about it? How can I fight back? Protect myself from myself? At this Vivian ran her hands over her friend's tormented, ash-blond head and said: This, Hansi, is part of a veritably protracted civilizing process that just manifests itself when dealing with contradictions.

By the same token, sexist advertisements produce a similar effect as pornography, which Drucilla Cornell had described through literary theory as a mode of recording extremely illuminating stagings of phantasmatic scenarios (pointing beyond two-dimensionally behavioristic stimulus-response schemata to which pornography was often reduced from a conservatively feminist perspective) that ought to be interpreted as a symptom of male resistance derived from the fear of castration. Barbara Vinken summarized this à la Lacan as follows: Women in pornography are the projection of that which men fear to be, namely the castrated Other, at worst reduced to a fragmented body, a bleeding hole. Only man's always optimally-lit perennial erection in pornographic films assures him of the literal opposite, namely of being himself, of being a man. Vivian had considered—but kept to herself from Hans—whether (if it wasn't going to be possible to fight with an orgasm) critical dialogue could be entered— since it was a matter of having disguised as being—with an erection. As a man, but of course. Her mother had owned a book of Alberto Moravia's about this that bore the title Io e lui, I and He. While reading it Gerlinde had laughed resoundingly again and again. Too bad that I never gave it a feminist look, the master's candidate with the bob thought. Barbara Vinken in her foreword to Drucilla Cornell's The Temptation of Pornography: Desire cannot be expressed by the subject; rather, it marks the borders of the subject whom it simultaneously foils. Other keywords on a light-gray slip of A4 paper she had drawn up after Hansi's late departure, just before going to bed: untangle literalism as phallicism in Catharine MacKinnon. Fuckers and fuckees, the object as subject in Drucilla Cornell? The latter's idea of an unfettered female production of pornography that was supposed to present the fetishized female body as an artificial construction, thus femininity as a masquerade. Could that be sold over the counter at Beate Uhse? A massive inflatable doll? Made of flesh and blood?

A few days later Vivian received from Hans Richard Wagner's letters to his modiste from 1864 to 1868, published in 1906 in book form, with a sticky note from the bygone medical practice on it that read: Do you know Hanns Fuchs' book Richard Wagner and Homosexuality with Special Regard for the Sexual Anomalies of His Characters, published in Berlin in 1903? P.S. Even Beethoven—according to Magnus Hirschfeld in any case—was only able to compose successfully in his dressing gown. And what all the clothes-horse Wagner had had made by his (before she was to betray him so hatefully later) exceptionally tolerant modiste Goldwag: long-flowing dressing gowns in pink silk, lavishly ruffled, adorned with little ribbons and provocatively lined on the inside, coquettish frilly chemises for hundreds of Guldens, silk booties in white, pink, blue, yellow, gray, and green. Vivian found it mysterious that these letters, which if nothing went into nearly fanatical detail, had been printed in a Viennese newspaper during Wagner's lifetime, in 1877, as Hans had added. To what end and for whose benefit for that matter? For the sake of general amusement? Goldwag's vengeance? To expose the anti-Semite? Perhaps even to show him respect? And respect for what? The genius? The woman? In the man? Vivian Atkinson, who had just been standing pensively at the window, her gaze riveted on the fuzzy forest-green gorges of the moonlit Odenwald, plopped herself down in front of her little gray Texas Instrument at her pink Rococo workspace and, full of curiosity (as so often: about herself), booted it up. Within an hour the college girl had hammered twenty-two hitherto unimagined lines of inquiry regarding the crisis of categorization into the liquid crystal.

It was Friday, late evening, and Frauke Stöver on the line: We're driving to Mannheim and going to HD 800, wanna come? Who's we, the étudiante asked, ripped from Rudolph Stratz' penultimate chapter. Angela and I, of course, the doctoral candidate replied. Apparently she was now married to Angela, whereby the Italian was, quite legally, called Stöver. Vivian hadn't heard anything from those two for ages, and so accepted somewhat enthusiastically (Mannheim was always fun actually) but then crept back, for just five minutes, to her two books, the paper one that had in fact found its way into her studies, and the electronic one in which she fixed her studies, for Meta, initially harboring a decided disinterest in men, had just—that is, a hundred years ago, in a bestseller anyway—fallen in love with a male feminist, Mr. Boniser, while Erna was having her falling-out with John Henry. Erna, in the stairwell: Here he comes, along with Meta Wiggers. Hello, Mr. Boniser. With a slight greeting, Ms. Bauernfeind slipped back into her room, latched the door, and paused very contemplatively. In and of themselves, the two she was observing through the window, the suffragist and the philologist, afforded nothing in the way of conspicuousness; whereupon the Windows 95 spell check in fact actually recommended the correction of the term suffragist to suffragette. Microsoft Word. But one thing did not escape Erna's sharp eyes: they had furtively linked their pinky fingers together while walking. For the cool blonde that was revealing, very revealing. And thus Stratz let his heroine continue brooding: If the cool blonde removed her pince nez to shed tears unimpeded, or even—though with touching clumsiness—attempted to exchange kisses, then it must be very far along indeed. To the extremest pinnacle of possibility, to engagement. Like Else Jaffé—Vivian noted on her computer screen—Meta Wiggers was now drawn to Upper Bavaria: We want to marry as soon as possible and then relocate to Munich. There I'll continue my studies of course and take my exams, just with more leisure than before, and he will dedicate himself entirely to the question of women's rights, theoretically, in writing and speech. Heidelberg and Munich, every GI's wet dream, thought the brunette army brat, quickly changing clothes and reapplying her eyeliner, then Angela and Frauke were already buzzing downstairs, traveling since their return trip from Venice and the Po Basin in their own car, a battered Lancia, cardinal red, which they had managed to smuggle through the Baden DMV with the help of Heidemario.

What was a man, and what was his gender? Along with a pleated cheerleader miniskirt in white, Angela had on a royal-blue top knit from nothing but sheer lace, extremely tight-fitting, and—absolutely unmissable—not a thing underneath. Run down from her own previous perceptions, Vivian Atkinson noticed this evening for the first time that Angela Stöver, née Guida—Angelo Guida, that is—was totally flat-chested, had no bust at all, not even the hint of one, much less a removable one. But I have Frauke's breasts, she might say when spoken to about her fateful, (in a traditional sense) thoroughly legible anatomy. And what a social construction Frauke Stöver was parading around in front of her: in a stretchy, low-cut crop top of crimson-iridescent sequins. Now what sort of garment was that, the invitee wondered, and what was it concealing? Her breasts? Only to reveal her navel instead? What in the world did a décolleté mean? An asymptote probably, Vivian agreed on with Frauke, who was a math ace. Where then had the corresponding discourse on men's clothing left off? Had men as it were deterritorialized the so-called feminine—their feminine—besieging it so vehemently with significance that no one hit on the idea any longer of scrutinizing their territorial masculinity? But how could there even be a discussion about masculinity, on the one hand, without walking into the reactionary, repeatedly phallocentric traps of Critical Male Studies on the other hand? Was there any way out here at all? Even the discourse on the feminine was in most cases formulated as a male one about the Other of the masculine, while the masculine itself—as the site of utterance—remained tacit, proverbially out of the question, thus inviolate, even inviolable. Of course it stills hold true to speak about women in the sense of their cultural construction and thus the gender relation of relative genders, Frauke said summarizing the matter, though Angela had long since disappeared onto the dance floor, there's nothing else to say about men for the time being, and that's that. Below the waist Frauke Stöver was dressed butch as usual: camo pants, combat boots.

The Italian, meanwhile, was twirling over the dance floor with a skirt hem flying almost horizontally. Vivian caught herself keeping an eye out for her penis and asked Frauke: is that Lacan? Lacan's penis as the object of female fetishism? The self-declared lesbian replied: exactly. Disputing normative, thus invisible female fetishism would mean mistaking heterosexuality (read: feminine desire for the phallus on the male body) for natural law. That Angela Stöver's cock was gendered female did not make the matter less complicated: might Vivian's gaze have been a lesbian one? If bodies could be read, then they were also translatable. But never the penis into the phallus, Lacan said. No one possesses the phallus. Tricky, tricky, extended silence, man oh man. Lacan's theory as a comedy of human delusions and confusions, of tragic deficiencies in realizing an identity. Why then had he gotten himself involved so exclusively with Freud's linguistic system? At least the DJ managed a nice cross-fade. Crazy blouse, by the way, that Angela's wearing, Vivian remarked, sipping on her cola. For God's sake, that's not a blouse, the other retorted, it's a teddy. Angela got herself that teddy—how oddly Frauke stressed this word and repeated it again—that teddy on our prenuptial honeymoon in Verona. The Two Gentlemen of Verona, the soldier's daughter said, associating William Shakespeare and his adolescent female impersonators who—as girls on stage and, over and over again too (as per the piece) as boys—could not reveal themselves as such, but got to (so to speak) dress up two and three times over, but she said nothing else, at which point Frauke Stöver, her head suddenly lowered askew, trotted toward the dance floor. Probably a posture she had inherited from her family and brought with her from Travemünde, thought Vivian Atkinson, and not particularly elegant. More as if heading into a pool.

HD 800 took place on Fridays above a leather bar in the rear wing of MS Connexion, one of the biggest gay discos in Europe, Mannheim, Neckarau, near the harbor, Angelstrasse, Kolbehalle, with significant involvement of Source people from Heidelberg.

On Saturdays it was possible that Frauke, Angela, and Vivian as women wouldn't even have been let in; that evening, for instance, ran under the title Pleasuredome, and Stefan George would have taken sheer delight here, perhaps even sheer madness, for male society and male society could be two completely different kinds of affairs. When, Vivian wondered, did a man's forced antifemininity also signify his homoerotic fixation? Hans Mayer expressed it for Otto Weininger as follows: friendship instead of sexuality; male society instead of the eroticized female cultural forms of the theater or ballet; folk dances instead of the sexual ersatz actions of can-can and waltz; loden clothes and not velvet or silk of concealing exposure; masculine philosophy instead of feminine psychology; Germans and not Jews. By the same token, couldn't a man's femininity accordingly be rated a possible reference to his heterosexuality? Frauke Stöver had once published a sensational essay in which she interpreted the feature films of the Frenchman Éric Rohmer—Claire's Knee, Boyfriends and Girl-friends, et cetera—as documents of female identification, Rohmer's voyeuristic gaze, his desirous camera, as sweepingly lesbian. I wonder whether that's really tenable, Vivian thought, and what would there be to say about Godard? Hans Mühlenkamm and Vivian Atkinson had once been dressed as women at a Bikini Kill concert where men weren't admitted. Vivian in her tailored suit, Hans in an ill-fitting stewardess outfit of Austrian Airlines. Had they not sort of formed a female society for an evening? Which symbolist paths had Charles Baudelaire—for whom, according to Walter Benjamin, the lesbian epitomized the heroine of modernity—trodden under the pseudonym Manuela de Monteverde? What was awaiting the onomastic transvestite on the Internet? If a one could wear a name like a chemise, what then was a pseudo-chemise?

Five o'clock in the morning, and no end to the questions. The battered Lancia parked next to a high, overgrown brick wall. The countless lights of the nearby large power station towering over the whole neighborhood twinkled picturesquely in the dawn. Was then all self-production—itself just virile display (Marjorie Garber had reasoned, with Lacan)—feminine because it is artifactual, displaced, and exhibits its lack, its doubt, its anxiety? Lacan's attendant construction went like this: to have the phallus, which is what, in fantasy, men do; to be the phallus, the object of desire, which is what, in fantasy, women do; while on a third level next to having and being (namely by seeming, at the same time a substitute for having, and protection against loss) the cross-dresser (call him Elvis, call him—just this once as far as I'm concerned—Angela) represents and nothing but represents—not woman and not man but—his own phantom, got it? Ugh, said Vivian Atkinson, as she in fact did every time she encountered Jacques Lacan, with whose analyses her expansive master's thesis was, despite all firmly post-Lacanian interrogativity, (so to speak) parasitically interwoven: OK, the phallus as extremely possible signifier of an impossible identity. The greater the lack, the more emphatic the male parade. Right, said Frauke, who sat next to her at the wheel; Angela, in the back seat, had fallen asleep back in Seckenheim. But what, Vivian asked cautiously when the sign for Edingen flashed in the Lancia's tremulous headlight beams, is the difference between phantom and subject? Roland Barthes wrote, Frauke Stöver attempted to backtrack, that our body signifies nothing as a merely sensual object, in fact that it is incapable of signifying anything; only clothing ensures the transition from the sensual to sense, and I now add, Vivian, to the supersensible. To the supersensible of underwear, if you will. Let me out first at my tobacco warehouse, the front passenger said at the last minute; Frauke Stöver would have thundered through Edingen on the B 37 almost nonstop. Apparently, Vivian mentioned while getting out of the car, the Savior's foreskin is supposed to reside in the cathedral in Hildesheim. Which Frauke had no ear for at that moment, however.

A relative surprise then to run into Pat Meier at daybreak on Edingen's deserted Hauptstrasse. I park over there by the gymnastics club, she endeavored to provide assurance, smiling awkwardly, and had already disappeared on the other side of the road. On her right wrist one could make out a small plastic bag, black, opaque, discreet. Just like from a sex shop, Vivian thought, turned around, and saw that very second Mr. Petersen's light turn off upstairs. Weird, really weird, the homecomer thought while opening the front door. In her apartment she opened a bottle of Eichbaum beer and recalled the previous night. In contrast to Venus Xtravaganza, whose energies for survival—before she was murdered in cold blood, probably by a john—were directed wholly toward social assimilation, Angela Stöver's autonomous performance in HD 800 could be judged as quite politically destabilizing. On the other hand, in her inability to bear children as the (so to speak) better woman, in a sexist respect—this Hans had highlighted— she afforded, to the chagrin of the Vatican, proverbially boundless sexuality without consequences. Jennie Livingston was charged from certain corners with having made money with her film Paris Is Burning off of the misery of the marginalized as well as from the multifarious symbolic contradiction in Venus Xtravanganza's sad existence. No small objection. Assommons les pauvres, Baudelaire had written back in 1869 in Le Spleen de Paris, having lived in the slums himself. Spleen, according to Walter Benjamin, as a dam against pessimism. Siegfried Kracauer had emphasized furthermore: Society clothes the sites of misery in romanticism in order to perpetuate them. Vivian had only recently stumbled upon this complex in an Austrian art journal. The happier ones who, like Angela Stöver, could deal with their elements of hybridity in a constructively decanonized manner and, once again, especially those who could appreciate such things in others were now accused of culturally leftist bastardophilia in the same place. The latter as overcompensation for sexist or racist hate. Or as the postmodern blather of a Peter Weibel. Whereby we would then all be completely inhibited, Vivian thought and went into the bathroom and then at once to bed.

The following Saturday morning she rang the bell of her neighbor Bodo Petersen of her own accord. Did he have facsimiles of advertisements from the sixties in which the then-brand-new synthetic materials of BASF were praised on female skin, she asked him politely. But he only said: huh? Perhaps his ears were still ringing from the night before with Pat Meier. He did in fact still have on his pajamas at eleven. Light yellow. Conspicuously stained, Vivian thought. Had the two chemistry fans experimented around in bed with some juices? No hard feelings, Mr. Petersen, the college girl said and scurried back into her apartment. She found Bodo Petersen strikingly repulsive this morning. The hairs growing out of his nose and ears alone could turn a woman into a lesbian for the rest of her life. The way Petersen was looking, Vivian thought, he could easily be a cop, even the interior minister. Or hiring for a new German feature film production company where he—beside the Hun-like Nazi goddesses who had been cast in all female starring roles for some years now—would have made a highly suitable figure. Somewhat pimply, cheerful, and awkward. Like the Federal Republic on the international stage.

OK. The slip of paper that prompted the twenty-four-year-old to buzz her neighbor contained, on both sides, the hard-to-decipher notes from a seminar years ago whose primary thought of homeovestism, the disguising of woman as woman (which hadn't appeared in that form at the university) was to be taken up in Vivian's master's thesis. To that end a citation from a salacious trashy book found at her Hanau grandmother's called Eroticism and Lace Panties, 1964: Recent years have brought synthetic fibers like Perlon, Nylon, and others onto the market. For this reason lingerie has shrunk to a diminutiveness one could easily hide in a closed fist. Women look attractive in them as never before. A few BASF ads—photocopied, recontexutalized—would have fit there nicely; perhaps even the ominous Pat Meier would have some fluttering around at home. An unpleasant thought, however, to call there. In the August issue of the journal konkret, Otto Köhler had written that the Buna rubber factory in Auschwitz had been planned from the Ludwigshafen BASF site in 1941: an extraordinarily beautiful landscape, in the southern part of the town a concentration camp with a workforce of twenty thousand.

From the Ladies' Brevier, 1949, regarding the female whereabouts of popular trousers after the lost war: Men's pants are becoming only for very slender women and young girls. Women with pronounced feminine curves, strong hips, and full breasts ought to dispense with them. Trousers are a masculine garment and simply do not suit too much femininity. And why should they, who else is supposed to wear all the many lovely typically feminine things? On the other hand: Girls will be boys and boys will be girls. It's a mixed up muddled up shook up world except for Lola. The old song by the English beat band The Kinks, yet somehow androcentrically androgynous, as it were, cleaving to binary praxis: there probably wasn't much more to it in 1970. On the same slip of paper, the same page, again below: the crisis of categorization as a purely male crisis of signs which only the male cross-dresser in a ball dress is capable—as a privileged man indeed—of acting out without consequences. Scribbled vertically next to that in pencil: who to this end may make use of the demeaning code of femininity, its utterly inferior object-status, performatively; whereas the transvestic woman—in peacetime dressed in a man's suit—truly does the forbidden, namely reaching subject-status and making her career. Could question marks be put here reasonably? Could there, after all is said and done, only be female homeovestites or even male homeovestites? Open bracket: the feminine as repressed desire as the erotic; close bracket. Upside down, at the bottom of the page in Korinna's handwriting the names Lyotard, Derrida, Deleuze, and Guattari. In her own: Foucault's dispositif. The master's candidate in fact had difficulty remembering exactly what she had wanted to get at with her notes from the previous winter semester. It's best to write everything out right away.

Iring Fetscher interrogates Ernst Bloch in 1967 about his youth in Ludwigshafen. First: hungry boy, second: the double existence on the same river. Ludwigshafen and Mannheim as a collision that produces music, grindingly, at the same time oddly roaringly. This collision of Ludwigshafen and Mannheim was, now, one could say—says Bloch, who by his own account read The Phenomenology of Spirit erotically—a collision of Hegel and Marx, next to each other on the banks of the Rhine; the old culture over there and the future here, the raw, new, Wild-West-like, fair-like future, this living Karl May scenery, with taverns called Son of the Wilderness or The Executioner, at least realistic titles for pubs, Bloch thought. His attitude back then: I only know Karl

May and Hegel; everything else that exists is a dirty mix of both; why should I read it? The next stops for the philosopher: Munich, Berlin, Heidelberg. Bloch: Heidelberg became important to me for its own sake. I didn't have anything special to do at the university, I was already a young doctor in Berlin. In Heidelberg I met my old friend Georg Lukács again, whom I had gotten to know in Budapest. Then there was the circle around Max Weber. There was a lot of fun too with figures we didn't regard very highly. Withered wasps among women and drunken railroad engineers among the professors who raved and wanted to be as journalistic as even the feature writers couldn't be; shortly after that: But it was also a genius loci that suspended the proximity of Heidelberg to Ludwigshafen and made Heidelberg so distant, almost like Moscow or old Spain. At the same time the desk in Garmisch in Upper Bavaria. Ernst Bloch: The written beginnings my philosophy originated in Garmisch, too, a Bavarian birth, as it were, with the will to be worthy of the Alps that I had before my window. There we have it again, Vivian Atkinson thought, turning her face cautiously to the rock quarries. Was Pat Meier sitting up there right now?

Georg Lukács to Fetscher regarding Bloch's prose: A mixture of Hebel's Schatzkästlein and Hegel's Phenomenology. The Principle of Hope, part three: Wishful Images in the Mirror. Making Ourselves More Beautiful Than We Are. Vivian copied down excerpts by hand: Naturally no man can make of himself what did not already begin in him. Underlined begin and notated with an arrow the word processual next to it. Sex as process. In the same manner he is only attracted by beautiful coverings, gestures, and things to what has long been living in his own wishes, if only vaguely, and thus what likes to be seduced. Lipstick, makeup, strange feathers

help the dream find its way, so to speak, out of the cave. Out of
the closet, as they had said in the Patrick Henry Village. Then
he goes and poses, enlivens the bit of extant material or styles it
into something phony. But it's not as if one could falsify oneself
entirely; at least one's wishing is genuine. The urge of the petit-
bourgeois: To seem more than one is. To be more than one seems,
however, the Ludwigshafener writes, this reversal is not imitated
by any grooming; for which reason there is never so much kitsch
as in the class that endures itself as not genuine. What is ours as
unfading, apart from the necktie it is still little worn. The student
had to think about that for a few minutes on her sofa. Next section: What the Mirror Tells Us Today. Vivian's reference: What
the mirror once told the girl-friendly Lewis Carroll. Buy his book
Through the Looking Glass. Then: New Clothes, the Illuminated
Display. No one can shed his skin. But can easily slip into a new
one; thus all grooming is in fact getting dressed. Women put on
a new part of themselves with their garb. The same woman as a
different one when in another dress—to speak with Bloch: in the
fine froth of feminine finery.

A metallic squeaking issued from the direction of the Schwa-
benheimer Hof, the other, barely active shore of the Neckar that
belonged to Dossenheim. A robust retiree had once ferried Vivian
to that side with his boat Odin. Upstream not a bridge for miles,
downstream only the old-time ferry between Neckarhausen and
Ladenburg. The collegian laid The Principle of Hope aside, walked
to the window briefly (aside from a cargo ship mooring just now
there was nothing special to see), and took a seat in front of her
dark-blue, glowing computer screen: What could a so-called racy
woman do with herself? Was there even such a thing as feminine self-hatred? Like the Jewish self-hatred depicted by Theodor

Lessing? Lessing, who in 1930 refused assimilation in favor of Zionism, had written: You are becoming one of the others and seem fabulously genuine. Perhaps a bit too German to be completely German. Auschwitz or Israel, as Hans Mayer later condensed it. On the other hand, could the Jewish intelligentsia (example from today: Daniel Boyarin) in a certain respect not be given positive credit for having developed a dialectical difference to the category of race? Or can this thought only be expressed once again with anti-Semitic connotations? As in Otto Weininger, who had wanted to overcome his Jewishness in order to become more German than the Germans. Wasn't Weininger also a feminine self-hater? So feminine self-hatred does exist? Never had Vivian heard of German self-hatred; the nation was, in a literal sense, invested exclusively in identity. In territoriality. In a horizontal sense. Here Vivian made a cross-reference to Tel Aviv, Herzl's Spring Hill (in German: Altneuland, Old New Land). OK. German self-pity, German twilight of the gods, German world war: in history's hall of mirrors, the German fatherland was capable of unleashing the utmost destructive force out of the bittersweet feeling of eternal lack. Apocalyptically wrenching itself along into the abyss, that was the German specialty; as such, German sentiment thus did in fact form a variant of self-hatred. How did Thomas Mann's famous troubles with Germany comport with this? As disgust or enjoyment? Melancholy? The anti-German position of a Hans Mühlenkamm could not be counted among the complex of self-hatred because the anti-German was automatically excluded, himself no longer German. Un-German. Hans Mühlenkamm was no German. Duh.

Vivian Atkinson had taken the OEG via Heidelberg toward Weinheim and disembarked shortly before the Handschuhsheim business park, the Burgstrasse stop. As she buzzed at the door to Ilse Schoolmistress' shared flat, no one answered. Ilse had perhaps traveled away for the entire summer vacation, the married Stövers were God knows where, and Pat may actually have been holed up in her conspiratorial crow's nest. So Vivian boarded the next OEG to Weinheim and only two stations later was out in the fresh air again where the west wind broke along the Odenwald bluff, turned onto the Bahnhofstrasse to Dossenheim's city hall, and continued up the Hauptstrasse to the rock quarry road. Now it was really steep uphill-going, a narrow little asphalt street, initially lined with homes, soon only with mulberry hedges. Then a turnabout, the end of the pavement, and a few minutes later, on the left side, gigantic archaic conveyors, by and large overgrown, heavily rusted. A small group of workers slashed their way through the undergrowth with machetes, uncovering some sort of steel cables, a couple others stood high above on the iron ruins and worked on these with sledgehammers long enough for individual fragments of the ramshackle mechanism to come crashing down, which were then loaded onto a dented-up truck with remarkable sloth by two other workers. Above this scenery, orange and enormous, semicircular, the northernmost of the three large Dossenheim rock quarries soared into the sky.

Seized by sudden curiosity, Vivian stepped up to the workers and asked whether the rock quarry was going to be shut down now. Two didn't give her any reply at all, a third, in broken German, referred her to the foreman, an older man in blue coveralls who at that moment—next to an old sand-colored VW flatbed truck without registration plates—was peeing quite unceremoniously into the dusty bushes. It likely did not happen often that a female person strayed up here, Vivian thought, Pat Meier doubtless took another route to her position over the escarpment. Warily, the foreman approached the college girl. No, the rock quarry would be abandoned in three, four years. Until then entry into it is both extremely dangerous and strictly prohibited. Behind the flatbed truck, below the unmoving tippers, the stranger recognized a U.S. Army Jeep, also unregistered (that is, without license plates), with running motor, slowly rolling by. She shivered a bit; the open animosity of these men prompted her to say a quick farewell and continue on uphill. After a few minutes a corroded viaduct of the former plant siding, dizzyingly high above the dark forest path, with a switch in the middle, thus bent up like a divining rod. Then, on the left-hand side, the flat ground of the rock quarry, the ascending access road, an open gate lined with numerous prohibition signs which Vivian didn't bother about. Her heart pounding, she entered the massive arena that had so often lit her way home in the evening, and tilted her head back so as to be able to perhaps make out Pat and her gadgets up there. Although, as people say, only what is known can be seen, the lady from Darmstadt had obviously camouflaged herself so well that the army brat, even after looking closely for a while, couldn't even recall where exactly she had stumbled upon Pat's hideout with Bodo Petersen on Pentecost. There was only one possibility left: climbing up along the edge of the rock quarry until she ran into Pat Meier. And all this just for the sake of illustrating her master's thesis?

Not really. It was more a solemn longing that drove Vivian on, at first deeper into the rock quarry which had yet another, more elevated plateau. When she reached its level by way of a wide pit road reinforced with banks for heavy machinery, she spotted from there what hadn't been visible from below, what had been in her blind spot: a whole fleet of disused vehicles, trailers, and containers of the U.S. Army with insignias sloppily painted over, parked in rank and file, for what purpose? For whose edification? Had her daddy Rodney Atkinson hawked these government issues, oldtimers of the glorious Seventh Army, to this place? Vivian instantly decided to have a closer look at this ghostly fleet—cemetery rather—and walked up to a martial-looking vehicle, wanting—as she had as a tomboy of old—to climb up over its man-sized tires into the cab. At precisely that moment she heard behind her the sound of a motor, craned her head in fright, and recognized the foreman's sand-colored flatbed truck approaching her at an idle and stopping about twenty yards behind her. The college girl endeavored to adopt an as insouciant-seeming a demeanor as possible and returned in a wide arc, with emphatic slowness, to the pit road and finally to the still-open gate. The creepy Volkswagen stayed on her heels throughout at an always uniform, creeping distance. If she stopped, it braked. If she turned off again to the left into the rising forest path at the end of the forbidden compound, the flatbed truck rolled down off to the right in neutral to the old conveyors.

Vivian Atkinson exhaled, accelerated her pace, crawled under a barrier to which the embittered foreman most certainly possessed a key. But it wasn't forbidden at all to wander into the Odenwald here on a marked path; only when she, curious, yet again broke out to the left, past dented shelters rusted through, over the slip rock—the sediment from blasts ages ago—into the thicket, and right through under the barbed wire up to the steep ledge was she once more on prohibited ground. It was already three o'clock. In pious chords, the bells of one of the three Dossenheim houses of God rang out. Perhaps those of the New Apostolic Church?

Was asking questions, she mused, now flushed, in fact part of the confessional canon, or did it represent a cultural technique that could also be instrumentalized atheistically? Faith does not mean knowledge, it was said. Or even (in a word): ignorance. Was it even conceivable to pose questions knowingly? Or deliberately? What bullshit to brood about so-called last things up here on the exposed bluff, young Atkinson decided, tying her blouson around her hips and standing there half-upright in the thicket before the abyss in a ripped NVA muscle shirt and blue jeans. Not daring, however, to sit down and let her legs dangle from the rock quarry, for she could see the men bustle about down there, could even hear their voices. Further off, very clear, actually close, the Edingen water tower as well as the high, newish Kling-Malz silo; next to it, considerably smaller, her domicile, the tobacco warehouse. And yet: the mountains seemed more tangible from the plain than the settlements sprinkled throughout the lowland did from the mountains.

Not far from the stone zenith, Vivian Atkinson reached Pat Meier's foxhole, the sought party not personally present, her gear stowed in various wooden crates and locked, well hidden under all the branches, only noticeable at all, even to the well-informed, from right out on the exposed ledge. Maybe Pat would only show her face up here at nightfall. Perhaps she took up her position only on Sundays and holidays, when no one was working at the rock quarry. So Vivian laid down recumbent in the grass forming a stripe just before the edge of the underbrush and tried to envision what a guerrilla existence would actually entail for a woman. Just yesterday she had read an article in the music journal Spex about the Eritrean women fighters of the EPLF, one of whom had emphasized: We never deigned to be

women, and we never allowed anyone to humiliate us. Weird way
of putting it, Vivian had thought, lying in her bathtub, but then
the telephone had rung, and Korinna Kohn was on the line—
having just come back from a jaunt to the Holy Blood Altar of
Walldürn, site of the universally authenticated Blood Miracle
of 1330—super wired, remarkably jabbery. All the while Vivian naked in the middle of her room in an expanding puddle of
bathwater.

From Vivian Atkinson's Weininger excerpts: All those women
who really strive for emancipation, all those women who have
a genuine right to fame and are intellectually somehow extraor-
dinary, always display many male features. That a homosexual
love affair even honors women more than the heterosexual relationship. That the tendency to lesbian love in a woman flows
directly from her masculinity, which in turn is a condition for her
superiority. George Sand's affairs with Musset, the most effeminate of poets, and with Chopin, whom one could even call the
only female musician. Mme. de Staël's sexual relationship with
August Wilhelm Schlegel, the homosexual private tutor of her
childen. Klara Schumann's spouse would be considered a woman
instead of a man according to his face during certain periods of
his life, and even in his music there is a lot—if not always the
same amount—of femininity. And as for emancipated women: it
is only the man in them that wants emancipation. Free admission
to everything, no hindrances in the path of those whose true psychic needs drive them, always in accordance with their physical
type, to masculine occupation, for women with masculine features. But down with the formation of parties, down with untrue
revolutionizing, down with the whole women's movement, which
creates in so many an unnatural, artificial, essentially mendacious

aspiration. The greatest—the only—enemy of the emancipation of women is woman.

At the end of August 1997, Princess Diana from England sped into a concrete pillar in a Paris tunnel, along with her lover and her chauffeur. Chased headlong into death by a band of photographers obtrusively claiming her for their own purposes who— by dint of the mass-hysterical ceremonies instantly unleashed in London—were able (in hindsight, so to speak) to see themselves legitimated. At least that's how Grete Mühlenkamm—who had been lodging with her brother for a week, in plainclothes, in the Untere Strasse—saw it. She had just asked for the sugar to be passed again, for at four cubes she apparently still didn't have enough in her tea. Vivian, positioned Indian-style between the two siblings, handed her the cardboard Südzucker box and blatantly yawned aloud. Since Hans had cleared away the colorfully vegetarian table—Grete's much-praised subtropical breakfast to which the student had been invited on short notice—she sprawled out with the others in front of the television. Yet she certainly had better things to do than to police (as Grete put it with emphatic cultural criticism) those stupid programs on the so-called private channels SAT 1, RTL, and Pro Sieben flickering across her friend's screen this afternoon. Sonja, for example: At my house, men pee sitting down. Then Bärbel Schäfer: And you call that a bust? And at the same time—while Grete switched channels back and forth hectically during the respective commercial breaks that she policed at other time slots—Arabella Kiesbauer: My bust makes me sexy. Was the German populace actually sexualized by these kinds of programs (which also demanded Korinna Kohn's thoroughly scientific attention) about their (as they were called in Anglo-American) private parts? Mobilized? Lambasted?

Disenfranchised in the Foucauldian sense? Sure, of course, Grete
Mühlenkamm opined; yet at the same time she seemed to Vivian
Atkinson almost symbiotically bound up with the object of her
studies. Still, you had to give it to the resolute stewardess for having infected her gentle brother with her analytic fancy way back
in his Offenbach days. Why then was this mid-twentysomething
still living at home with her parents?

Her current and actually first extended visit to Hans could be
traced back to reading the new issue of the women's magazine
Amica, in which it had been ascertained (and statistically ascertained at that) that Heidelberg, governed by a mayoress, was
the most women-friendly city in Germany, followed closely by
Korinna's Electoral Karlsruhe, Göttingen, in third place as the
sexiest of all cities; Potsdam in fourth as the one with the most
daycares; poor Dortmund as city of assholes and caboose in thir-
tieth place. Amica's criteria for this had been safety first, job and
career second, shopping third, child-friendliness fourth, quality
of life fifth, and—not in competition because of its subjectiv-
ity—sex and romance. Just read the outrageous explanation for
shopping, Grete said when the television had finally been turned
off, and Vivian read away over Hansi's shoulder: Here one might
accuse us of again reducing the life of the woman to the three C's:
career, children, and now consumerism. We think: these three do
play an important role for women. We weren't able to investigate
all shopping sectors, so we concentrated on the number of fashion
and cosmetic stores. The number of sales personnel on the one
hand, that of perfumeries, women's wear stores, salons, and lingerie stores per fifty thousand residents on the other hand. That's
nuts, said Vivian. Grete may have had to wear makeup during
work but showed, aside from an always finely drawn eyeliner, no

undue interest in feminine cosmetics otherwise. And the mostly Far-Eastern fashion she wore in her free time would certainly not be available in any of the businesses listed in Amica. Hans Mühlenkamm's older sister had thus arrived to contradict the gender topography of Heidelberg as charted by the ostensible women's magazine with her own on-site cultural studies. Fear of entering a designer temple? Totally normal if you aren't always circulating in that milieu, the Munich professional psychologist Dr. Anna Schoch says in Amica's comparative city test, for example, recommending: just go in. Amica's follow-up question: Only to be looked up and down by condescending sales clerks? Dr. Schoch's reply: If that really happens, remind yourself how much a sales clerk makes and what kind of an education she's had. It just gets worse and worse, laughed Vivian Atkinson. She began to like the woman in the kimono.

And the winner is: Heidelberg, first place in matters of child-friendliness, second in shopping, fifth in sex and romance, seventh in quality of life, twelfth in safety, in career prospects for women (its weakest point of all) fourteenth out of thirty slots. Every criterion—minus of course the heterosexually coded sex and romance (which was after all a matter of taste)—weighted equally. Leipzig, with the allegedly best career prospects for women—but because of its lousy shopping offerings for (in Hansi's harsh words) gussied-up cows—in only twentieth place, not to mention Leipzig's thirtieth-place finish in sex and romance. Amica's Göttingen, by contrast, was the absolute leader in matters of sex because it was able to offer, numerically, the most men per thousand women, namely nine hundred fifty-six, almost ten percent more than Würzburg, for example. For why else were men around at all? For fucking, Grete said mockingly. But Amica had also counted the number of marriages and how many men saw the feature film Romeo and Juliet. The best location in Heidelberg for flirting: the Neckar meadows, around Uferstrasse, Neuenheim. To meet new people, bring with you: Frisbee, volleyball, or diabolo. Among the feminist achievements of the mayoress with the name Weber, according to the Amica interview: the elimination of unsafe spaces—Vivian first read unsafe races—as well as the establishment of safer parking spaces for women. Also in Grete Mühlenkamm's rollerboard: the new issue of the magazine Emma with a conversation between the authors Elfriede Jelinek and Marlene Streeruwitz in which Jelinek had dropped exclusively masculine pronouns probably a hundred times. Obviously redacted by Alice Schwarzer, was Grete's opinion in this regard.

Heidelberg we'll spare, because some day we'd like to live there. To this day the legend of the leaflets with this exact wording—which had supposedly been dropped on the city in the spring of 1945 by American military aircraft—survived among the populace; and yet even the Odenwald publisher Pieper had at no point been able to get his hands on one. When the Yanks were finally moving closer, a small Heidelberg delegation drove to meet them in order to negotiate the sparing of their city, but not its capitulation. Dr. Dieter Brüggemann was there and forty years later, on March 30, 1985, told of it in the Hotel Prinz: Around nine in the evening we began our march. We were driving in an open military utility vehicle. The bridge here in Neuenheim was still undestroyed. We were now heading out of the city slowly on the Handschuhsheim country road toward Dossenheim. The last German outposts were on both sides of the street at the cemetery. They waved to us—of course they were informed—and then we went into no-man's-land. The interpreter unfolded a large, makeshift white flag.

Now, according to international law, a bugler should have been with us to sound a trumpet signal to announce our arrival to the enemy. But who had a bugler toward the end of the war? There hadn't been any for a long time. As a substitute, the interpreter called out loudly and continually, walking alongside the now idling vehicle: peace negotiator. Peace negotiator. Peace negotiator. Not long after, we arrived at the American outpost. They received us, and—the first surprise—we weren't blindfolded. We could see candidly what was happening there. Of course as an officer from my own camp I was very interested in what I got to see. And the reason why they let us go unblindfolded was soon clear to me. Lined up toward Heidelberg on the road was one heavy Sherman tank after the other. We saw it, and we were obviously supposed to see it.

That same night, at the proverbial last minute of the war, Heidelberg's Old Bridge, celebrated by Goethe—the Karl Theodor Bridge—was detonated by the Greater German Wehrmacht, more precisely, by the NCO of the Pioneers Schlicksupp from Mannheim-Neckarau, where today Heidelbergers run HD 800. A few years later it was rebuilt. The Judenanlage, the Jewish Installation, where we're standing here, on the corner of the Philosophenweg and Hirschgasse, was not given back its original name and is still called the Hölderlin-Anlage to this day, Vivian Atkinson lectured, though Jewish Installation, Jewish Lane, et cetera, had probably also been marginalizing designations. Grete and Hans paused briefly, their gaze resting on the old city across the river, thinking they even recognized Hansi's garret. The easing of the prohibition of contact between Americans and Germans was then welcomed primarily by young girls (then called Fräuleins) as well as by intellectuals and workers. GIs playing with kids on every street corner. Only the openly displayed militarism that moved into the city with the headquarters of the Seventh Army undermined the population's trust in the U.S. Army as a (so to speak) civil armed force. Soon most of the locals' bars were off limits. The OEG began operating again, even over into the totally destroyed squares of Mannheim. One even derailed because two nine-year-olds had laid rocks on the tracks: one dead and eighteen injured, according to Werner Pieper's investigations. The later Bundespräsident Heuss and a communist with the melodious name Agricola as the founders of the Rhein-Neckar-Zeitung. In it, local historian Pieper had found a letter to the editor according to which women in men's pants ought to make the latter available immediately. Karl Jaspers returned to the university. At Christmas of 1945 the peaceful illumination of the castle ruins by the occupiers living on the Molkenkur. Hans pointed the Molkenkur out to Grete. To the left of it, the house in which Sissi, the Austrian empress, had lived. Grete was now wearing a Kawasaki leather jacket, open, over her kimono. The unemployed part-time physician's assistant in oil-smeared coveralls from Ford Kurpfalz in Mannheim, the advanced master's candidate in an unassuming summer dress from H&M. Before long the three neared the Neuburg abbey, the old Benedictine convent. Why is it so unnaturally warm in this area, Grete wanted to know. Vivian's answer: because of the emissions from BASF.

Aha. Smokestacks. Phalli. Of course, said the stewardess, always hard and perennially horny. Exactly, the chimney fucks the climate and gets to come continuously, Hans said, seizing on Grete's idea for the fun of it, but his sister immediately followed up critically: Can you have an erection and not think of rape at the same time? Can you think your way out of an erection? Do you know bell hooks' essay Power to the Pussy: We Don't Wanna Be Dicks in Drag? She quotes Madonna in it: I wouldn't want a penis. It would be like having a third leg. It would seem like a contraption that would get in the way. I think I have a dick in my brain. I don't need to have one between my legs. The small-framed nonworker shrugged indecisively and looked over to Vivian for help. This complex had indeed been occupying the soldier's daughter frequently, essentially since her sex-obsessed mother had apostrophized the nice GI Amos from the genteel house next door on San Jacinto Drive as a limp-dick, reserving for him the words: the boy really is totally inhibited. To this day Vivian was not inclined to reduce men all too simply to their martial percussive energy. For this reason she then endeavored, at the foot of the old cloister (on the lovely south-facing slope, heavy with fruit), to answer in Hans's place by freely summoning Drucilla Cornell's thoughts on pornography a second time. To Lacan, the assistant in its construction (and possibly a misogynist like Weininger, Freud, and Žižek on top of that), a special significance is again accorded here because he insisted that the masculine and the feminine were signifiers and that male identity will always misfire in its uniformity because it is dependent upon the phantasmatic object Woman; whereupon Grete was able to contribute an inscrutably weird episode from her time as a tambourine-beating rock 'n' roller in a Japanese hard-rock band. The vilification and denigration of women that is so vividly shown in pornography articulates a split in man that persistently obstructs his access to the truth of his phantasm. This barrier prevents, quite tragically (Atkinson said, summarizing Cornell), fond dealings with the Other, which he actually desperately yearns for.

Pornography is thus not what men want, but the substitute for the lack and split in men which the structure of male identity imposed upon them occupies. Not male power, but the lack of security about who they really are is portrayed in pornography. It probably really is a great deal trickier to have a dick as opposed to a pussy. Didn't Grete also think that the latter, in comparison with the monumental singularity of the male doofloppy, boasts an almost phenomenal plurality? So is it castration anxiety—Grete Mühlenkamm tied in as persistently as she did earnestly—when the USA boycotts the international climate convention? Why in the world has American philosophy, in contrast to European philosophy, continually attacked psychoanalysis until recently? And why does it face very concrete threats today, Vivian added, of being eliminated at German universities? I think your sister definitely ought to meet Frauke, she later remarked when Grete was strolling alone through Heidelberg's pedestrian zone retracing Amica's footsteps. Do you really think, Hans asked with surprise, that she's ready for Angela Stöver, née Guida, too? Mentally?

It would be completely at my discretion to write a chapter about this dry rose here if the object were worth the effort. It is a flower from last year's carnival. I picked it myself from Valentin's greenhouses, and that evening, an hour before the ball, I went, hopeful and pleasantly excited, to Madame de Hautcastel's to give it to her. She took it, laying it on her dressing table without looking at it, indeed without even looking at me. But how could she have paid me any heed: she was busy looking at herself. Fully bedecked, she stood before a large mirror and put the last touches on her array. So much was she occupied, so completely was her attention directed toward the ribbons, tulles, and bobbles of all kinds piled before her that I was granted not even a look, a sign. I surrendered myself to this: humbly I held pins all readily arranged in my hand, but her pin cushion being closer at hand, she took them from her pin cushion. And when I extended my hand, she took them indifferently from my hand, and if she wanted to take them, she groped for them without averting her gaze from her mirror, fearful of losing sight of herself. For a time I held a second mirror behind her so that she could better scrutinize her finery. And when her face was reflected from one mirror to the other, I beheld a series of coquettes of whom not a one paid me heed. In the increasingly sprawling stage of her master's thesis, Vivian Atkinson was now discovering connections almost everywhere. Even the old-time General de Maistre was suddenly able to be converted for gender-related having, being, and seeming.

The woman in the mirror, 1794. Four chapters of his Journey Around My Room later, de Maistre was, however, also capable of climbing behind the confounded mirror. Vivian copied out for herself the following passage about the author-general's so-called Other: At any rate, it was awake, and wide awake at that, when my soul loosed herself from the bonds of sleep. For a long time now the latter had shared, if vaguely, in the sensations of the Other; but she was still shrouded in the veil of night and slumber, and this veil seemed to be transformed into gauze, lawn, or Indian canvas. My poor soul was thus wrapped up in all this material, and in order to hold her more tightly in his domain, the god of sleep added tresses of blond hair, bows of ribbon, and pearl necklaces to his own fetters: it was a pity to see her floundering in these nets. The agitation of the most noble part of myself conveyed itself to the Other, and this by turns acted powerfully upon my soul. I had gotten myself altogether into a state that was difficult to describe when my soul found a means through perspicacity or coincidence to free herself from the gauze smothering her. Whether she noticed an opening or whether she, which is more natural, simply dreamt up a way to eliminate it, I do not know; the fact is that she found her way out of the labyrinth. The shaggy tresses were still there, but they no longer presented a hindrance, but instead an expedient: my soul seized them as a man about to drown holds on for dear life to the grass on the riverbank. But the pearl necklace broke at a touch, and the pearls slid from the string and rolled onto the sofa and from there onto the floor of Madame de Hautcastel; for, because of some whimsy whose reason was difficult to specify, my soul thought she was at that woman's house. A large bouquet of violets fell to the ground; at this my soul awoke, returned home, and brought with her reason and reality again.

Here Vivian broke off her transcription, walked past the map of Ohio to her bookshelf and drew from it the memoirs of the lovelorn Abbé de Choisy, an authentic curiosity from the seventeenth century, around a hundred years before Xavier de Maistre, with the original title Les Mémoires de l'Abbé de Choisy habillé en femme. Vivian looked for the passage where the clergyman (a womanizer in a double sense) expounds upon the reasons for his compulsive predilection for complicated feminine clothing and toilette. I have considered, François-Timoléon de Choisy wrote, where such a bizarre desire comes from, and this is the result: It is the nature of God to be loved and worshiped; man aspires, as much as his weakness allows, to the same aim; since it is beauty that arouses love, and since that is usually the inheritance of women, men try—when it seems that they could possess or think to possess a bit of beauty that could awaken love—to enhance it with feminine attire that is very favorable. They then feel the ineffable joy of being loved. Several times I have myself felt what I say in sweet experience, and whenever I have been at balls or the theater in a beautiful dressing gown, diamonds, and beauty spots and heard them saying nearby: that is truly a very beautiful woman, then I felt in myself a delight that cannot be compared with anything else, so great is it. Vivian, from her own hetero-sexual experience in turn, was not completely able to follow the Abbé in the fact that feminine beauty was supposed to be the only beauty that could be loved, and classed this quotation, together with General de Maistre's reverie transcribed a mere quarter of an hour before, with Lacanism.

On the other hand, the gallant Abbé in the provocative silver moiré had screwed one damsel after the other; both heterosexual and homosexual women and men had succumbed to his alluring charms. The reputedly mental erotic desire revealed itself to the reader here entirely as an exterior construct, as the happy conse-quence of performatively seductive processes under (as it were) society's supervision that could be located, least of all, in a fixed core personality. Would Vivian ever possibly be able to soften herself to Hans if the latter approached her not in disaffected work clothes but in the contemporary equivalent of François-Timoléon's embroidered bodices and black-gold dressing gowns, with—as the Abbé had implemented—white satin trimmings, a corseted belt with a big bow on the butt to show off the waist-line, a long train, a heavily powdered wig, drop earrings, beauty marks, and a little ribbon bonnet? Would she have to be regarded structurally as a gay macho man if she fell head over heels in love with a Hansi Pompadour done up so complicatedly à la femme? Or even—and here it was difficult to make headway—the latter as a lesbian? Monique Wittig had of course written in Le corps lesbien in 1973 that lesbians are not women since the category woman—as the historical product of compulsory heterosexual-ity—denotes a gender exclusively based on men. But wasn't the system of homosexuality just as fatally entangled in the binary? Didn't the homo already possess a far more identity-determining character than the hetero? Had Richard Wagner—the other way around (Vivian Atkinson's head was buzzing)—perhaps worn, when he slept with his Cosima, a concubine's clothes, tailored ones? And how was Friedrich Nietzsche dressed when he handed Lou Andreas-Salomé the whip?

According to Luce Irigaray, femininity and melancholia had a common structure. Let's go, one more time to the bookshelf, and one more time back to de Maistre's century: Karl Philipp Moritz's theatromanic anti-hero Reiser—caught up in a pathogenically modified, melancholic vicious cycle out of which the book's subject can no longer deal with his topic—was only not unhappy at that moment, had only not felt despair in that constellation from lack of existence, only not had the feeling of being trapped in self-contradictedness, and only not shown signs of paralysis of the mind when he (Anton) got to perform Clelie (a young girl) on stage. Vivian's fleeting keywords for this, soon to be posed as questions: the Other as the Proper. The Proper in the Other. The Other in the Proper. The Proper as the Other. The melancholic entanglement of the external world and the self. See also: the hypochondric gaze into the river. Pietistic self-observation as an early exemplum of de-subjectified writing. The necessity for reflection as the deepest melancholia of every genuine and great novel. Georg Lukács. And that's it for today because in about five minutes a locomotive was going to pass through Edingen, in which Hans Mühlenkamm was supposed to be sitting. He had called on short notice, whether Vivian might want to join him, head to Mannheim to stroll around, just because, she knew. For days now Grete has been back in international air space, serving crêpes to random business people with a smile, a shit job actually, said Hans as Vivian took her place next to him punctually, he didn't even know how exactly the high social and sexual reputation of stewardesses had survived for so long. All the same, you, too, threw yourself into a stewardess costume for Bikini Kill back then, the twenty-four-year-old with the grown-out bob interjected. Oh, whatever, said the little man next to her in the big UPS jacket, under which he was wearing a lime-green Nyltest shirt. Unusually annoyed. Vivian suspected that Hans Mühlenkamm once again had no money with him, but also didn't want to borrow any from her. So she mentally prayed to the heavens above that they both wouldn't end up at the uncomfortable police station again as on their last errand trip to Mannheim.

The student from the tobacco warehouse simply didn't have the nerves of a thief. Never did, not even as a tomboy in the Patrick Henry Village. To be sure, she had gotten her Hansi off the hook very eloquently at the precinct so that there was nothing else for the policemen to do ultimately but release Hans and Vivian again from the station with best wishes for the rest of the afternoon, but before, at Engelhorn & Sturm, she had been pale as a ghost as her friend, as cool as ice, bagged all the Ralph Lauren polo shirts, one after the other. Today for the first time it seemed to her that Hans was also nervous. Edingen-West. A horde of schoolkids boarded. Neu-Edingen, business park. A drunk from Mutterstadt with an unmistakable Palatinate idiom and a rickety bike, noisily spouting off sexist blonde jokes. A female migrant with a gigantic skai purse. Well, Grete was living, Hans explained, with their parents because she's hardly ever in the country at a stretch. She had a boyfriend in Kuala Lumpur, right at the foot of the world's tallest building, yes, a steady boyfriend, for years now, he'd seen him once before, on a video film, what should he say, just one of those men, in the so-called best years of his life, well-built, white suit, aviator glasses, a Dutchman or something, no, an Englishman. Assuredly not a suffragist.

Three hours later, engulfed in the inspection of their stolen goods, Hans and Vivian loitered around in front of the Electoral Palace, which housed Mannheim's university. Mannheim's Germany university—for Mannheim also hosted the University of Maryland of the American military in whose cafeteria Heidemario had once worked as a dishwasher. Munich's University of Maryland, where Vivian's cousin Snooks had studied, had been closed after the Cold War, and Snooks had moved with a redheaded Aschaffenburg girl to New Orleans where he became the bassist in a very busy band called Petticoat Government. Hans Mühlenkamm assured Vivian Atkinson of the political correctness of all of his appropriating deeds, to the extent he could review them; only then did she allow various, not-all-too-expensive accessories for her electronic Texas Instrument (which had long since fallen asleep on the name Lukács) to be handed over. No store security guard seemed to have examined the svelte freebooter and his attractive wingwoman sauntering next to him with wary eyes at all today. Was it because of Hansi's jacket? Vivian's bilious green velvet corduroy tube dress, that extravagant souvenir from the Bauland that she was wearing again for the nth time at the side of her ash-blond admirer? They weren't sure. I don't know how you can walk in that dress at all, Hans had remarked again. Finally, they both vanished for two, three hours into a well-assorted record store where Vivian spent all her cash and after closing time found themselves once again in the Electoral Palace's garden, which was traversed by numerous on- and off-ramps to the big Rhine bridge, with a view of the river and Ludwigshafen on the other side, Bloch's mixed, undisguised proletarian-capitalist reality, the desolate Walzmühle, left to be demolished—Vivian's ex-boyfriend and DJ had often spun records there—and, northwards, the flourishing chemical factory. Ernst Bloch: The hard, peculiar, crackling harmony between the future to the left of the Rhine and the antiquarium to the right of the Rhine pursued me rather plainly throughout my whole philosophy. To plunder the old, assembling something new, works best from the standpoint of such cities.

Thinking of the Marxist's nymphs in the reeds of the riverbank, Hans told Vivian of the alchemical water sprites of the Odenwald forester Fabricius that regulated electrolysis in the forest floors so that hydrogen ions would corrode the rocks and oxygen could weather them, of ethereal creatures that created razor-thin films of water on the surface of soil kernels in which millions of the tiniest animals lived, of figures from the intermediate realm who as mermen provide for the oxygen content of the waters in the rustling of brooks so that they can furnish fish with a habitat, who as nymphs protect the springs, and as nixies the particular elements of the forest at ponds and lakes. Fabricius: In the evening we visited the nymphs of a spring pool deep in the rocky hollows. They led the horses to water amicably and quieted the deer that came to drink so that they wouldn't be disturbed by us. No wonder the psychedelic Werner Pieper had published the spiritualist works of the Weinheim forester. In German fairy tales, however, the forest often stands for the world as an impenetrable confusion, regrettably and also totally wrongly, Hans Mühlenkamm explained, raving about witches, fairies, and maidens as not so long ago about Irmgard Möller. An Intercity train thundered over the Konrad Adenauer Bridge, the gas flares of BASF blazing menacingly in competition with the setting sun.

Vivian Atkinson didn't quite want to be so arrogant as to dismiss Hansi's tales bubbling forth in view of the stirring Rhine as unscientific and thus posed a few questions about the fabulous nature of the pixies, dryads, sylphs, and whatever they all were called. Of the backwards-speaking dwarves from the boulder field who so tormented the drug dealer Heiner, however, Hans had never read a word. Of the Odenwald custom of tickling to death, though, likely. He knew for example about the Wildeleuthäusel, an area of craggy cliffs in the Sensbach Valley where, as the name suggests, wild people—little, ugly, ragged, nearly unclothed, mostly outcast characters—were supposed to have dwelled. One day a wagoner traveling from Gaimühle to Hebstahl threw rocks into the Wildeleuthäusel and was subsequently tickled to death by a wild woman. On top of that a Germanic priestess from Waldkatzenbach supposedly withdrew into the Wildeleuthäusel upon the introduction of Christianity. Did she or her spirit tickle the wagoner to death perhaps? Some two and half miles (as the crow flies) northwest of the aforementioned craggy cliffs, in cool Rindengrund near Unter-Sensbach, was the Wildfrauenstein, the Wild Women's Stone, from which the saga of death by tickling also originated. South of Hassloch near Gross-Bieberau, too, there was once supposed to have been a similar Wildfrauenstein. Another legend told of an Odenwald farmer's wife who had tickled her own husband to death after he had shouted at her: you're all dried up. Vivian had had no idea how well her friend knew his way around behind the porphyry quarries. She immediately made plans with him to drive into the mysterious mountains together as soon as possible. I'm curious to see what you'll wear then, Hans Mühlenkamm remarked, giving his woman in green a friendly jab in the ribs.

From Vivian Atkinson's Weininger extracts: Just as we have always been indebted only to men for truly valuable disclosures regarding the psychic processes in women, so too have men alone depicted the sensations of the pregnant woman. Correspondingly, we remain dependent on just one thing: what is feminine in men themselves. In a certain sense, the principle of intermediate sexual forms proves to be the precondition for every true judgment man renders upon woman. In anatomical build: the prominence of male genitalia that so completely takes from the man's body the character of a vessel. For woman, the condition of sexual arousal only denotes the greatest intensification of her total existence. The wedding night, finally, the moment of deflowering, is the most important one, I would like to say the point of bisection of the woman's whole life. Woman is only sexual; man is also sexual. The morphological detachment of male genitalia from the man's body could again be regarded as symbolic for this relationship. Thus, man can confront his sexuality and consider it in isolation from others. In women, sexuality cannot be isolated from a non-sexual sphere by a temporal boundary of its eruptions, nor by an anatomical organ in which it is visibly localized on the exterior. Put bluntly: the man has the penis, but the vagina has the woman.

Weininger: Women lack any and all consciousness of immortality. Absolute woman has no ego. Man has everything in himself, and may only foster in himself this or that in particular. He can reach the highest heights or degenerate to the lowest of forms, he can become an animal, a plant, he can even become a woman, and therefore there are feminine, effeminate men. But the woman can never become a man. A female genius is thus a contradiction in terms; for genius only ever consisted of intensified, fully developed, higher-level, generally conscious masculinity. Just as the human genius has everything in him, so too does he have woman in him; but woman herself is only a part of the universe, and a part cannot contain the whole in itself, as femininity cannot contain within itself genius. The principle of all conceptuality are logical axioms, and women lack these; for them, the principle of identity is not the guideline which alone may give the concept its unambiguous determinacy, and they do not take as their norm the principle of contradiction which alone demarcates it against all other possible and real things as a completely self-sufficient concept. Therefore, because women's thinking is chiefly a kind of tasting, taste in the broadest sense remains the loftiest feminine characteristic, the highest thing a woman may achieve on her own and wherein she may develop a certain degree of accomplishment.

Mudau municipality, September 25, 1997, 8:30 a.m., Edingen area code: 06203. Korinna Kohn had awoken in her white double bed bathed in sweat and had run straight to the telephone. She had dreamed she had to edit the Routledge reader announced for October Re-thinking Abortion (Routledge as the publishing house where the books of Judith Butler, Donna Haraway, and so forth appeared). When exactly was she due, the army brat asked after having listened sympathetically to everything, and the convict's bride answered: the end of January, beginning of February. Apropos of Donna Haraway, Mary Shelley begins her preface to Frankenstein with the words: The event on which this fiction is founded has been supposed, by Dr. Darwin, and some of the physiological writers of Germany, as not of impossible occurrence. Had you known that? I was flabbergasted too; but it makes sense. And since you're on the line anyway, I'd like to ask you really fast if you think it'd be reasonable to characterize listening to Exotica records as racist. Likewise, putting a pineapple in the living room as colonialist? What's more reprehensible here: ornament or consumption? Vivian, however, had just woken up—because of Korinna's phone call, that is—and promised to call back later, threw on her American summer dress, and ran down to the kiosk where she purchased some candy, the Rhein-Neckar-Zeitung, and the entertainment magazine for Mannheim and Heidelberg. Two old men with narrow-brimmed corduroy hats were conversing in front of the refreshment stand about how Edingen's SPD mayor had flown to a new sister city in Turkey, causing the great discontent of the local CDU, to which the two beer-drinking old men obviously belonged. That the man behind the kiosk may have been a Turk did not seem to bother them further. The Indian summer, which this year was called High Pressure Area Ottmar, had driven up the mercury columns in the thermometers to over seventy degrees Fahrenheit. Beside the entrance to the tobacco warehouse lay the free local rags and weeklies, now from Mannheim, now from Heidelberg, in the mailbox a letter from Daddy Atkinson, on the mat upstairs in front of Vivian's apartment door Petersen's pre-read Mannheimer Morgen. A cup of coffee, brewed; the two candy bars ought to do for breakfast.

Vivian brushed a strand of hair out of her face. Her bangs had gotten so long that she had been trying for weeks now, mostly without success, to comb them into a side part. Would she have to procure a barrette and temporarily look like a girlie? Better to squint through the fringes awhile longer as she was doing then at the sunny kitchen table, and like Chan Marshall that time on the dim stage. We need supervised drug clinics and the controlled distribution of heroin: The Drug Society of Mannheim celebrates its twenty-fifth anniversary; tomorrow a courtyard festival in K3 to this end. The redevelopment of the Edingen's town center: The new Messplatz was inaugurated. The cockroach plague over in Ladenburg under control. Personals: Emanuella, hot like the Amazon. Teeny Aileen, eighteen and blonde. Mistress Lady Mona with lady playmate. All this Mannheim and Ludwigshafen. In the Heidelberg area: glowing lava, forty-seven-inch bust. Trans-Gabriela from Brazil, well hung, bust size 31B. Next to a man she would probably be read as a woman, and next to a woman as a man; the strictly binary police records department was hetero-sexually determined through and through. Top model Melanie, twenty, coffee-brown, bust size enormous, shaved, super service. Outstanding in Ludwigshafen: transsexual Chanel, mega boobs, well hung.

New in Bruchsal: Antonella, catchy figure, piss play, scat. Mega boobs new, named Sandy, twenty, luxurious legs. Daniel, the love-shaft for Her and Him. Jasmin from Mexico, exotic, back again. Vivian choked on her coffee. Sudden thought: What had actu-ally really happened with Korinna? In the Heidelberger Amtsan-zeiger: Women's Emergency Hotline in Heidelberg: Prevention of Sexual Violence. A Series of Events Sponsored by Mayoress Beate Weber. Personals: Angelika, blonde Rubens model, tender cuddle-sex or bizarre eroticism. Directly under that, bold-faced and bordered: Two hundred forty pounds, beautifully wrapped, twenty years old. Neckarsteinach: More new international girls in all skin colors, with individual, leisurely service. The Snickers bar was melting between Vivian's fingers. Was poor Korinna going nuts in the Bauland? Another from Neckarsteinach: New girls are here. Cora, lady in suspenders, white and black studio. Pornography, according to Judith Butler: symptoms of the always misguided imaginary relationship between the sexes, showcasing the unreality of gender roles. What was Donna Haraway showcasing? Would she label a paraplegic person in an electric wheelchair a cyborg? Tasty treat and hottie; fine-print below: ISO female colleague. Rethinking prostitution? Filipino girl Gie-Gie, Sundays and holidays too. Where had Korinna Kohn gotten her Routledge catalogue? Maybe Vivian shouldn't even call her back, just drive straight there.

The Rhein-Neckar-Zeitung reported an automobile accident in the merging lane of the L 600 to the Patrick Henry Village caused by a twenty-six-year-old female Honda driver. John Deere's innovative final assembly for tractors, done up big in the Mannheimer Morgen. Smaller: A masked man ambushed a fifteen-year-old girl in a clump of bushes, threatened the schoolgirl with a butterfly knife, and forced her to undress. The victim gave the unknown man a kick in the pelvic area. After that he went on the run. In the evening hours on Tuesday an approximately twenty-four-year-old man exposed himself to a young woman. He approached her from the connecting foot path between Rheingoldstrasse and Nibelungenweg, initially touched her from behind, and when the woman turned around exposed himself indecently. A report with photo from the local riflemen's ball in Edingen. Mouse on Mars tonight in Heidelberg's Schwimmbad Musik Club; one could go there with Hans. During her wild tomboy years (tomboys: girls who play outside) Vivian—then still in nothing more than swimming trunks—had been pinched in the breasts, just then beginning to show, by an adolescent lifeguard trainee at the Heidelberg outdoor swimming pool. After that she had preferred to bind them. On the other hand: ancient krautrock with Guru Guru in Heidelberg's Karlstorbahnhof. Their legendary drummer Mani Neumeier, replicated, in a wax museum in Tokyo. Vivian decided to look up a telephone number in the far reaches of the Odenwald, but for now continued flipping through the Rhein-Neckar-Zeitung. On September twenty-seventh at eleven o'clock in the morning, the women-friendly mayoress would open the Heidelberg Old City Festival with the Baden wine queen Andrea Galli, and the castle dwarf Perkeo, for which reason blues rock with East of Leimen would echo through the Untere Strasse from three o'clock on. For weeks now the city hall chief's convoys had trekked through the old city scraping off so-called illegally posted bills, etching away student graffiti, and so on. The homeless were removed from the city without a trace, trailer communes dragged away, anarchist centers were facing their immediate closure. On October twenty-fourth, yeah, finally Sleater-Kinney live in Karlsruhe. And with that enough of the morning press review. Already past ten thirty.

Vivian walked to her wattled clothes chest and picked out a pair of underwear. What would've been the difference for the men at the kiosk if they had known that the tall, young woman with the two chocolate bars wasn't wearing anything under her dress? The student tied her Buffalos and packed Jacques Lacan's Encore into her backpack. The book had to be returned today; by no stretch of the imagination had she understood the essay God and the Jouissance of the Woman anyway: highly peculiar translation beholden to French syntax, Greek letters, and cryptic formulations all over, the definite article before Woman in the title even diagonally crossed out. Lacan: Thus we term it, this jouissance, however we can, vaginal, we speak of the posterior pole of the cervix and other cuntfusions, it goes without saying. If only she would feel it and wouldn't know anything about it, that would allow quite a few doubts to be raised on the part of the famous frigidity. Straight talk, by contrast, in the second nearly-overdue book that had to be returned to the library today. Valerie Solanas, in 1968, in her manifesto of the Society for Cutting Up Men, abbreviated S.C.U.M., which recognized but one member, namely the author herself: the male is a biological accident: the Y (male) gene is an incomplete X (female) gene, that is, it has an incomplete set of chromosomes. In other words, the male is an incomplete female, a walking abortion, aborted at the gene stage. To be male is to be deficient, emotionally limited; maleness is a deficiency disease and males are emotional cripples. In contrast to the version disseminated by men that women are rudimentary men, not being fully formed in the decisive detail, the clitoris. Was that sort of thing sexist? Even racist? Donna Haraway did find it racist to advocate against genetic manipulation. Vivian, quite to the contrary, thought it interesting to consider when the genetic engineer was acting in a racist manner: when he bred a lower or higher species? What would a genetically improved man even be? One who no longer raped and murdered in any case. But where did male violence begin? Was—Silvia Bovenschen had asked back in 1976—logic already a piece of virile perfidy? Once again, photocopied by Vivian, the Germanized manifesto of the solipsistic Society for Cutting Up Men, paper-bound in bright yellow, a macho man on the cover—naked save for briefs, helmet, and sunglasses—who is very drastically firing a gun into his underwear (which looks like a diaper): When he believes he's a woman, he then achieves a continuous diffuse sexual feeling.

Screwing is, for a man, a defense against his desire to be female. But sexuality is itself sublimation. The man must always compensate obsessively for not being a woman. Valerie Solanas decided that he had transformed the entire world into a pile of shit and pulled her trigger on Andy Warhol of all people. Classic case: phallic woman.

Barbara Vinken, University of Hannover, had gotten to the heart of the matter: The woman wants what she lacks, and therefore she confirms that the man has it. See also Frauke and Angela. Angela's gotta have it. Gender-based having, being, and seeming on all channels of perception. Vivian briefly considered whether she should also pack clothes, but then decided that underwear was sufficient, perhaps a few tights for potential fall weather. Eroticism and Lace Panties, 1964: Sheer panty hose are considered highly erotically charged clothing. That's why preteen girls do not wear them, but instead wear neutral ones. They are not yet mature sexual partners and thus ought not to be falsely distinguished as such by clothing. Thus the Boston players of the 1917 Hasty Pudding dancing girls are girls in heat? The stern censor's mature sexual partners? Nonetheless, even such sheer stockings were credited with a warming effect, and Vivian Atkinson packed a few of them. Next to her bed lay, still as good as unread, Caroline Walker Bynum's book Fragmentation and Redemption. How, Vivian suddenly wondered, did Frauke Stöver make her living exactly? Did her father earn so much money in the Schleswig-Holstein marmalade factory that he was forever able to support his soon-to-be-thirty-two-year-old daughter, dissertating around in circles now for semesters on end about Jesus' foreskin? Or had Ilse Schoolmistress waived the rent? Did perhaps Angela Stöver bring in all the money from the lesbian pizzeria? It occurred to

Vivian that she hadn't the foggiest idea and had also never thought about how old Angela Stöver even was. An ageless woman, maybe already over forty? Frauke, on her as-good-as-wrinkle-free wife: she is much more vain than I am. She always has all twenty nails painted perfectly twenty-four/seven. Juridically speaking, Angela was probably Frauke's husband. Health insurance would carry them that way too. Therefore: He is much more vain than I am. He always has all twenty nails painted perfectly twenty-four/seven. Like the Abbé de Choisy. Was the woman from Travemünde thus subjecting the sissy boy from the Po Basin to a dichotomous worldview or not? At the OEG station a giant poster hung touting the October issue of the women's magazine freundin. On it a print, seemingly dashed off, of a woman in the mirror, at home, from behind. Shot blurry from below the right arm, akimbo on her hips. Black bikini, a part of the bare back, the mirror image unfocused, golden band, concentrated application of lipstick. Next to the photo a paperclip, both denoting the workplace and attaching an oversized slip of paper on which, brazenly, the typed words stood: Women look in the mirror more often than men. Space. After all, there's more to see. Uh oh, said Vivian, only half-amused; the railcar had almost pulled away without her.

The previous day Bodo Petersen had slipped under Vivian's door an illustration of a German living room from the time of the Economic Miracle in which almost all of the plastics used were named individually and in contemplation of which the master's candidate was now immersing herself on the interurban tram: the high-density polyethylene of the coffee cups, the Trolitul of the egg-cup set, the Lupolen of the breakfast basket, the greasy father's no-iron Perlon dress shirt, his more durable Diolen business suit, the wash-n-wear Perlon play dress of the dutiful child, the stiff Trevira combination of the submissive mother, her Cupresa ladies' hose; the kitchen unit with Hornitex laminate and black linoleum baseboard. Apart from that, Hostalen buckets were flying around, Stratoplast bowls, impact-resistent Polystyrol dustpans. So what? Petersen had copied this illustration, according to his handwritten addition, from a nearly twenty-year-old, obviously more nostalgically than analytically-minded book entitled The Puberty of the Republic. Not really what Vivian needed although possibly interesting as a quasi de-Nazified epilogue to the heavily inauspicious Karl Aloys Schenzinger—that is, his and his kindred spirits' idea of the mobilizing production of national plastics from the spirit of tragedy.

The continuity of the Third Reich in the flourishing Federal Republic of Germany had prompted Beate Klarsfeld, characterized by the ruling public as an admittedly pretty but quite obviously unsatisfied young woman, to slap the then-Chancellor Kiesinger in the face on November 7, 1968. According to a photo—yellowed, hanging today in Pat Meier's room—the politician's nose had begun to bleed upon this formidable quittance; see also Sigmund Freud's and Wilhelm Fliess' erotic correspondence on the nosebleed as menstrual equivalent. Below that Pat had taped a page torn from Stern magazine with Sebastian Haffner's annotating comments on it: There was a time when a slap was understood as a challenge to a duel, and in very old-fashioned circles it likely still means this even today. Perhaps Ms. Klarsfeld envisioned something like this kind of yellowed code of honor. But it applied or applies only among men; even emancipation has changed nothing in this regard. A woman cannot challenge a man to a duel. Which is why, under the old code of honor, a woman is or would be allowed to slap a man only in a single situation, namely to ward off sexual harassment. What emancipation, Vivian Atkinson pondered as the OEG Weiblingen passed by, could Haffner have meant in 1968? That of the man from his past?

The books were returned swiftly; the train into the Neckar Valley left the central Heidelberg train station at one o'clock. Little clouds of steam curled over the surface of the Neckar. After a half-hour train ride spent without any sort of conversation and without any book to read: arrival in Eberbach. Five minutes there for the transfer into the waiting BRN 821 bus that, full of commuting schoolboys and schoolgirls, was driving to Mudau by way of Waldkatzenbach, Strümpfelbrunn, Mülben, Wagenschwend, Scheidental, Waldauerbach, Schlossau. Almost another entire hour of travel time there, through the gently rolling dizzy heights of the Bauland, Odin's woods increasingly interrupted by expansive farmland. The student alighted at the old train station taken out of service in 1973, surveyed the disused narrow-gauge steam locomotive in front of the building while strapping on her backpack, oriented herself briefly, and finished the rest of her unannounced journey on foot, again wandering out of the midday quiet of the small town, at the periphery of which Heiner's spick-and-span, snow-white estate lay. Korinna Kohn—now obviously pregnant, in a brown caftan, irrepressibly surprised by Vivian's lightning visit, thus immediately showering her girl friend with kisses—had only just come back from her female gynecologist in Amorbach, Bavaria; the historic Tatra sedan still stood glowing and ticking in the tarred driveway.

Right away the two classmates swapped stories about how, tellingly, women's doctors were still predominantly male; even their mothers, as if it were self-evident, made pilgrimages to rakish, expensive-sportscar-driving gynecologists to have themselves (exposed from head to toe) frisked, opened up, inspected, and measured, quite often painfully. Where could the equivalent of a (what one might call) men's doctor be found who pathologized healthy boys' bodies? Well, nowhere. Thus, early on, being a woman had been taught to Vivian and Korinna as a sickness that regularly needed treatment for matters of fertility or, as the case may be, copulation. Their femininely sexualized bodies—impure scenarios of nearly endless penetration and outflow—had no limits at all that prevailing hygiene would have spared. Standing to comparison was the pure, masterfully hermetic, at best sperm-donating model of male sexuality: no filth, no blood, no secretions, no milk. Have you ever noticed, Korinna Kohn asked, that menstrual blood is always shown as clinical blue on commercials? Blue like the little band on my tampon, Vivian Atkinson added. She also knew that light blue had once been the color for little girls and pink for little boys. Yet how had the tables turned? There were gynecological textbooks—Frauke Stöver had one from the seventies—that talked about the proverbial superfluity of the mammae as soon as a woman no longer breastfed. For the efficient prevention of breast cancer, prestigious gynecologists had recommended, in all earnestness, early surgical removal of the dangerous mammary glands, even in the emergent girl. However, before the sadistic doctor was able to thrust his body-part-fragmenting, body-island-isolating, organ-dissecting knife through the surface of the woman, the superfluous, wily body part had sought a new task; it served henceforth as a sex symbol.

The two classmates had learned that bodies initially have no gender. They were only ascribed a culturally specific gender through social knowledge, practices of perception, representation, and thematization. On that note, I absolutely have to show you something, Korinna exclaimed, running inside. Vivian took a seat on the patio. Everything here still looked as if Heiner had only just been arrested. Why didn't the tennis player throw all that white tat in the trash? But there she came again, had an old issue of Spiegel from the sixties in her hand opened to an article titled with the words And We'll Show Our Breasts to Anyone. Four photos were taking up more space than the whole text. Defendant Ursula Seppel before the court: a young woman with a bob, Rodenstock glasses, and large, globular breasts under a dark, transparent flounce-collar dress. College-girl striptease in the courtroom: six young women with bared torsos, reading pamphlets aloud; in the foreground three men, one unrecognizable, one student-like, smiling, one bourgeois, affronted. Defendants, police: two uniformed guards, between them—her body in profile with face turned away—a bare-breasted woman. Removal of a female student from the courtroom: at least three uniformed officers tearing at an blurred person of indefinite gender. As if they wanted to quarter her/him.

Korinna Kohn, in a deck chair, read aloud: And we will show our breasts to anyone, six collegiate women of the SDS Task Force Emancipation sang last Thursday in Hamburg district court, doffing sweaters and blouses. The cue for the solidarity striptease was inadvertently given by the court before which the student Ursula Seppel had to answer for trespassing for not complying with a demand from the police to leave the courthouse during an earlier student trial. Although Ursula Seppel had appeared in a see-through blouse with no lingerie, judge Wolfgang Schneider, forty-one, had opened the proceeding without inhibition because he considered the black-veiled bust a fashionable gag.

But when he announced, as the girls had expected, that the challenge on the grounds of bias brought before him by the defendant was overruled, the female auditors who had come without brassieres as a precaution formed themselves into a topless sextet. Ursula Seppel, too, exposed her breasts, lept over the barrier, and sang along in the Ballad of the Asexual Judges, based loosely on Brecht. Judge Schneider—open quotation marks: This manner of bias I'd like to preserve for myself because I'd like to continue to feel something in the face of toplessness, close quotation marks—called the police and had the girls conducted away. My mom would definitely have liked to have been there, Vivian Atkinson remarked drily, even issues of konkret showed topless girls on the cover back then. Not my ma, Korinna replied, rose clumsily out of the deck chair to take the Spiegel magazine back inside, but then stopped in the patio door and asked abruptly: Are you wearing a bra under your summer dress? No, Vivian answered, are you under your caftan? Also no.

So then, what does the gynecologist say? Everything's fine; in Plessner's words: I am a corpus, I have a body. She holds the fallacious belief, though, that the fertility imputed to us women for a certain period of life is the origin of all binary conceptualizations of bodies and in turn not the effect of polarizing powermongering. Speaking of, I have a book for you, from down in Amorbach, Korinna disclosed. It's upstairs next to my bed, it's yellow. Vivian took her backpack, went up, and discovered amid a pile of books beside Heiner's and Korinna's double bed a huge yellow tome with a violet inscription: Comedienne, Harlot? The Artiste's Life and Love in Light of Truth, by Medical Councilor Dr. Bernhard A. Bauer, Specialist for Gynecology in Vienna, published by Fiba, Vienna and Leipzig, 1927. Thanks a million, Korinna; wasn't that much too expensive? Oh no, my gynecologist found it in the attic, with her char, after recently acquiring the practice, and just gave it to me to take when I spoke of you. Funny word: char, and what was there to tell about her, Vivian, the master's candidate wanted to know. Well, your thesis topic, Korinna retorted. And your topic, Vivian countered, do you still have it, or does it now have you?

For weeks now (as she candidly admitted) Korinna Kohn had been boning up on (particularly since finishing the collection of historical material on the transsexual tennis champion Renée Richards) Sir Galahad, Bertha Eckstein-Diener in civic life, acknowledged authoress of the first female cultural history in the German language (albeit under the male Grail-Knight pseudonym: Mothers and Amazons, 1932, proceeding from Bachofen's Mother Right) but also of the idiosyncratic Idiot's Guide to Russian Literature of 1925 and several other curiosities, only one of which—a cultural history of silk—was published under a woman's name, the pseudo-name Helen Diner, during the Second World War. Didn't Sir Galahad want to be a woman? Far from it, Viv, the magistrate's daughter declared, paging hastily through the authoress' first novel The Conic Sections of God from 1920. Listen, here: But being an entirely solitary self, malleable only from within, has its silver lining too. One closed oneself off and just loved whatever found its way inside. Huh, what, the visiting soldier's daughter probed, and loved what? And just loved whatever found its way inside, repeated the tennis player in the brown caftan, it goes on: For example a borzoi—you know borzois, right, those Russian greyhounds?—Upon first sight of the incomparable animal walking strangely and resignedly behind his Viennese master, she went into rapture for days, became bleary-eyed from the (watch out,

Vivian) harp of this body on which the ribs shone through like strings, nor did she rest until she actively possessed the drawn-in flanks of the Russian greyhound on her own body. One exercise was especially good for this, Korinna continued reading: While recumbent, suck the body into a crescent shape and pour out the jar with the goldfish into the depressions. If the fish were then able to swim around beating their fins without touching ground in this pelvic dish, everything was all right and produced the dearly desired contour on the upright body, exclamation point. No kidding? Vivian thought it was nuts that Korinna had found a body island that presented itself as a body of water. She would have liked nothing more than to hammer this passage directly into the liquid crystal right then.

To me Sir Galahad's behavior seems extraordinarily morbid, she said to her friend. Could it be that here, in the purebred dog, the German gods witness their twilight? You yourself lent me Maria Groener's 1927 The Science of Woman months ago, without which I would never have stumbled across Sir Galahad, Korinna Kohn answered, but apparently you didn't read it, because the book comes with the same objection, from the far right. The expectant mother ran upstairs to fish The Science of Woman: On Woman's Well-Being and Man's Power (written in St. Ilgen near Heidelberg, published by Verlag Psychokratie, in Hattenheim, Rheingau) out of her pile of books, returned breathless to the patio, took a seat in Heiner's beloved canopy swing—for which a Heilbronn garden center manager had allowed himself to be compensated with a sack of Ecstasy pills—and let it rip: Primordial time, seen as the nurturer of small, racially pure, and unchallenged families of peoples, was very well able to hand power to the woman (Groener here referring to Bachofen) but when a nation is to be destroyed for ever and always on account of its achievements (she writes) then only man, who alone is the bearer of the thought of the metaphysical obligation to honor his race and who thus can dictate a degree of persevering and defiance of death—which is remote from woman's nature—can steer a nation to victory and self-assertion. The Karlsruher paged further: Woman is thus now—liberated from all things, even her maiden name, which is to say that of her father—the spiritual bearer, the nameless one, symbol of the eternal tat tvam asi of the divinely unnamable coalescence; have you ever heard such a thing? Vivian also didn't know what tat tvam asi was. The blissful characterlessness of the woman, writes Maria Groener—herself a woman, to the extent (the listener interjected) that that's not actually a male pseudonym—as the test of strength of luminous male domination. Domination as Grandma Hanau's most frequently employed curse word for damnation. Let that much be said in advance before she makes Sir Galahad pay the piper.

It is Jewish sexuality, too, that fills a book which is perhaps the most widely read one in Germany right now: Sir Galahad's Conic Sections of God, Albert Langen, Munich. If the information about this book is correct—which is being spread as an open secret—that is, that the author is a woman, then we probably must see the self-portrait of the author in the woman Sibyl. Read it yourself, Vivian. Korinna handed The Science of Woman over to her classmate. After the first quixotic=god-seeking connection with an hysterical=occultist Aryan, this woman, having grown up without manners, but with the starving spirit of the decadent form-intoxicated aesthete, falls for the perversely vivisecting Jew. Fleeing from him, she kills herself in the arms of the Hindu arrested for bigamy because of her. Twelve lines below, Vivian Atkinson got stuck on the formulation that Sir Galahad constructs a sexual fairy-tale India before our eyes that exists nowhere but in the mind of a Jewess or a Jewified woman. Groener quoted Sir Galahad word for word where the latter seemed to her most shameless, that is, the sinful, (so to speak) gynecological enlightenment of an innocent, virginal gentlewoman regarding the breathing of the womb, closing and tensing, counter-swelling, to strengthen the hidden inner walls through lissome practice in such a way that from them the lunar wave casts itself toward the solar flood during the tides of Eros; to close back the flower-sleek ring into unspoiled virginity after every ray of love as if with magic inner forceps. What is there to do, Maria Groener countered here, to save our people from the nets of the corrupter? Ending The Science of Woman one page later with Goethe's words: Man obeys. Woman serves. Serving, however, means coming first. Goethe, Goldoni, and Woman-Hating. Vivian cleared her throat. Korinna was painting her toenails Prussian blue. In the appendix, the publisher Greifenverlag zu Rudolstadt advertised for Ms. Groener's hominibus bonae voluntatis, The Book of Woman in the Light of Schopenhauer: People of German inwardness, read this book, pass it along and spread it wherever you can. This, however, Vivian and Korinna found interesting: German inwardness in the light of the Thousand-Year Reich.

If the Aryan god is to be born in our souls, Maria Groener had written in St. Ilgen, then the god Jehovah must be dashed to pieces, and in order to realize a god, everything that constructed a god must be destroyed. Funny concept of construction and also of religion, remarked the only-child from the Patrick Henry Village, but her host's thoughts dwelled anew on the idolatrously corseted Sir Galahad. When in 1899 she bore her first son Percy—from

Perceval, the piercer of valleys, Wolfram von Eschenbach's Parzival, to Richard Wagner's Parsifal—people were taken by complete surprise. In her own words, the authoress with the iron wasp waist had in fact: always lost exactly as much weight herself as her fruit swelled. The fine, hard sinews drawn in tautly, without slackening, doused with volition. The noble depression only just filled out. Hopefully Korinna Kohn didn't have such bees in her bonnet too. The lunar-white depression between the borzoi flanks: a flat mirror. Then finally the inevitable caesarian section. The first sentences of Mothers and Amazons, Sir Galahad's book about gynaecocracy: In the beginning was Woman. Man first appears later in filial form as the biologically younger and later one. The woman as what was given, the man as what became; women's rights could not be successfully contended in this way. But Vivian had to leave one thing to Korinna and her crazed Grail-Knight: if Sir Galahad, with Bachofen, understood woman as nature, she herself—alias Bertha Eckstein-Diener—had become something more in any case, culture, noble depression, a park with a goldfish pond.

True to form, Dr. Bernhard A. Bauer—Specialist for Gynecology in Vienna, whose work Vivian studied over the course of the following days, mostly lounging around the garden, but also on the Schneidershecke, that stone Limes foundation in the forest near Schlossau from which she, alongside Korinna, was letting her legs dangle—proved to be a thoroughly misogynist gynecologist too. He wrote: We do not wish with Weininger to divide the female sex separately according to its manner of lifestyle into the two types mother and harlot, but rather we want and must have the courage to admit that these two types exist collectively in every woman. Should one of these two components be missing, then the woman is simply no longer a woman, but a hybrid thing; the woman without a propensity for harlotry just as the woman without the desire for motherhood. Vivian hadn't been able to stop herself from reading this passage aloud and thereby yanking Korinna from her reading of Womanizing Nietzsche, the book published two years ago by the philosopher Kelly Oliver at the University of Texas that the expectant mother was currently plowing through together with Richard Ekin's distinctly easier-to-read Male Femaling. You do know, Vivian suddenly asked, that the winter semester begins today? And both classmates immediately tried to imagine how their professor might be riding his bike over the Karl Theodor Bridge just then.

May I? The twenty-four-year-old Heidelberger read over the twenty-seven-year-old Karlruher's shoulder and initially understood next to nothing at all. I agree, Kelly Oliver wrote, with the diagnosis of philosophy's need to try to become woman in order to avoid the crisis of the Enlightenment subject, man. I will not only diagnose philosophy's desire to become woman, but also philosophy's success at opening itself onto the feminine. Becoming woman always in quotation marks. Nietzsche and his reader Derrida, Korinna explained, had opened up philosophical discourse for other voices, multiple voices. Vivian thought she had read about the female gender of philosophy in Daniel Boyarin, couldn't quite really get the exact circumstances together, and, stirred up, jumped down off the Roman brick masonry. Found the nearest tree with a white L painted on it and ran along the former demarcation line first to the left, then just as many paces to the right. But by then Siegfried had grown into his manly powers, she declaimed. He went out into the land, caught bears and lions, and hung them up on the trees as a mockery, whereupon everyone was amazed. This Siegfried was no philosopher,

Korinna called over from the remains of the watchman's post. But had there ever been lions here? Were those tormenting Heiner in his cell even Nibelungs?

And what's with Male Femaling? That does sounds kind of promising. Dressed in a light Southwest-African safari costume from Mother Kohn's stock, Vivian snatched the open Ekins from the brick wall and instantly got caught up in a passage where the author, director of the Northern-Irish Trans-Gender Archive, commended to his interested readers, if they like, to skip the scientific section—which he had captioned Mainly Theory and hadn't arranged very epistemologically anyhow—and proceed directly to Mainly Practice, all the bizarre case studies of which the archivist was so proud. That's just like in old sex-ed books, Vivian thought, where science had formed the smoke screen, lifted at all the right places, that only legitimated the reader's wanton lusts. Or like in current male philosophy, the collegiate woman in the caftan (a charcoal-gray one today) said in agreement, this discipline that has largely deteriorated to pragmatism, which I encounter in the lecture hall at most as a more or less pieced-together history of philosophy. You're right, said Vivian, this Ekins is obviously anything but a literary scholar; but Judith Butler, does that mean she isn't a philosopher? Right now she has, as you know, a professorship for rhetoric, Korinna informed her classmate and went on: I find that my mother's little Namibian safari dress, especially over the Riefenstahlian teddy, makes you exceptionally attractive; I'm already looking forward to being able to wear both next summer again.

Speaking of Male Femaling—Vivian could not be dissuaded— didn't Rainer Werner Fassbinder make a rather grim feature film about how a homosexual man parts with his penis so he can be together with a heterosexual man? And do you think Judith Butler has seen this film? How do you in fact convey the common denominator of performance and impersonation in German? As representation? Embodiment? Personification? To distinguish it from imitation? If Angela Stöver doesn't want to align herself with Butler's idealized notion of parody—I also don't find anything parodic in that sense in her feminine habitus—she still doesn't have to be a case for Richard Ekins. Or rather: can we even be Butler disciples without signing off on her—as I deem it—superfluous chimera of parodic repetition? Now don't you worry yourself about that, replied Korinna Kohn, testing a fat mulberry for worm-eatenness. Also, I received a postcard last week from Frauke in which she raves about Angela's latest fancy, male impersonation. That must really be a case of parodic repetition then, the woman in the safari dress laughed aloud in surprise. On those days she calls herself Angelo, her girl friend explained, looks like the author Annemarie Schwarzenbach, and works MS Connexion until the cows come home—though until the cows come home needs to be untangled etymologically. Angelo's favorite expression when someone fucks with her, as Frauke writes: You clearly do not know who you're talking to. Though it would be instructive to know whether Angela wears feminine undergarments under Angelo's masculine outfit. And since we're on that topic already: there's news from Frauke too; since her father discontinued his longtime payments, she's been working as a hostess, but leaves us in the dark about what her specific occupation consists of. Frauke Stöver, ending up with an escort service? Mainly Practice? Vivian Atkinson couldn't possibly imagine that. Had that perhaps been why she hadn't received a postcard about this? Korinna Kohn rummaged around in her duffel bag for a hairbrush. Since being pregnant, the striking dark blonde had been spending a comparatively large amount of time and effort on her hairdo; today it was that of Rita Hayworth, glammed up, 1953, in William Dieterle's Salome.

Here, read this. The woman on the Roman wall, deep in the Odenwald, handed her friend a bent-up, red-black rororo volume, and Vivian read, first quietly to herself, what the other had pointed out: But frequently he still felt something like a burden on his back: those were his complexes; he wondered whether he shouldn't seek out Freud in Vienna: I'll travel without money, on foot if necessary, and tell him: I don't have a penny, but I am a case. That I'm familiar with, the woman on the forest floor said right away, The Childhood of a Leader by Jean-Paul Sartre, then paged to the beginning, and read aloud: I am adorable in my little angel costume. Your little boy looks good enough to eat. He is simply precious in his angel costume. What's your name? Jacqueline? Lucienne? Margot? My name is Lucien. Lucien, the light one, like Lucifer, the bringer of light, the fallen angel. Sartre: He was not quite sure about not being a little girl. Here, Korinna, it's also about the gender of angels. Many people had kissed him and called him mademoiselle, everyone thought he was so charming with his gauze wings, long blue little dress, naked little arms, and blonde curls. He was afraid that people would suddenly decide not to take him for a little boy anymore. He could struggle against it as he liked, no one would listen to him. He wouldn't be allowed to take off his dress anymore, except for sleeping, and in the morning it would lay at the foot of his bed, and whenever he had to go pee during the day, he would have to hike it up like Nénette and squat down. Everyone would address him as my sweet little girl, and finally the time had come: I am a little girl.

Vivian Atkinson flipped straight to the end and read: The change was complete. An hour ago a lovely and insecure lad had walked into the café, now it was a man who left it, a leader among the French. But who then—the reader added—still decides out of caution to grow a mustache. And earlier, more toward the the beginning of this leader's childhood, the following passage: What would happen if we took Mama's clothes off, and if she put on Papa's pants? Maybe she would grow a black mustache on the spot. Crazy. Insane dialogue, too, between the father and the mama's boy; paging through again, Korinna Kohn squinted through the foliage at the sun. Will I be a boss one day? But of course, my little man, that's why I brought you into this world. And who will I command? When I'm dead, you'll be head of the factory and will command my workers. Sartre later has a homosexual man say to him: You are Rimbaud, he had your big hands when he came to Paris to meet Verlaine, he had this rosy face of a healthy farm boy and this long, slender body of a blonde girl. Urges the future boss to remove his collar and unbutton his shirt, leads the confused angel in front of the mirror, and allows him to admire the—Sartre writes—delightful harmony of his red cheeks and the white top of his breast. That is exactly the passage I was looking for, Korinna said.

Try this on. Korinna Kohn, on account of her womb, could no longer imagine at all how this sexy tennis dress—which she had worn on the occasion of a championship whose title she had won—actually fit. And it fit well, both found, on Vivian Atkinson's slender body. Just a touch looser around the top and at most shorter by the one half inch that Vivian was taller than her girl friend. White terrycloth socks, white sneakers—the same model as those of Martina Navratilova back in the day—completed the picture. The visitor wondered whether Heiner had potentially met Korinna on the tennis court, both entirely in white, but it was somehow impossible to talk to the Karlsruher about her jailed friend. Apart from that, Korinna Kohn (save for this morning in a blindingly white Nyltest hairdresser's smock) only ever really wore white on the tennis court. While standing for a moment alone in the living room, Vivian suddenly thought that it might in fact have been better to bring her own clothes with her to the Odenwald. But then Korinna was already coming back from the bathroom with an Italian dressing case and pulled out of it a white porcelain bottle with a gold screw cap. Label: Versace White Jeans Woman. His first posthumous eau de toilette, the tennis player said solemnly and had already spritzed her friend in her mightily short tennis dress with it. Next, Vivian was made up by her classmate, namely in the style of the twenties. Just lemme see, Korinna said, warding off all objections from her gradually more impatient victim, how I looked in 1988 on the day of my greatest triumph. The whole procedure, however, reminded Vivian Atkinson of how her German mother had dressed her up every year for Carnival as an Indian chief and made her up in the newest ladies' fashion as well. Then when she had finally been allowed to determine her own costume for herself for the first time, she chose that of the Lonesome Cowboy without any makeup at all. I'm cold, Vivian said to Korinna, and shortly thereafter she had on a white fabric-softened sweater over the tennis dress. Traces of powder, mascara, rouge, and lipstick stuck to the V-neck, so hectically (as it were) had it been slipped on by Korinna, now busying herself with a hot curling iron and sticky hairspray on wisps of Vivian's hair, too. And now, the acquiescent woman asked finally, bedecked contrary to her taste, all dressed up and nowhere to go? Quite the contrary, laughed Korinna, disappearing again into the bathroom.

A short time later Vivian heard the shower curtain drawn upstairs, the splatter of the shower, the automatic power-up of the gas boiler. She went into the kitchen to dab off the outrageous cherry-red lipstick her friend had applied on her, and when she saw her reflection in Heiner's silly Coca-Cola mirror, she thought perhaps for the first time in her life: that's an American girl; less: that's me, more like: that is I. I takes a seat. And so on. Lewis Carroll: In another moment Alice was through the glass, and had jumped lightly down into the Looking-glass room. Was America behind Heiner's looking-glass? The last chapter of Through the Looking-Glass was called: Which dreamed it? Alice asked her cat: WAS it the Red King, Kitty? You were his wife, my dear. See also the woman as the cat without a tail in Virginia Woolf's A Room of One's Own. Venus Xtravaganza in Paris Is Burning had not only wanted to be a woman, but—which for her was connected inextricably with the Other—white, too. Was multiplying gender by race a means of augmentation for the Other? Or by species? Wasn't there a motion picture with the title King Kong and the White Woman? Even at postcolonial Southeast Asian transvestite beauty contests there was no question that all even remotely promising candidates had to look white, Anglo-Saxon, Protestant, middle-class, heterosexual—in a word, like Western American women: the global American Otherness, imagined the world over, conjured the world over.

What, however, was—especially after the hapless loss of the Union of Soviet Socialist Republics in the east—the American's Other? The alien, Vivian thought, could at best substitute for the exterior Other; but (though it also sounds paradoxical, it can nevertheless be said) since its discovery, America had always, if not known, then had the interior Other as well. See also the

Indian, Vivian thought, his clothes, his war paint, his makeup, his (according to Weininger) feminine hairstyles. Indians, Indian, derived from India, which Columbus thought he had discovered with a western course to the Far East. These days, after the almost complete eradication of the (well, exactly:) effeminate, American indigenous peoples, the Asians in particular, next to the ever-stigmatized African Americans, were those who brought the both sexual and racist Other to the congruence which was felt, Euro- and androcentrically, to be sinister and threatening. Why this more-than-ethnographic concentration (mayhap a perfidious projection) on the Far East? Because in Thailand, Malaysia, and the Philippines, so-called secondary sex characteristics, both the biological and the social ones, were more negligibly absent? And therefore the ambivalent slogan There's nothing ambiguous about ambiguity was obviously easier (read: more appealing, more acceptable) to visualize? Could this graffito be carried over to Heidelberg, Germany, too? And what was with Vietnam? Or even Israel? Vivian was desperately jonesing for her Texas Instrument, which she hadn't laid a finger on in a week and a half anyway. Yet couldn't the possible difference between the Other and the Alien also be untangled on a paper napkin like the one with which she had just dabbed her American-German lips? Lipstick had even been sticking to her incisors. And finally: was the alien in general always the enigmatic, too?

Immanuel Kant had been firmly convinced: Woman does not betray her secret. And Otto Weininger had prefaced his chapter on male and female sexuality with precisely this motto. Sigmund Freud had fantasized in a lecture with the title Femininity: At all times humankind has speculated about the enigma of femininity. You, too, will not have excluded yourselves from this speculation insofar as you are men; one does not expect it of the women among you, they are themselves these enigmas. Gynecologist Dr. Bauer in his tome on the Life and Love of the Artiste in the Light of Truth: Woman is capable of playing all the thousands of metamorphoses in her life so well because she, as a whole, is a singular metamorphosis. While sitting so provocatively tarted up in Heiner's kitchen, Vivian recalled Silvia Bovenschen's emphasizing that the naturally beautiful does not simply lurk underneath the patina of the cosmetic industry. It becomes difficult, the literary scholar had written, when attaching the idea of the beautiful not to an image of woman created by man's hand, but to an empirical woman. Marilyn Monroe—product of artifice, myth of femininity, and victim of an inhuman culture industry in one—could not be split ex post facto into a natural and an artificial woman according to the pattern of leaving one part to Normal Mailer, sticking the other in jeans and protesting for women's lib. The whole woman belongs on our side, Bovenschen—who allegedly never wore jeans herself (it'd be interesting to know if not even white ones)—had written in the seventies. If jeans counted as natural, however, they were indeed the most female of all articles of clothing, Vivian recalled the slogan: woman equals nature, man equals culture. Typical, she thought: the synthetic baby doll as man's invention for the female body he fetishized. No lady would ever collect men's briefs. Or men's shoes. But why did women collect closets full of high heels, without any fetishism?

I'll be right there, Korinna Kohn screamed over the drone of her electric hair dryer. On the other hand—her girl friend reasoned further—hadn't Levi Strauss' cotton twill workman's pants long since been recoded as leisure pants? And what, again, did that have to do with emancipated womanhood? Silvia Bovenschen, on the self-staging of the smooth body of late-period Marlene Dietrich, as if draped in an unknown plastic: the performance of a representation of a woman's body. In British English Strumpfhosen were called tights, the confined things. In American English panty hose, panty approximating pansy, a colloquialism for weakling, sissy. Tights denoted femininity via their surface character. Even those girls' jeans designated explicitly as such for the denim girls of the sixties and seventies had always been the tightest-fitting ones. When Vivian the tomboy began to get curves—as her mother wisecracked back then—not a single pair of traditional blue denims (read: boys' jeans) would fit her at first. How did Elvis the Pelvis even fit into these things? Answering herself much, much later as a student: he only performed his pelvis in the gender-fuck hip-swing. Like Willi Ninja, the Vogue-ing employee of the Madonna Road Show. Today's stretch jeans—which Vivian (who instead wore the common, less well-fitting jeans from the men's department) found primitive—not infrequently accentuated the labia of their wearer.

If woman was the beautiful one, the one who is, but man was the signifying one, the one who is to be—Vivian wondered, gazing at her expressively, almost expressionistically (as in a silent film) made-up face in the blade of the bread knife while Korinna crimped her hair upstairs in the bathroom—what then did a mother-to-be symbolize? According to Ortega y Gasset the vocation of woman consisted in being man's concrete ideal, his enchantment, his illusion. Womandom. Had Angela chosen for herself this thankless artifice with the help of her bigoted Monika published monthly in Donauwörth? Did she even work in the Handschuhsheim pizzeria regularly at all anymore when Angelo wasn't around doing odd jobs in Mannheim? Or had Ortega y

Gasset alluded to Hansi Pompadour's fairies about which the nasty gynecologist Bauer contended: the best thing fairies take away from the little creature when they give it beauty in exchange is its heart? Beautiful women usually had no heart. Korinna Kohn, from upstairs: do we need jackets? I don't think so, her visitor answered, as meanwhile the sun had since come out over the farming landscape, warm autumn light flowing through the drug dealer's kitchen with the imitation Art Deco mirror and the Islamic kitchen clock inherited from the mysteriously perished previous tenant. But then the pregnant magistrate's daughter had already thrown a big pile of textiles down the steps.

The two classmates now found themselves on the country road, via Reisenbach, Eberbach, and Hirschhorn toward the Hirsch spring between Heddesbach and Heiligkreuzsteinach, where Korinna Kohn filled up an entire case of empty mineral water bottles kept in the trunk of the Tatra. For Heiner, she said monosyllabically, while holding one bottle after another under the calm fountain, Vivian for her own good not even bothering to ask why. Instead, though: are you going to smuggle that stuff into jail, or do you have someone else for that sort of thing? Someone else, Korinna answered tersely, Lutz, nickname Lucifer, from Neckarkatzenbach, he comes by every third Thursday and heads off straight to Heiner afterwards. He's the one who's taking care of Heiner's mastiff too. Vivian Atkinson shivered despite the V-neck sweater on top of the tennis dress, despite the eggshell, fitted, knee-length poplin fall coat she had thrown over her shoulder when she had left the car, despite the nude Lycra stockings she had even put on shortly before departing, while gazing at the streaked sky. Heiner's world simply gave her the shivers. A quarter mile later, behind the fogged-in top of the pass in the clouds, the driver stopped yet again. Down there is Heiligkreuzsteinach, she said—today wearing a judge's robe altered to be a maternity dress—and pointed to an idyllic-seeming little village in the valley. Smoke climbed vertically from various chimneys; in the inner Odenwald, the heating season had already begun weeks ago. On a street corner stood two older men in hats. At Vivian's and Korinna's feet a Palatine boundary stone from 1791. An open hut for hikers. Beads of fog rolled down Vivian's lacquered hair, stopping on her fake eyelashes. Only one or two miles to go to Altneudorf, Korinna said promisingly. Altneudorf. Tel Aviv. Altneuland. Theodor Herzl. Daniel Boyarin too. West of the village the Steinach River, the slopes, the Judenwald, the Jews' Woods.

The branch off to Schriesheim, the upper village, the camping site Steinach Perle, Altneudorf a one-street village, the Tatra crawling along in second gear, the dozen bottles in the trunk clinking brightly. Now the lower village, the Deutscher Kaiser Inn on the left, guest rooms. Korinna and Vivian ascended the stairs and entered the inn's lounge. Two groups of two old men sat silently at two different tables. The hostess bustled around mutely behind her counter. On the left-hand side a massive Hammond organ. Next to it a board on which was written the word today. A pretty tremendous electric buzzing, bordering on the unbearable, filled the room, having probably swelled unnoticeably in the course of recent decades, long since edited out by the heads of the locals, no longer perceived by a soul. What tension, remarked the woman in the tennis dress. Then Korinna ordered two cups of tea. The men at their tables began murmuring, probably about us, Vivian whispered to her friend. No, about Golems, homunculi, androids, cyborgs. The hostess described to them the way up to the Judenwald. Korinna paid. A short bit in the Bernauer bakery to buy provisions. A phone call to the ob-gyn in Amorbach from the telephone booth at the sports center of the SV 02; in the meantime Vivian ought to wait outside, Korinna's belly was far too big for two in one booth. Finally the ascent.

The she-man. The she-male. The phallic woman. The lesbian phallus. Don't be afraid, Viv, said Korinna Kohn as she pulled the dildo from her backpack, this here is also a sign of my personal acceptance of heterosexual paradigms, call me, like Frauke Stöver, heterosexual by compulsion, if you will. Vivian Atkinson remembered having read in Judith Butler not long ago that with the symbolically lesbian phallus the relation between the logic of exclusionary contradiction and the legislation of compulsory heterosexuality is attacked on the level of symbolic and corporeal morphogenesis. I know, I know, said Korinna, and she also writes that the insertion of the lesbian phallus opens a discursive space where the tacit political relations are scrutinized which constitute the division between corporeal zones and the whole body—my topic, Vivian—between anatomy and the imaginary, corporeality and the psyche, and which endure in these divisions. The magistrate's daughter thus lifted her metallically sparkling crimson robe and strapped the permanently erect, clay-colored plastic penis to her naked body.

The dumbfounded soldier's daughter in the white tennis dress laid herself into the wet leaves of the Judenwald, the V-neck sweater spread out underneath her head. Without saying a word, she pulled off her tights, her panties too, the only articles of clothing which belonged to her. The bisexual tennis player employed her tenderness first at those body islands of the American-German woman classified as erogenous zones, now plunging the fetish object visibly into the lower abdomen of her submissive partner. The belly, the breasts of the pregnant woman swung rhythmically over the hollow, over the svelte, unfertilized body, over the pointed nipples of the provocatively made-up Vivian. Divergent bodies. Wandering eyes. What about homosexuality is supposed to be more perverse than heterosexuality with contraceptives? Where would Daniel Paul Schreber's immaculate conception have to be categorized in this dichotomy? May the dildo be considered the deconstruction or the reconstruction of the masculine costume, and what is actually stuck inside me: a penis or the phallus? The memory of the penis or the parody of castration? Has the Judenwald been opened as a discursive space? And what speaks from Korinna Kohn's coital construction: the double-edged intermediate product of organic penis envy or the synthetic cyborg's proverbial autonomy? Both Frauke and Angela Stöver understood Angela's penis as something supplementary. Copulation was always a phantasmatic or perhaps phantasmagorical resignification on the coordinate system of having, being, and seeming, too, that's obvious. Would Vivian Atkinson later be able to describe this memorable sex act being consummated at this moment? And in whose words?

The fleeting sight of the former synagogue of Neckarsteinach, between the Neckar and Steinach, then on the B 37 to Heidelberg, barely twelve miles to Edingen, where Vivian Atkinson, feeling besmirched in the dirt-smeared tennis dress, the torn tights, the tear-stained makeup—Korinna's dress, Korinna's makeup, Korinna's tears—wanted to put on something else, something of her own before returning with her university friend to the Bauland. The latter parked her Tatra in the fire lane in front of the tobacco warehouse, preferring not to come up at all. But then she was sitting on the edge of Vivian's bed and watching the quickly rinsed-off woman change clothes: uncomplicated black flared pants, Sleater-Kinney T-shirt; in a week and a half the sensational trio—having moved from Olympia, Washington, to Portland, Oregon—would perform in Karlsruhe, Baden-Württemberg. Over that a gray cardigan from Benetton and Korinna's fall coat that she had hung up in the forest on a broken-off branch. Black lace-ups. And now I would finally like to see where you're actually from, said the crimped-haired classmate in her eccentric robe while waiting on the elevator. OK, take Hauptstrasse up to the left, after the church turn on Grenzhöfer Strasse, go through Grenzhof and Plankstadt, after that at the intersection, don't head toward Schwetzingen, but take a left toward Heidelberg and right before the Autobahn, again on the left (you can hardly miss it), turn into the Patrick Henry Village. Can I just go in without any problem, and aren't you coming along, Vivian? Fine, the latter grumbled and glided into Korinna's Tatra with a rollerboard of Rodney Atkinson's, disused for eons, and still-wet hair. The army brat hadn't been to the Patrick Henry Village in years.

When the two women were just approaching their military objective hardly a quarter of an hour later, they saw in the wide, sandy fields to both sides of the country road large, hand-painted wooden signs bearing the word Pumpkins. Of course, right, it'll be Halloween soon, Vivian exclaimed, the day before All Saints' Day. My parents also always bought their pumpkins from Baden farmers; and now please take a left in here. Welcome, Korinna, to the Heidelberg military community, Vivian Atkinson pronounced. Here's the first school right here, and to the right behind the sports fields on South Gettysburg Avenue the next one. But first here come proletarian tenements from the fifties, almost endlessly, my Hanau grandmother always calls it the skid row of the Patrick Henry Village. Korinna Kohn let her Tatra roll slowly along Lexington Avenue. All around them, exclusively, cars with American military plates. At a rather busy intersection, a friendly African American MP regulated traffic according to the rules of the German Traffic Code. Why doesn't he stop us, Korinna Kohn asked diffidently, are we somehow on German territory? The FRG provides the U.S. Army with the land, Vivian replied coolly, only in times of higher alert do they still do thorough checks. Even back in my day there were public festivals held regularly on the compound, for Germans too. Today all of these here are still, as far as I know, quarters of the United States Army Europe, which is the same thing as the illustrious Seventh Army. Whose status after the end of the Cold War, despite extensive withdrawals and relocations, hasn't really changed. The strategic headquarters of the Seventh Army are located around two miles east of here, under strict surveillance, in the heart of the Mark Twain Village, as are, incidentally, the headquarters of the multinational NATO ground forces of Central Europe. Wow, Korinna Kohn said, looking at her friend from the side. A big banner stretched over the entrance to a parking lot was pointing out the Holiday Bazaar in the village pavilion; here, finally, there was a military checkpoint. Just keep on driving past that, Korinna, Vivian said, we're almost to the better areas of the town: the curving little streets in the north, San Jacinto Drive, where I grew up, with its small, free-standing houses. Korinna Kohn turned into the northerly San Jacinto Drive. Idyllic villas, finely mowed lawns of saturated green before them, little flags, kids' toys, the winding street canopied by shade-giving treetops. In the background, only half a mile away, the periphery of Eppelheim.

THOMAS MEINECKE

Shortly thereafter the two collegiate women tramped through Lexington's Grill and the jam-packed Book Mark, both on the same square, across from the cinema, next to the tennis center, where there were things for the Karlsruher to see. The scattered tennis players, though, stared over with no less interest (Vivian thought: completely thunderstruck) at the metallic-purple robe of the large pregnant woman. In the Burger King the two were not served hamburgers because they did not possess U.S. Army ID cards. What sort of ID check would ever let identity pass as an effect of discursive practices? No matter, Korinna Kohn adjudged, outside we'll get ourselves two thick Amerikaners with icing. Once they had done this soon after in a small Kirchheim confectionery not far from the Golden Rose in which the 411th Base Support Battalion held its regular German-American social table—and had drunk tepid peach iced tea too—the friends drove toward Heidelberg's inner city in the evening twilight through Rohrbach's Römerstrasse, on both sides of which lay the Mark Twain Village, at its edges harmlessly merging into German residential areas, centrally, armed to the teeth, secured behind very high barbed wire. The nerve center of the European U.S. Armed Forces. It was rush hour on the Römerstrasse; at least every fifth car, Korinna noticed, had a U.S. Army license plate. Where are they all going, the magistrate's daughter asked, why do I never see these people in the pedestrian areas? At most their wives shopping with their daughters, buying European clothes, Italian pumps, French lingerie. Why, the college girl complained, did I always only see zillions of students when I was living in this city? Korinna Kohn had almost rear-ended a military ambulance that was languidly pulling up to a traffic light. My last bit of info, Vivian Atkinson said, is that around sixteen thousand soldiers,

employees, civilians, and their family members belong to the Heidelberg military community, in a total Heidelberg population of
one hundred forty thousand. Half of them live in the more than
two hundred houses of the Patrick Henry Village, the PHV, as
well as here in the MTV, the other half, as we say, on the economy,
that is, with Germans under one roof, or rather, next to Germans.
And don't forget that Mannheim also has its big housing areas; I
did tell you how I was deflowered in the Benjamin Franklin Village there. Had we just turned right, by the way, you would have
seen the Nachrichten Kaserne, the U.S. Army hospital where my
daddy Rodney got his appendix removed.

Did you know in fact, Vivian remarked, that Adolf Hitler's furniture from the Berchtesgaden branch of the Reich Chancellory
(which fell into American hands in 1945) has been here in Heidelberg, in the European headquarters of the U.S. Army, since last
year? Hitler's furniture? And is not just standing around, but—
don't ask me how—being used? Korinna had never heard that
before. In all, my father says, said Vivian, there are twenty-three
desks, chairs, even paintings; twenty-four other pieces supposedly went to the Munich Head Financial Administration, meaning we've once again redrawn the old, magic triangle between
Heidelberg, Munich, and the Alps. Then on Tom-Sawyer-Strasse
Vivian Atkinson routed Korinna Kohn past a beauty shop where
her mother had once been an enthusiastic customer, and subsequently, beyond the hermetically sealed Campbell Barracks to a
German-American industrial park in the middle of which stood
an austere Baptist church. As a little girl she had strewn flowers
here at a small wedding; the marriage between a Bostonian and
a woman from Schwetzingen, however, had been dissolved after
not even two years. Apparently I've crossed over to your side

completely, Vivian said, suddenly all pensive, turning around on her own axis as if looking for something, in fact I have no contact whatsoever anymore with the military community. And I haven't missed it either. Come on, get back in the car, said Korinna. She found even the Handschuhsheim industrial park—at whose perimeter Ilse, Pat, Frauke, and Angela lived—more inviting than this one. It occurred to Vivian that Bodo Petersen's Edingen mailbox was overflowing. Was the man perhaps lying dead in his apartment?

From Vivian's Weininger excerpts: And thus the woman is also never naked or always naked, whichever you will: never naked because she never really achieves a genuine feeling of nakedness; always naked because she lacks that other thing that would have to be present in order ever to make her conscious of the fact that she is objectively naked and which could thus be an inner impulse for covering. And a woman is objectively always naked, even under crinoline and the bodice. If one asks a woman what she understands by her ego, then she is incapable of imagining anything else by it than her body. Her exterior, that is the ego of women. The joy that seems to ensue, even in the ugliest girl, both in touching herself and in examining herself in the mirror, and in many sensations of the organs. The female manner of vanity can be explained by the lack of intrinsic value of human personality. The absolute woman is analyzable, is an aggregate and thus dissociable, cleavable. Thus for this reason, the living, naked woman can never be deemed beautiful by anyone because the sex drive renders impossible the purposeless observation that remains the unavoidable precondition for all judgments of beauty. The naked woman is more beautiful in individual aspects than as a whole; as such, namely, she inevitably arouses the feeling that she is looking for something and causes the viewer more feelings of aversion than desire. This moment of being purposeless in herself, of having a purpose outside herself, emerges most strongly in the naked woman standing upright; naturally it is mitigated in the recumbent position. In all love, the man loves only himself. He projects onto another human being his ideal of an absolutely valuable being of which he is incapable of isolating in himself. To heap everything one would like to be oneself and never quite can be onto an individual, to make this individual the bearer of all values: that is love. The introjection of the soul of man into the woman. The attempt to find oneself in woman, instead of just seeing in the woman only the woman herself, necessarily presupposes the neglect of the empirical person. The sex drive negates physical and psychic—eroticism always the psychic—woman. Vulgar sexuality sees in woman a means for onanism. Madonna is a creation of man, nothing corresponds to her in reality. A completely new creation of woman. Were there any beauty in the woman per se, she would not continually extract assurances from the man that she is beautiful.

Weininger, continued: The phallus is what renders the woman absolutely and definitively unfree. It is also exactly that part which rather mars the body of the man, which alone renders the naked man ugly, the same one that most excites and most intensely arouses the woman, doing this right when it presents what is likely the most unpleasant thing of all, when it is erect. The need to be penetrated may be the most intense need of the woman, but it is only a special case of her deepest, her singular vital interest that comes after coitus; of the wish for as much penetration as possible, by whomever, wherever, whenever. Women have no existence and no essence, they do not exist, they are nothing. One is a man, or one is a woman, depending on whether one is somebody or not. Because there is no ego, no I in the woman, there is no you for her either, for which reason, by her view, I and you belong together as a pair, as an undifferentiated entity: that is why the woman can bring people together, that is why she can be a procuress. The woman seeks her consummation as an object. The man is form, the woman matter. The nullity of women who can be impregnated by anyone at all. The woman is nothing, and for this reason and this reason alone she can be everything; while the man can always only be what he is. From a woman one can make what one wants; the man may at most be helped in becoming what he wants. Women do not have this or that quality, but their quality rests upon their having not qualities at all; that is the whole complexity and the whole enigma of the woman, therein lies her preeminence and inconceivability for the man. The woman does not sin—for she herself is sin—as possibility in the man. A hollow vessel, for a time covered over with makeup and veneered. The woman is the fault of the man.

Weininger still: Just as one only loves in the other what one would very much like to be and yet never is, so does one only hate in the other what one never wants to be and yet always partially is. Whoever hates Jewish nature, hates it first in himself: that he persecutes it in the other is only an attempt to separate oneself from Jewishness in this way. This is why the Aryan owes thanks to the Jew; through him he knows what he is guarding against: against Jewishness as a possibility in himself. The real Jew, like the woman, has no ego and thus no intrinsic value. The real Jew and the real woman both live only as types, not as individualities. Men who act as procurers always have Jewishness in themselves. Procuring as the blurring of boundaries. The Jews would first have to overcome Jewishness before they could be ripe for Zionism. Nor is it a coincidence that these days chemistry lies to such a great extent in the hands of the Jews. Absorption by matter—the need to have everything absorbed by it—presupposes the lack of an intelligible ego and is thus fundamentally Jewish. Certainly, however, the organic can never be explained by the inorganic, the latter at best being explained by the former. What is inaccessible to the real Jew for all eternity: immediate being, God's mercy, the oak tree, the trumpet, the Siegfried motive, the creation of himself, the phrase: I am. Between Jewishness and Christianity, between commerce and culture, between woman and man, between type and personality, between worthlessness and worth, between earthly and higher life, between nothingness and the godhead humanity once again has a choice. Those are the two poles; there is no third empire, no third Reich.

Korinna Kohn came downstairs for breakfast in a kind of tunic, possibly a drape; on her uncombed hair she wore a fur cap: was it that of Freud's father or that of Sacher-Masoch's mistress? For more than a week the two classmates had lain in bed with a fever (each in different rooms, albeit on the same floor), even missing the Sleater-Kinney concert in Karlsruhe; since yesterday at least they had started getting up for meals. Frauke and Angela Stöver— who still didn't know that Korinna was pregnant—had called from Handschuhsheim and reported excitedly that Corin Tucker of Sleater-Kinney shaves her armpits (shaves out her armpits, as Angela said). That sounded like chafed out, Korinna thought. Also, the new drummer Janet Weiss is heterosexual. At the university, a Californian exchange student—up to his ears in a German-studies report on Laurence Rickels' thesis of Goethe's Werther as history's first Beach Boy—had brought materials of a research project with him on the unbelievable bebop Nazis who, to the exclusion of the forcibly coordinated public, had both developed Jewish psycho-analysis further and declared homosexuality as curable (that is, of a neurotic origin) and listened all night to jam sessions from Minton's Playhouse recorded on acetate records: Dizzy Gillespie on trumpet, Thelonious Monk at the piano, Charlie Christian on the guitar, Kenny Clarke on the drums.

In the foyer of the lecture hall building, Frauke Stöver had cautiously expressed misgivings about whether in the end such schemes had not also fostered that of the Auschwitz lie, thereby, however, only reaping the Californian's disdainful guffawing. In the university plaza, posters announcing the performance of a Baron von Richthofen in the German-American Institute. Hans Mühlenkamm had called back after Vivian ended up on his answering machine and told enthusiastically of how he had located the practice space of the Monks—a proto-punk band from the years 1965 to 1967 comprised of American GIs—and had, practically around the corner, purchased extremely rare records by the Mannheim modern jazz legend Wolfgang Lauth. A part of the industrial building around MS Connexion had been torn down; completely new, unfamiliar vehicle access to HD 800. The dining car and its occupants on the trip from Mannheim to Frankfurt as aesthetic purgatory. A sumptuous ball night with Grete in Offenbach's velodrome; and so forth. Hans also wanted to talk with Vivian in detail about why to this day a sissy boy (an effeminate lad) received so much less respect—even from enlightened adults, to say nothing of adolescents—than a tomboy (a boyish girl). As soon as Korinna and Vivian were well again, Frauke, Angela, and Hans wanted to stop by sometime finally, perhaps with Ilse. No, Pat has been missing for weeks now.

The twenty-four-year-old noted down: an alabaster silk tunic, in part with black horizontal stripes. Sand-colored, long cotton vests on top of light Georgette trousers and a jersey teddy, nutmeg cotton blousons. Indian shirts, a jersey-devoré sari, a chestnut-brown, long safari coat over khaki pants, a sand-colored wrap skirt with bustier. An eggshell silk-tulle wedding dress with lightly draped, deep décolleté and appliqué on the back. Long, tight-fitting jumper with English embroidery. The delicate ivory on the thighs interrupted by a six-inch-wide transparent inlay, going down to the floor below that. A short, draped jacket in a black allover floral pattern, four jacket buttons with real pressed flowers, deep front collar, high in the back, with a stole-look, with square embroidered insets, the whole thing studded all over with little gold pearls and sequins, worn over a cream-colored silk chiffon dress covered with yellow, sky-blue, red, and violet diagonal stripes, furnished with black criss-cross stripes on the back and on the sides with shimmering inset work. Millinerial resplendence. A black crown of thorns. Brassiere. Bustier. Vivian Atkinson was sitting at the kitchen table in Belgian pajamas borrowed from Korinna and, while she let her herbal cold-tea steep, excerpting from an extensive article by Alfons Kaiser in the Frankfurter Allgemeine Zeitung of October 20, which the Amorbach gynecologist had left there a few days before. Titled Prêt-à-porter in Search of Ethnic Correctness, it summarized the ninety Paris fashion shows, among them, merely mentioned, one by Lolita Lempicka as well. Did she perhaps descend from the painter of the Chemise rose?

What, Vivian asked Korinna, is a Cul de Paris exactly? Quite simply a bustle that emphasizes the posterior part, worn on the butt under a rearward poofing dress, a pillow on which only gazes might rest, answered her friend, adding: you do know that there's a municipality here in the Odenwald with the name Weiten-Gesäß, wide buttocks? But the master's candidate had already immersed herself in an ad insert that had fallen out of the newspaper whose text disclosed the following wording: An eyecatcher for your legs. Refined, opaque fine pantyhose with Lycra, very fashionable in plaid, diamond, or crotcheted patterns. The desirous male gaze was ensnared here again on the surface of the female covering, Vivian thought. Korinna turned on the radio, intricately lifted her fur cap in order to tuck the now-oily locks underneath it better, likewise brewed herself a cup of tea, and disappeared for a moment in her study. The weather report heralded a so-called atmospheric inversion. And here Korinna was on her way back with a folder under her arm. A perfect beautifull Woman must have an English Face, a German Body, and a podex from Paris, the Valet of Beauty (the collegiate woman possessed a facsimile of it) had demanded back in 1747. Having no or a bad backside is always an aesthetic misfortune, Friedrich Theodor Vischer had ascertained in 1878; Korinna was working on finding out, among other things, what exactly Vischer had wanted to denote with the remarkable formulation: no backside.

Then, on November 9, Frauke, Angela, and Hans had actually turned up (without Ilse, as was to be expected, and with a stopover in the Sensbachtal at the Wildeleuthäusel), spent a beautiful fall day together with Korinna and Vivian in the Katzenwald, and argued animatedly about the varying social valuation of sissy boys and tomboys. After Frauke and Angela had first been taken by complete surprise in light of Korinna's pregnancy. At the same time they themselves were about to move into a single-family home in the western portion of the Handschuhsheim industrial park. The Offenbacher more sedate, with only feigned astonishment. Vivian simply hadn't been able to keep her mouth shut to him. In the evening, when the Lancia was already running (with the help of a jump from the Tatra), Hans Mühlenkamm, who was to begin a new job in a radiology practice on the Boxberg promptly the next morning, had decided rather spontaneously to stay for a few more days in the Bauland with the convalescing girl friends. Making camp downstairs in the living room, he slipped into his greasy blue coveralls from Ford Kurpfalz every morning, under which he wore—laid out fresh daily by his lady host—Heiner's significantly too large, snow-white underwear. Today it was storming and raining outside, Vivian was evaluating her Weininger excerpts by the tiled stove, Hans and Korinna had driven in to the dollar store in Mudua for an hour or so. On the kitchen radio the report about a man who applied exclusively for women's jobs and was standing trial in Mannheim for fraud. Vivian pricked up her ears and went over into the kitchen. Said man, a law student from Trier, had applied for positions all over the country that had been advertised for female secretaries and switchboard operators, among them one in the Franciscan nuns' convent in Neuwied. Whenever the respective employers had rejected his application with the justification that he was inappropriate for the position in question as a man, he demanded three months' salary in compensation. Seventeen times in total had the twenty-six-year-old appeared before labor court to sue for his demands. Four times it had come to a settlement by which the student had been able to rake in two thousand deutschmarks each; most often, however, his suit had been dismissed. Now the tables had turned, and the man had been charged with seventeen counts of having abused the ban on discrimation enshrined in the Civil Code. Vivian Atkinson let that melt in her mouth for a moment: abuse of the ban on discrimination; that really was an interesting case. Hey, listen to this, she thus shouted, turning the radio up when she heard Hansi's and Korinna's approaching clatter, hurry, hurry, a really interesting case.

A few days later it was Korinna Kohn who, waving a wadded-up issue of the local newspaper from the day before in which a head of lettuce had been wrapped, burst into the well-heated living room where Hans was still fast asleep and Vivian was sitting with her smoothly purring Texas Instrument: the Wall Street Journal, cited in the local rag, had announced on its front page that the toy manufacturer Mattel wanted to give its world-famous glamour doll Barbie a new look in 1998, a so-called more natural design. The legendary bust size will disappear, Korinna read aloud, and in turn Barbie's waistline would grow a bit, at the same time with considerably slimmer hips. Her still-hyperfeminine head of luscious hair will be tangibly softer and (heretofore blonde, of course) darker, with only scattered gold strands in it, tending toward the brunette range. And now came what for Korinna Kohn constituted the actual revolution in the Mattel company: Barbie's quintessential, perennial smile since the seventies was to be scrapped, virtually without substitution. Have you, Viv, ever really thought about the difference between smiling and grinning? In Lewis Carroll there's this passage where the Cheshire Cat's grin appears without the body of the cat. And: have you ever pondered the congruence between the dimples on the face and those on the butt? The continual linguistic identification of jowls with cheeks, but never of ass cheeks with ass jowls? Hansi Pompadour opened his blue eyes and for a moment had no idea where was. White ceiling. Withered gladiolas. A flower window. In it a misty mountain range. Low-hanging wisps of clouds. A high-voltage pylon. Hans raised his head up and discerned Korinna standing in the arch-way in her mustard-yellow caftan with an attractively crimped, almost ordinary mane as well as enormous quartz drop earrings. And here, if he turned to the side, his beloved, Vivian Atkinson, was sitting right in front of him too, at the low coffee table, in an adventurous, red-velvet leisure suit, bent over her electronic notebook. Bonjour, ladies. Not thinking, Hans tossed back the wool blanket he was lying under, and abruptly the two women caught sight of his morning erection. The imperious urgency of this male bulge, Korinna Kohn remarked disparagingly and in hushed tones, does it not represent the paradigmatic symbol of the perpetual rape of the woman? Lord have mercy, replied Viv-ian Atkinson, and then Hans Mühlenkamm was already coming back from the can.

In the fax machine the photocopy Frauke Stöver had sent of a report in the Süddeutsche Zeitung about the comeback of the fashion designer Wolfgang Joop with comeback photos of the supermodel Claudia Schiffer, pale face, almost without makeup, the hair sleek. Joop working up enthusiasm before the SZ: Doesn't she look ethnic? And provided the answer himself. A white black woman. Crazy. Korinna immediately tried to counter-fax her Bar-bie article to Handschuhsheim, but the wadded-up page gooed up with snail slime just didn't want to go through the machine. Instead, she inserted a copper engraving that illustrated the per-foration of nipples with which Parisian gentlewomen had once sought to accentuate—and not seldom also to enlarge—their bust. The subtitle of the gallant little picture read: Yesterday I had the honor of piercing the breasts of a princess of royal blood. Infants in any case couldn't extract another drop from mammae manipulated like that. Even Angela (possibly while still Angelo) had had her (or his) meager nipples pierced in order to be able to thread rings through them and stretch a chain between them on special days. Korinna did find it (so to speak) technically quite interesting, but had never wanted to do those kinds of things to her breasts, not even before her pregnancy. Hans—who had quickly gotten dressed and was still wearing Korinna's light-blue Cat Power T-shirt under his coveralls, over one of Heiner's wife-beaters, on account of the colder time of year—expressed with amusement the presumption that Angela Stöver was probably the absolute only Monika subscriber who wore such special jewelry. Vivian inquired from what political positioning on the catego-rized body a ring could be designated as intimate jewelry, or as special at all. And Korinna added: if even functional erogenous zones depend on primitively negotiated pacts—thus are nothing but political issues—how I can still safeguard my, well, personal sensation of pleasure under these circumstances as—at the very least—my spoils, my private property? An almost embarrassed silence seized the study, the midday bell pealing from Mudua could be heard outside, then the three amiga/os (the slash-o because of Hans) abandoned the fax machine they had been standing around the whole time, seated themselves together at the breakfast table, and again agreed upon the (in Baden-Württemberg no less than in Ohio) extreme dubiousness of the contrivance of so-called primary, or rather, secondary and ter-tiary sex characteristics.

From Vivian's rollerboard: Fragmentation and Redemption. Even back in the Middle Ages, the mind was generally considered male, the body female. Caroline Walker Bynum saw in this identifica-tion of woman and flesh, however, not only a basis for misog-yny, but also a correlation between the woman and the body of

Christ. In this way Hildegard von Bingen had been able to see the masculine as the symbol of Christ's divinity and the feminine as the symbol of his humanity. This conjunction lay at the heart of Hildegard's repeatedly voiced position that women were rightly refused the priesthood since they could unite themselves with Christ in another way. See also ecstasy during the Eucharist. As brides of Christ, women were not just Christ's representatives but entered into an unio mystica with his body. Frequently, the flesh of Christ was even regarded as something feminine, at least in its redemptive functions, bleeding and nourishing. That, the medievalist wrote, sheds light on why more women than men imitated Christ physically, especially through stigmatization. And brings us, I say, said Vivian, to our problem of impersonation. In another respect also to the unmasculine Jew Daniel Boyarin. Perhaps even to the hippies; my mother's first boyfriends, according to the stories of my Grandma Hanau, supposedly looked strikingly like Jesus. To continue, though: Since Christ, mindful of Mary's Immaculate Conception, had no human father, his entire body came from Mary and was thus closely linked with female flesh. I don't accept though, Korinna Kohn said with agitation, that my maternal body has to be coded female. That's right, said Hans, primarily in light of the social implications that what is coded female carries with it these days. In the Middles Ages, however, Vivian continued, it was possible for nuns, female mystics, but also clergymen like Anselm of Canterbury to view Jesus as mother. When he nurses them in the Eucharist with liquid gushing from his breast, when he gives birth to the Church from his side. You all know I got all this from Frauke, right? Soon to be Dr. Frauke Stöver. Korinna was enthused about how medieval nuns undercut the gender binary. And on top of that there was something else entirely.

A large part of the debate surrounding the resurrection of the body and the relationship between body and soul in the twelfth and thirteenth centuries revolved not around the opposition between body and soul, but around the continuity of the body. Questions about the resurrection of embryos, foreskins, or fingernails, about the subtilitas of the glorified body, questions about if and how God would reconstruct the amputee or the fat man, as questions about the reassembly of body parts. Caroline Walker Bynum now asks: On what, Korinna, does the identity of the earthly and the resurrected body depend? What of me must rise again so that I am the resurrected body? You can imagine what words were placed in quotation marks here. On images of crucifixion from back then, the wound in Christ's side is frequently depicted as an independent body part, detached from his body, floating freely, vulva-shaped. The viewer, male or female, plunges into this wound as into a maternal womb. Vivian flipped open a few illustrations in Fragmentation and Redemption for Hans and Korinna. And in this vein I'd like to read to you a passage from Willa Cather's novel Death Comes for the Archbishop, 1927. A loan from my professor, incidentally, after I had come to his office hours for the third time.

Come, I know a place. Be quick, Padre. The bishop was blind and breathless, panting through his open mouth. He clambored over half-visible rocks, fell over prostrate trees, sank into deep holes and struggled out, always following the red blankets on the shoulders of the Indian boy, which stuck out when the boy himself was lost to sight. Suddenly the snow seemed thinner. The guide stopped short. They were standing, the Bishop made out, under an overhanging wall of rock which made a barrier against the storm. Jacinto dropped the blankets from his shoulder and seemed to be

preparing to climb the cliff. Looking up, the Bishop saw a peculiar formation in the rocks; two rounded ledges, one directly over
the other, with a mouthlike opening between. They suggested two
great stone lips, slightly parted and thrust outward. Up to this
mouth Jacinto climbed quickly by footholds well known to him.
Having mounted, he lay down on the lower lip, and helped the
Bishop to clamber up. He told Father Latour to wait for him on
this projection while he brought up the baggage. A few moments
later the Bishop slid after Jacinto and the blankets, through an
orifice, into the throat of the cave. Within stood a wooden ladder,
like that used in kivas, and down this he easily made his way to
the floor. He found himself in a lofty cavern, shaped somewhat
like a Gothic chapel, of vague outline, the only light within was
that which came through the narrow aperture between the stone
lips. Great as was his need of shelter, the Bishop, on his way down
the ladder, was struck by a reluctance, an extreme distaste for
the place. The air in the cave was glacial, penetrated to the very
bones, and he detected at once a fetid odour, not very strong but
highly disagreeable. Some twenty feet or so above his head the
open mouth let in grey daylight like a high transom.

One rather patchy day in late November, Korinna, Vivian, and
Hans played croquet in the yard behind the house; Korinna had
discovered the game among Heiner's old things in the basement,
and Vivian was finally supposed to get away from the liquid
crystal into which she had hewn almost a hundred ready-to-
print pages of her master's thesis—already deemed much too
extensive anyway—over the last few weeks. Adding to Versace's
disco dirndl, she had draped a fur stole of Mother Kohn over her
shoulders, and her stockings were opaque. Hans wore Heiner's
hideous, white (of course) leather jacket over the now thoroughly

washed coveralls and, as once when a little boy, had painted his fingernails blue. Korinna in a synthetic teddy-bear costume without the head, allegedly a souvenir of her father's from Leningrad (today St. Petersburg) that had until now been way too large for her. Korinna was in the lead big-time when the telephone rang and Frauke Stöver announced a university-wide plenary assembly for the coming Wednesday, including a strike vote. The day after, on November 27, a country-wide demonstration against cuts in education and social services was to take place in Bonn; forty deutschmarks roundtrip, did they perhaps want to come along? Korinna had immediately put it on speaker phone, but Vivian and Hansi, in the open patio door with croquet mallets in their hands, didn't make a peep. Korinna, too, in her so-called condition, didn't quite know what she should say and inquired sheepishly what was generally involved in a university strike. Oh, fine, Frauke pouted, you all obviously don't want to understand. Apart from that—she continued again blithely, though—you can soon expect imaginative initiatives like alternative lectures in the OEG, a striptease in the display window of the Vinyl Only record store, and so on; I'll call back, then.

On that same day in the Rhein-Neckar-Zeitung: the French sociologist Pierre Bourdieu had been awarded the Ernst Bloch Prize in Ludwigshafen, the American rapper Coolio had lifted clothes from a Böblinger boutique and punched a female sales clerk in the gut. The Indian Diana Hayden had been crowned Miss World in the Seychelles archipelago in the Indian Ocean, once discovered, as they say, by the Portuguese (later colonized by Frenchmen and Brits, Korinna Kohn knew). Heidelberg's university had not had a women's affairs officer for ten years now, though over half of the student body was of the female gender. The number of female doctoral candidates ran to thirty-seven percent, that of tenure-track female professors to fourteen percent. Ninety-four percent male tenured professors. The Mannheimer Morgen carried a somewhat more detailed report on the contentious crowning of Miss World; according to that, the victress allegedly maintained business relations with one of the jurors. The literary critic Marcel Reich-Ranicki had delivered a brilliant speech in the Eichbaum brewery. And the Ludwigshafen opening ceremony for Pierre Bourdieu merited a large color landscape photo for the Mannheimer Morgen. The cultural sociologist had called for the formation of a new International. Super essay also by Bourdieu on la domination masculine around which the editors Irene Dölling and Beate Krais had only recently assembled an entire reader on gender construction in social praxis, Hans Mühlenkamm recommended. It's lying upstairs in my rollerboard, Vivian Atkinson answered, a little red volume. Pierre Bourdieu in conversation: I had the impression that the idea of symbolic force was something that was still lacking in the theoretical foundation of feminist criticism. Not that I had thought that feminist criticism wasn't of interest, far from it. The more work by female historians, sociologists, ethnologists, and so on I read, the more I think that there is a wholly new, enormous empirical task with feminist criticism that constitutes a significant step forward in the social sciences. But it seems to me that a systematic and coherent theoretical construction is missing which could form the basis of all these results of empirical research. In my article, I attempted such a construction. What impudence, Korinna Kohn said, blew her nose into a tissue, and carried the little red volume back upstairs, bringing batteries back down because Heiner's Islamic kitchen clock had stopped.

As if the female croquet players and the male croquet player had anticipated it, the ensuing protest movements proceeded according to an extraordinarily measured pattern; the responsible politicians manifested understanding, even, for the demands of the zealous students, no SPC had been brought into being anywhere, not one police car set on fire, the whole concept of the political had evaporated, as it were. It now belongs entirely to us, Hans determined solemnly, I for example am working politically toward the day when I can affirm my heterosexuality with the same lack of self-evidence that Frauke does her homosexuality. The deconstruction of identity does not exactly mean the deconstruction of politics, Judith Butler says, but presents precisely those terms by which identity is articulated as political. I may have a broken relationship with power, but I'm talking about the same power that first permits me to say I. No longer can I simply view politics as a set of procedures derived from the ostensible interests of prefabricated subjects. In a word, identity formation, Hans said, only functions by way of the dirtiest procedures of exclusion. Look over my shoulder, kiddo, replied Vivian good-humoredly, having just booted up her Texas Instrument to weave the following prompts into the context of her master's thesis: Otto Weininger's phallogocentric formulation—that the man is feminine in the proportion in which he is not masculine—as the primary constituent of heterosexuality. Luce Irigaray: There is only one sex, and that is the male sex. Woman as the male sex which merely appears in the garb of otherness. Simone de Beauvoir: Woman is the Other, the second sex. Irigaray: The woman is absence, the absent sex. The ostensibly binary relation between the sexes as male cunning which completely excludes femininity. Judith Butler: Women are neither the subject nor its Other, but a difference from the economy of the binary opposition, itself a ruse for the monologic elaboration of the masculine. According to Claude Lévi-Strauss: The woman as man's ornament, object of exchange of male homosocial desire. Trophy wife. The bride reproducing the name of the husband reflects—in a relationship between men—male identity by representing the site of her absence. Lacan: Precisely for the sake of what she is not, she thinks she is desired and loved at the same time.

Hans Mühlenkamm had positioned himself behind the master's candidate and then allowed his gaze to rest on her screen. Vivian, in a light-blue, low-cut cocktail dress from Korinna's deep closet, was sitting on a beige Mauritanian pouffe at the coffee table littered with loose pages, diskettes, and opened books, and pondering how she could put Irigaray's critique of Lacan and Butler's critique of Irigaray to the service of her own interrogative argumentation. Luce Irigaray had, Hans read, unmasked the phallogocentrism of Jacques Lacan. No question mark. The proper names and the word phallogocentrism, unknown to the spell check of Windows 95, underlined with a red squiggly line. After two minutes, the words Vivian Atkinson's Screen Saver popped up, from the right. Vivian sighed and stroked her hair back with both hands. The unemployed part-time physician's receptionist became engrossed in observing the college girl from behind (her silhouette, her neck, her ear lobes?), went into a partial crouch, and braced himself on his thighs. His small-framed body wraith-like, faint on Vivian's automatically darkened computer screen. The blazing of the flames in the tiled stove. The ponderer felt the puff of Hansi's breath on her neck: he, possibly the somewhat obtrusive scent of her American shampoo in his nose. Hans, Cat Power T-shirt, wide-flared blue jeans, barefoot, strained his head forward a bit, then withdrew it again immediately. Had he forbidden himself from directing his attention to Vivian's neckline? The woman at the computer looked down impulsively at herself. Her hem, somewhat ridden up. The knees swathed in gossamer, skin-colored synthetic fabric. Flesh-colored, as Gerlinde Atkinson had always said.

Vivian Atkinson typed: Monique Wittig contends, before Judith Butler, that the category gender is always female under the conditions of compulsory heterosexuality. The woman functions as a term that stabilizes a binarity and an oppositional relation to a man. A lesbian is accordingly not a woman and also has no gender. Do you have a gender, Hans Mühlenkamm asked cockily, still behind her, are you a woman? The army brat inquired back immediately: Do you? And handed back to him—I tore it out of the newspaper last week—another report on the topic of men in women's jobs. Hans read: Can a man be executive director of the charitable organization for mothers, the Deutsches Müttergenesungswerk? Since Friday the labor court in Nuremberg has been addressing the question of possible sexual discrimination against a man. A forty-year-old jurist had sued the Müttergenesungswerk for damages because his application had been rejected. A woman had been explicitly sought for the position. Just as Doctor Ancelet and in fact all previous employers of the ash-blond Hansi had sought a cute female receptionist. The conciliation proceedings between the parties had ended without a rapprochement, the DPA reported. Not quite an everyday case, which may yet be addressed by the European Court of Justice, the labor court judge summed up. The decisive factor is whether the plaintiff was rejected exclusively because of his gender. Which the Müttergenesungswerk absolutely disputed. The applicant simply did not conform to the job profile. Hans took a deep breath and riveted his gaze again on Vivian's computer screen. Butler's critique of Wittig: If lesbianism defines itself in radical exclusion from heterosexuality, it deprives itself of the capacity to resignify the very heterosexual constructs by which it is partially and inevitably constituted. As a result, that lesbian strategy would consolidate compulsory heterosexuality in its oppressive forms.

Vivian had Hans brew a cup of tea, arose, and went to the telephone: if a lesbian wasn't a woman, then Luis Trenker could in fact have been a lesbian. Frauke Stöver was delighted at Vivian Atkinson's call, and the latter requested that the Stövers please bring Angela's Bible on their next visit to the Bauland; she absolutely had to excerpt something from it. I'll give you one from my collection, Angela called out in the background, grabbing the receiver. At home in the Po Basin, she had a big brother who lived in priestly celibacy and quite regularly provided his little sister with all sorts of ecclesiastical accoutrements. The waitress even had a threadbare cowl hanging in her closet in Handschuhsheim, though she hardly ever took it out. It was to be worn like a dress. So, too, were the ceremonial garments of her big brother; he had always generally been crazy about dressing up. But a clergyman in vestments isn't dressed up, Hans objected after Vivian had hung up the phone, and he is also (begging your pardon) by perhaps premature implication to your Monique Wittig—I mean this totally positively—not a man. Then Hans called upstairs about whether Korinna also wanted to drink tea.

Third Sunday of Advent. Facing a mirror—Vivian greeted Frauke and Angela—what would you two say: I'm looking into the mirror, onto the mirror, through the mirror, or is my gaze bounced back in reverse onto me, or rather, onto itself? Frauke had no answer right away and stopped dead in her tracks. Angela curtsied and found that the Catholic church represents a reflective surface which allows the pious gaze through. Donna Haraway had finally also brought about the downfall of Darwinism with her realization about the narrative character of the so-called natural sciences, the postmodern dissolution of the modern subject having enabled the resurrection of the soul. Proof of the existence of God, Angela Stöver beamed. That's right—Korinna (with crazy hair and a golden tunic) called down from upstairs to Heiner's front door—Foucault even said that one doesn't say that the soul is an illusion or an ideological concept. And Judith Butler added—Frauke said in addition—in this sense the soul is a superficial designation that contests and displaces the differentiation between interior and exterior. The oh-so-stupid subject-verb-object formulation: for Hans and Korinna, too, the root of all evil. I am a woman: this in effect cannot be said in that way, Vivian said. You aren't a woman, Frauke added, presenting the brunette with a fat bouquet of flowers, but you act like a woman. Man, that was complicated. But let's let Frauke and Angela at least come inside; that'll do with the quiz on the property's driveway. The platinum-blonde coiffed visitors—once again in Hemingway's partner-look—rid themselves of their jackets, under which they were wearing stiff, lined loden clothes, rubbed their hands together, and said in unison: nice and warm here. Evidently the heat in their Lancia didn't work. Never did, Frauke laughed. And how the Cuban coffee aroma wafted to the coatrack.

Angela had the Bible she had brought along—an antiquarian, to some extent well-preserved piece from South Tirol, even wrapped in a sheet of pink tissue paper on which she had

written in her purple lipstick Love—and Vivian had to act all fes-
tive before she could get at the desired quotation. At the other
end of the table, Frauke was meanwhile insisting to Korinna that
she finally ought to give back her expensive dildo. Did she need
it for her ominous deployments as hostess? Hans, Ganymede to
the hilt today, served defrosted quark pastries from Walldürn
with the coffee. OK, the apostle Paul's first letter to the Corin-
thians, 13, 11 to 13: When I was a child, I used to talk as a child,
think as a child, reason as a child; when I became a man, I put
aside childish things. At present we see indistinctly, as in a mirror, but then face to face. At present I know partially; then I shall
know fully, as I am fully known. So faith, hope, love remain, these
three; but the greatest of these is love. Thus spake the Bolzano
book of books. And do you all know, Vivian asked while the others bit into their jelly pastries, what came to Augustine's mind in
De trinitate almost one thousand six hundred years ago in his
cell? Angela crossed her immaculately shaved legs and clapped
her manicured hands, anticipating the message. They—Vivian
Atkinson, five-foot-eleven, recited solemnly while standing—see
indeed a glass, but do not so far see through the glass Him who
is now to be seen through the glass, that they do not even know
the glass itself which they see to be a glass, i.e. an image. Do you
think, the master's student asked the group, that's too religious as
a motto for a scientific work? Not at all, Angela Stöver thought,
and the others agreed with her for once.

Well. And yet—Vivian read aloud from another passage from
Aurelius Augustinus that Angela obviously knew—they who see
in this glass (ergo, the dative case) and in this enigma, as it is permitted in this life to see, are not those who behold in their own
mind the things which we have set in order and pressed upon

them; but those who see this spirit as if an image, so as to be able to refer what they see, in some way be it what it may, to Him whose image it is, and to see that reality also by conjecturing, which they see through the image by beholding, since they cannot yet see face to face. For the apostle does not say, We see now a glass, but, We see now through a glass. Right on. What a construction, the collegiate woman closed enthusiastically. What a religion, Angela (whose big brother had purportedly memorized Augustine completely) cheered. Then for two, three minutes there was complete and utter silence in the room. The radio that more or less ran constantly in the kitchen reported that around two thousand citizens in Ludwigshafen on the Rhine had been evacuated because of an acute, extremely risky defusing of a bomb from the last world war.

From around the world: In the USA a single-engine Piper Comanche had flown two hundred fifty miles, steered by the autopilot, after the pilot had fallen unconscious. The latter, a doctor, had been on a flight from his home town Hoisington to Topeka, one hundred sixty miles away, when he lost consciousness from inhaling exhaust fumes that had made their way into the cockpit. The small aircraft remained on course and flew more than two hundred fifty miles into the neighboring state of Missouri. There it went down in a field after the fuel was used up. The four-seater plane skidded over a harvested wheat field and was stopped by a tree. When the pilot awoke, he detected only light lacerations and a broken wrist. Cockpit—Vivian said, answering Hansi's question on this matter—might best be translated into German as Hahnengrube, pit of roosters. On the North Sea coast the dismembering of numerous stranded sperm whales was taxing the minds of the volunteer helpers. The director of a sea aquarium stated in a direct quote, during the agonizing days when he had dismembered these wonderful, powerful mammals, some pretty crazy thoughts went through his mind. Possibly also the difference between slaying and dismembering, Korinna remarked drily. She paged through the TV guide she had spread out on her knees halfway under the table and picked out for herself the vilest talk show afternoon of the coming week. After a few pages she struck gold and declaimed to general scholarly amusement: first SAT 1 at one p.m., Sonja with her topic: Big and sexy, colon, three hundred seventy-five pounds in lingerie. Then, two p.m., on RTL and Pro Sieben simultaneously, Bärbel Schäfer with the well-known trope: Having babies ruins the figure, and Arabella Kiesbauer's perennial hit: Trouble with the boobs, respectively.

OK, one more time, Angela (for Angela, male and female impersonator, now really wanted to know, and Korinna had fetched her German copy of Gender Trouble, Das Unbehagen der Geschlechter, Gender and Its Discontents): For women to be the Phallus means, then—Butler said, summarizing Lacan—to reflect the power of the Phallus, to signify that power, to embody the Phallus, to supply the site to which it penetrates, and to signify the Phallus through being its Other, its absence, its lack, the dialectical confirmation of its identity—be and being in quotation marks of course, Korinna Kohn emphasized. By claiming that the Other that lacks the Phallus is the one who is (this last word in italics) the Phallus, Lacan clearly suggests that power is wielded by this feminine position of not-having, that the masculine subject who has the Phallus (has is here in quotation marks now) requires this Other to confirm and, hence, be the Phallus in its (more quotation marks now) extended sense. Vivian could not recall at all that

Judith Butler, summarizing Lacan, had ever actually employed the term subject. Frauke could though. But how does a woman appear—in quotation marks, oddly, Korinna Kohn said looking up—to be the Phallus, the lack that embodies and affirms the Phallus? According to Lacan, this is done through masquerade, the effect of a melancholy that is essential to the feminine position as such. But how should even a man, Angela Stöver countered cheerfully, be able to strap on a dildo just like that? Vivian wasn't sure—and expressed this to those present too—whether Angela had now understood everything or nothing at all. Upon arrival, her conspicuously learned passing remark on Donna Haraway.

Who had invented the SS officer in garter belts and when, Angela, Hans Mühlenkamm drilled down, and who had the gartered nun glamorized all over the country? You've got me there, Angela Stöver began after collecting herself, and then Korinna Kohn interrupted her, speaking about body-island-signifying and -testing and (poof) -colonizing function of the elastic garter, about lace-trimmed lines of demarcation, mined suspender belts even, and the frequently invoked strips of snow-white flesh between the Allied occupation zones of pitch-black and blood-red nylon. Those are the colors of the Reich's War Flag, Vivian interjected. The Dyke's War Rag, Korinna punned, out of breath. Angela had in fact never set eyes on the Greater German tricolor. In any case, the world-famous Helmut Berger, in a tight gartered corset, with a sensational wasp-waist (though with rather ugly, hairy legs), was—the waitress rhapsodized—one of her earliest idols as a phallic Marlene Dietrich. La caduta degli dei, in German cinemas shown as Götterdämmerung, also The Damned, year 1968, an opulent film of Luchino Visconti that all had enjoyed seeing.

Did you work as an actress, Hans asked curiously, back then in
Italy? At first—Angela corrected the out-of-work man, tapping
him on the nose with her index finger—as an actor, officially, playing many leading minor parts in our sinful city, until one beautiful day a very young, drug-addicted go-go dancer—to whom I,
following an uncomplicated night of love, had lent my hitherto
exclusively private equipment—cancelled on the communists.
Got it, said Hans, from the tuxedoed Mary Magdalene Dietrich,
presto, to the gartered Helmut Berger. And back. And back again.
An oscillogram, Angela Stöver, née Angelo Guida, helped along,
in which one doesn't preclude the other. Especially not before
the altar: like the man, the woman is also the image of God; and
so we see God as in a mirror. Miss Guy, the Mistress Formika,
RuPaul, Joey Arias, Bambi Lake, Sylvester, Sherry Vine, Candy
Darling, Jackie Curtis, Mario Montez, Peki d'Oslo, Barbette, The
Only Leon, and the Abbé de Choisy, Angela enumerated happily,
they all made it unmistakeably clear to me: drag is pure male fantasy; why should women wear it? OK, then I'll just wear it too as a
man, Vivian (tomboy from San Jacinto Drive, today in a far more
womanly dress than Angela) retorted par for par. Your pretty
oscillogram may be able to release you from the constraints that
binarism places upon us, but it still remains binary itself. And so
I began working in night clubs, the addressee continued her life
story, at first in the Po Basin. And the rest is history, Frauke Stöver
said, springing up ostentatiously, abbreviating her unusual bride's
broader, downright turbulent history by way of the Brenner Pass
and Kitzbühel to Handschuhsheim.

Hans Mühlenkamm had wanted to pack his things, but besides
the little he had worn on his person upon arriving—the Ford Kurpfalz coveralls, a set of underwear, socks, and the sand-colored

Fila sneakers—hadn't had anything else with him. Whereupon it immediately occurred to him to stay a bit longer at Korinna's, she might perhaps need him, the unemployed part-time physician's receptionist. In fact: I will support you, Hans, my future nanny, the pregnant woman had said, and Vivian had darted upstairs on the spur of the moment as the Stövers were saying their goodbyes to pack her green rollerboard. Stowing it jauntily, to the surprise of all, in the trunk of the hissing Lancia. To check if everything is in order at home after all those weeks. Thus Frauke, Angela, and Vivian trotted off like Andy Warhol's Lonesome Cowboys, the American-German woman even with her full-to-bursting Texas Instrument. Her mailbox, too, was full to bursting when she got home, though not as hopelessly overflowed as her apparently still-absent neighbor's.

And she had quickly gotten settled again in the old tobacco warehouse. The master's thesis on the Rococo workspace was as good as written. Had also caught up on a lot of sleep at the same time. After an uplifting office hour—up by the castle in a romantic Korean joint while he scampered next to her down the Kurzer Buckel, the stairs to the old city, to the university—her professor had wanted to invite her on one of the next few days to Mannheim, whose State Museum for Technology and Labor hosted an exhibition called Body Worlds that had caused a worldwide sensation. In Japan it had been able to rack up one whole million visitors. Dead human beings, Ms. Atkinson, are exhibited for viewing, fragmented but not at all redeemed, preserved instead as never before with the help of a vacuum procedure, developed here at the University of Heidelberg, in which bodily fluids are replaced by special plastics. Let's stop for a second, take a breather. Although walking and talking, the professor said, really do go together beautifully. Off yonder the roofs of the German and Theological faculties, the Church of the Holy Spirit, the Royal Stables, Lecture Hall East, Lecture Hall West, the Marstall Café. The Neckar, the Philosophenweg, the Institutes for Physical Sciences, the little garden house. Medieval music in the immediate vicinity of those lingering about. Not localizable. Esoteric crescendos and decrescendos. No way the Middle Ages were like that. Let's keep going. All the body's cells, even their structure, are kept in their original form, that is, in the form they had during life, the exhibited specimens—ordered by bodily functions, from motor function to circulatory system to human development in the mother's womb, Ms. Atkinson—odorless and dry after the preservation treatment, graspable in the truest sense of the word. Some exhibits have actually been cleared for touching; can you imagine that. And in each functional area you can also see specimens with diseased mutations, from a heart attack or a bout of cancer, for example. Soon they're supposed to establish an entire human museum. I'd rather not go along, Vivian had said delicately to her professor, but maybe you could bring me back a catalog.

Monday, December 22, 1997. Altenstadt by Schongau, Franz Josef Strauss Barracks: Jewish women mocked with sex scenes. Big lead of the BILD-Zeitung; Vivian Atkinson had never bought herself one before. A sex photo, Nazi pictures as well as all the embarrassing details could be found on pages ten and eleven. The female student wanted to look at it after she was back in her apartment and had two more candy bars, a Snickers and a Bounty, handed to her from the kiosk. She was cold, had forgotten to put something on before impulsively leaving her rooms. The day after tomorrow she would travel for a few days to Hanau. In a few

weeks she would celebrate the end of her twenty-fifth year. Israel
would be fifty years old in 1998. The salesman quoted a price.
Vivian paid and, in passing, gazed down the Alte Neckargasse
to the river, recognizing the quarries in their wan morning pale-
ness through the bare tops of the trees on the riverbank. When
she returned to her warehouse, police vehicles stood in front of
her door. Having arrived upstairs, Vivian was startled by Bodo
Petersen's forced apartment door; several criminal investigators
were searching his cabinets, ravaging his furniture. A floor lamp
lay across the rumpled bed, its lampshade—the Brunsbütteler's
pride and joy—crumpled up, the shining sea depicted on it, dis-
torted. A lavish picture book of Japanese motorcycle saddlebags
on the carpeted floor, heedlessly crushed under foot. Random
ties, a cigar wrapped in cellophane broken in the middle. Some
old Playboy magazines. The Best of Reader's Digest, peanuts.
Nothing, a younger police officer reported to an older one, shrug-
ging his shoulders cluelessly, absolutely nothing. The older man
bent over for the cigar laboriously, unwrapped its halves from the
packaging, held it under his nose to sniff, fixing his countenance
(almost vacantly, Vivian thought) on Petersen's ceiling. Nothing was written there either. Havana, he finally surmised. Two
other officials stared out the window silently, looking toward the
Odenwald. Static crackle came from their radios. Vivian dropped
the BILD-Zeitung on the ground. That made a sound. The men
turned around. Vivian thought: now they see the brunette standing in the doorframe, grabbed the newspaper, ran into her apartment, and locked herself in.

The Altenstadt décor: swastikas, pictures of Hitler, soldiers of
the Third Reich in battle uniforms with steel helmets and assault
rifles. The music: hard rock. Location: the Franz Josef Strauss

Barracks. Starring: elite soldiers of the German army. Camera: comrades. The Terminator, a colossal private with the G3 army rifle, enters. Makes a threatening, racist speech. Knocks on a door. Sarah, a sergeant dressed as a Jewish woman, with head scarf, cigarette between her lips, opens the door. The Terminator, asking if her name is Sarah. The woman nods with fright. The following scene: the Terminator on his back, pleasurably fooling with an assault rifle, on a bed. Sarah crouches between his spread thighs, pleasuring him orally. Sarah as that name German authorities gave to Jewish women to be able to brand them as such. Wife of Abraham, progenetrix of Israel. Vivian, also Vivien: English form of the woman's name Viviane. Well-known namesakes: Vivien Leigh, English film actress, twentieth century. Vivian: English man's name corresponding to the French man's name Vivien. Viviane: woman's name, adopted from the French, going back to the name of a figure in the King Arthur legend. The fairy Viviane holds the sorcerer Merlin captive. She is the governess of the young knight Lancelot. Duden, Bibliographic Institute Mannheim, Vienna, Zurich. Vivien Leigh was actually named Vivian Mary Hartley and Blanche DuBois in Gerlinde Atkinson's favorite film: Elia Kazan's filmic adaptation of Tennessee Williams' stage piece A Streetcar Named Desire.

Vivian Atkinson watched, standing at her window, as the police vehicles turned onto Edingen's Hauptstrasse. Then she laid the Duden aside, went to her telephone, and called Handschuhsheim. They were already here too, said Angela. Ilse was far too obsequious with them. In the background: chamber music of the Mannheim school. The day before yesterday in MS Connexion: Logical Progression. Tomorrow: The Night of Angels. We could pick you up. I'll be ready, said Vivian. What will we wear?

ABOUT THE AUTHOR

Thomas Meinecke was born in Hamburg, Germany, in 1955. He is the author of six novels, all of which use an innovative writing technique similar to music sampling. This approach allows him to deal with a variety of topics, from popular culture, music, and gender roles to the German, Jewish, and African Diaspora in the United States. When he isn't busy writing, he plays in the experimental rock band F.S.K. (Voluntary Self-Control) and works as a club DJ in Berlin.

ABOUT THE TRANSLATOR

Daniel Bowles is a literary scholar and musician. Born and raised in Louisville, Kentucky, he holds degrees from Vanderbilt University and Harvard University, where he received his PhD in Germanic Languages and Literatures in 2011. His scholarly endeavors have earned him numerous fellowships and grants, including a Fulbright Fellowship, a DAAD Fellowship, and a Whiting Foundation fellowship, leading him to additional study at the Universität Regensburg, the Freie Universität Berlin, and the Humboldt-Universität zu Berlin. Beyond his research in contemporary German literature, satire, semiotic theory, gender studies, and music, Bowles is a teacher of literature, film, and language and a translator. He also remains active as a pianist and connoisseur of the aqua vitæ of his native Kentucky. Daniel Bowles resides in Cambridge, Massachusetts.